THE MIND'S EYE

SYNSK: BOOK 1

K.C. Finn

Clean Teen Publishing

This is a work of fiction. The characters, incidents, and dialogues are products of the author's imagination and are not to be construed as real. Any resemblance to actual events or persons, living or dead, is entirely coincidental.

The Mind's Eye

Clean Teen Publishing
PO Box 561326
The Colony, TX 75056

www.cleanteenpublishing.com

Cover design by: Marya Heiman
Typography by: Courtney Nuckels

ISBN: 978-1-940534-38-1

Content Disclosure

For more information about our content disclosure, please
utilize the QR code above with your
smart phone or visit us at
www.cleanteenpublishing.com.

The Mind's Eye

"Go and join in Leigh," I pressed, "I'll be all right without you."

My little brother didn't seem sure about that, but he took the opportunity he'd been waiting for all the same. I watched his skinny legs skip into the throng of children until I lost sight of his brown bowl-cut head of hair in the crowd. I looked around hopelessly, confirming once again that I was the only teenager on the train. I cursed under my breath. I'd forgotten to tell Leighton to take care of his label. It didn't matter so much for the other kids, now trampling on a sea of white paper name tags on the train floor, but our labels were important. Ours were green.

I took another careful look at the train. The guard had passed through our carriage quite some time ago, which meant that the children who had been initially well behaved had now worked themselves up into a frenzy. They were chattering excitedly about where they were being sent, asking the ones that were good at reading to read out notes from their parents, hanging their heads out of the window to catch a taste of the bitter September breeze flying by. They hadn't noticed me. Nobody really did. So they wouldn't notice if I were to do something odd.

I closed my eyes, lifting my arms until the base of my palms rested on my forehead. I took two slow breaths. In and out and in and out. I brought my hands gently down over my face until I could feel them casting a shadow against the light streaming in from the window. The chatter of the children faded into a low hum as I began to concentrate hard on Leighton.

2

CHAPTER ONE

Evacuate Forthwith

"Wish me luck as you wave me goodbye..."

That's what they were singing, all along the train. Hordes of children much younger than me, singing and dancing in their drab school uniforms, flinging their gas masks at each other like catapults. Some of them had lost the name labels that were supposed to be pinned to their lapels, those little white tickets that told the billeting officers where they'd come from and where they were going. But they didn't care; they just went on singing.

"... Cheerio, here I go, on my way..."

I didn't feel much like singing. It was all too sad and too sudden, leaving Mum at the station in London, being herded onto the great grey engine like cattle. Leighton didn't understand my thoughtful expression as he stood beside me, rocking with the motion of the carriage. He wanted to sing, I could tell. But he was only ten, a full five years younger than me; he didn't even know how to feel the way I did. He didn't worry about when we'd be able to see Mum again.

Or Dad, for that matter.

For Jackson Freeman:
Henri's biggest fan.

A cold shiver passed through me. When I opened my eyes I was four feet tall and standing in the middle of a mass of giggling boys and girls. One girl with curly blonde ringlets gave the shoulder I was attached to a push. I felt her pinchy grip.

"What's your name then?" She demanded with a lisp.

"Leighton Cavendish," I heard my brother's voice reply.

"Are you goin' on your own?" The girl asked.

I felt a little dizzy as my brother shook his head.

"No I'm with my sister, Kit," he explained, "she's back in the other part of the carriage."

"Oh yeah," said the little blonde girl, who I was beginning to think was a rather nasty piece of work. She screwed up her piggy face and shoved Leighton again. I felt the jab harshly. She had hurt him. "Where are you goin' then? I bet it's not as good as my place. I'm going to An-jel-see."

Anglesey, I thought, but I tried my best to keep it to myself. Leighton was fidgeting with his lapels, confirming my worst fears when he dropped his head down to look at them. Through his eyes I saw the pin that should have been holding his green paper label.

"Oh, um," he stammered, starting to look around.

I followed his gaze in deep concentration, trying to ignore the piggy girl's laugh as I helped him search the floor of the crowded carriage. I could feel the tension building in his little body, like he knew how angry I might be at him

3

for losing his paper after all the warnings Mum had given him that same morning. His glances became more erratic and harder to follow as he twirled around, but I caught a flash of something in a pea green shade on one of his twists. But I couldn't make him move back to it and he didn't seem to want to turn that way again.

Frustrated I thought harder, pushing myself deeper into his head, until I could hear him fretting so loudly in my skull I thought my head would burst. I let out a breath I didn't know I was holding, trying just to whisper the words in my mind.

Behind your left shoe.

Leighton turned, looking to see where the voice had come from.

Left's the other way.

He turned again and to my relief he immediately saw the paper on the ground. As my brother bent to retrieve it I let him go, sinking back into a dizzying blackness for a few seconds until I could see my own hands over my eyes. I let my arms drop, taking a lungful of oxygen in desperately. My head ached and my arms were limp at my side, but I smiled at the sight of Leighton skipping back up the corridor towards me with the slip of green paper in his hand.

"Kit, this came off," he said as he waved it in my face, "Can you pin it back on please?"

"Perhaps I'd better keep it until we get off," I suggested, after which he immediately handed the paper over. I didn't miss the look of relief on his face.

Most of the children had settled into sleepy little heaps by the time we finally crossed the border into North Wales, which gave me some time to recover from my little trip into Leighton's head. I wasn't supposed to do things like that in public places. Nobody had ever told me so, exactly, but then nobody else knew what I could do. I just knew that the closed-eye deep breathing thing would look odd to me if I saw someone else doing it, and God only knows what I looked like when my mind was otherwise engaged.

Probably like some great gawking ape, with my bristling curly hair the colour of ginger biscuits flying out in all directions, my indigo eyes dark and dead to all in my immediate space. I laughed to myself silently so I didn't disturb the sleeping masses. If those kids had seen me use my ability, then they were likely to forget it, perhaps write it off as teenagers just being odd and doing strange things. So long as no-one important ever caught me, I'd be safe.

The train guard re-entered the carriage with the jangle of keys, stepping gently down the central aisle and shaking his head at the carpet of labels under his feet. He caught my eye and gave a "Tsk, tsk". I just nodded politely whilst he approached.

"We'll be at your station in a few minutes, Miss Cavendish," the kindly old guard informed. He had a voice as smoky as the puffs passing the train window. "You'd best wake your brother and I'll help you alight."

5

"Thank you sir," I said with a small smile.

I could feel the tremble in my chest as I gave Leighton a little push. He was curled up on the seat beside me with his head in my lap. He unfurled himself like a cat and rubbed his sleepy blue eyes as I told him the news from the guard. When he'd got himself together he nodded and climbed off of the seat so I could shuffle over to the edge in preparation. Sure enough the train slowed a moment later and the watchful guard crouched down beside me.

"If you'll pardon me, Miss," he said as he put one hand under my knees. I said nothing, feeling terribly awkward as I put my arm around his shoulder, letting him lift me out of the seat. "Come along young Mister," the guard said to Leighton in haste, "you'll have to carry the chair."

The strong old guard took me down the steps from the carriage onto the platform. Over his shoulder I watched Leighton scrambling down in pursuit of him, clanking my poor metal wheelchair along behind him. It hit every step on the way down, making me shudder.

"Can you stand for a moment Miss, whilst I work out this fancy folding chair of yours?" asked the guard with a patient smile. I panicked instantly. Stand? Fall was far more likely. But Leighton saved me with an outburst.

"Oh it's easy!"

Leigh was already well away attacking the chair, pushing it to and fro until he could slam down the middle and put the tubular frames in the right places. The old guard looked relieved and impressed at the same time as he set me down into the seat. I felt the redness rising in my cheeks at his kindness. He patted me on the head and straightened up.

"I'll fetch your bags Miss," he said with a smile, "You wave those green tickets about until the billet man sees you."

I looked around the dirty, smoky railway platform into the mass of unlabelled children now wandering aimlessly along in clumps. The billeting officer wasn't hard to spot at all; he was the tall one in the middle of a particularly large clump of younger children, most of whom were crying. The billet man looked like he wanted to cry too. He was an older man, though not as grey and bristly as the train guard and as the bawling children were shuffled to and fro I realised that he was wearing a policeman's uniform under an open beige jacket. I waved my green label towards his field of vision just as the train guard said, but he didn't notice us. The green was supposed to signal us as a special case because of my chair. He should have been looking out for us, but now I could see he was too busy in the throng of cry-babies to even look up.

Eventually we were introduced when the guard took us and our one suitcase over into the eye of the child storm. I was wet from the explosion of tears instantly, pulling a handkerchief from the pocket of my knit jumper to wipe my face. It was always awful being at the same eye level as small children and large animals. On this occasion I would have preferred the large animals over this noisy mess of kids who had just realised they wouldn't be seeing Mummy again for a while now that their train adventure was over. I couldn't hear a word that the billet man said over the din, but eventually he took control of pushing my wheelchair and made off for the station exit.

I turned weakly in my chair to wave goodbye to the kind old guard, feeling the noise of the busy platform fade away. My head felt normal again at last.

"I've just got to transfer my duties to Officer Jones, then I'll be accompanying you two up to the village."

His accent was a terribly thick Welsh one and it was actually several minutes after he had gone back to the station before I could translate exactly what he had said and tell it to Leighton again. We were in a little car park where a cold wind nipped against my stockings, making my knees ache under my pleated skirt. I should have worn something warmer. Mum was always telling me to worry about the weather more. But then she wouldn't have abandoned me in a car park in the first place.

The flustered officer assigned to help us on Evacuation Day was Officer Lewis. When he returned, I was wheeled into the back of a large hospital car especially built for the purpose. I had to admit the shiny white car filled me with a little excitement. When Leigh came to sit opposite me on a bench inside the back of the vehicle, he looked around him with a big smile.

"Nice this Kit," he mused, "Do you think it means the people looking after us are rich?"

"No such luck young man," said Lewis from the front passenger seat, "This is the doctor's private car, this, you'll only see it when you're going up his office."

Again it took some time to translate, the way Lewis mashed all his words together into a melodious jangle was hard on our London ears, but I got enough words from the mix to know I shouldn't expect a chauffeur. Although I probably would be in this car quite often, given the circumstances. The pin in my jumper where the green label clung to me was starting to itch. I took it off gently, saving the pin against the fabric strap of my gas mask holder and tried to read the address we were destined for.

Ty Gwyn, Bryn Eira Bach

That was it. No borough, no postcode, not even a house number. I stretched forward to give the paper to Leighton whose little eyes were craning to see it. A lot of good it'd do him. He scrumpled his face at the address.

"Tie goy-un?" he asked, "What kind of address is tie goy-un?"

Lewis curved his head round his seat, looking at the paper over Leigh's little shoulders.

"Tie indeed," he tutted, "That's Ty Gwyn that is. Lovely big farm house on the edge of the village. You'll love it there."

He said it as Tee Gwin. I tried to remember it, murmuring it on my lips. It would be so rude to say it wrong to the people who were kind enough to take us in for the duration of the threat in London, perhaps even for the duration of the war. Tee Gwin. The thought of a farm house didn't appeal in the least to me, all I could think of was how cold and drafty it would be in the winter months, but Leighton was all over the idea, scrambling up the bench to

9

turn and talk to Officer Lewis.

"A farm!" he squealed, stamping his feet, "Will there be pigs and chickens and things to chase around?"

"I don't know if they'll appreciate you chasing 'em much, bach, but yes there will be animals about the place." Lewis's round face smiled at Leighton before he turned his brown eyes on me. "Oh it's a lovely village this, you'll have everything you could ever want in Bryn Eira Bach."

I felt a bitter taste in my mouth, but I smiled back before I looked out of the window. Unless this distant village could somehow make me able-bodied again and then give me a handsome young chap to go dancing with, I knew that Lewis's promises, and my hopes, couldn't ever come true.

CHAPTER TWO

Ty Gwyn

The doctor's private car took us an awfully long way from the station, over sparse grassy hills and down little brown roads that led to yet more hills. We had gone over so many bumps that I could feel the restraints on my chair starting to loosen, but just as I began to worry that I'd be flung out of my seat at the next bend, the car finally stopped. Out of one window I saw a mass of misty fields with the vague shadow of mountains in the background. From the other I just caught sight of a lot of out buildings ranging in shape and size. Barns and things, I supposed.

Ty Gwyn was straight ahead of us, so I didn't see the huge white building until I was properly out of the car. Officer Lewis started to wheel me up to it over the bumpy gravel path, jarring my spine with every pebble. I tried to keep smiling and made sure my clothes and hair were neat as we approached. When Lewis rang the doorbell the ancient sound echoed out of the cracks in the wood around the window panes. A few birds roosting in the eaves of the big white farm house suddenly took flight, making Leighton jump. He shuffled from foot to foot, biting his little pink lip.

The tiniest girl I had ever seen answered the door. She was short and willowy with huge blue eyes and tawny brown hair sticking up at funny angles. Her plain little dress was stained with something that looked like blueberries. She clung to its hem as she looked up at Officer Lewis, then she suddenly broke into a great beaming smile, showing off her stumpy white teeth.

"Ble mae Mam?" Lewis asked the little girl.

I tried to pick out the English as usual, but this time I couldn't. Leighton gave me a wide eyed look, scrunching his nose.

"Yn y gegin yn paratoi cinio," the little girl replied. I marvelled at the complex language falling out of such a tiny mouth.

"Dod â Mam yma!" Lewis added with a flick of his hand.

The little girl scampered away, leaving the door wide open. I would have waited, but Lewis seemed to take that as the invitation to go inside. He wheeled me in over the bumpy threshold of the wide farmhouse door and into a big reception space, adjusting Leighton until he stood up straight beside me. Everything in this part of the house was either black or white. Black tiles lined the cold stone floor. White lacy doilies covered the shelves of an old black dresser in the corner, next to an even older metal coat stand that was ready to fall over with the amount of coats flung upon it.

I looked at the steep, black stairs fearfully. If I was

expected to climb them every day and night, I would surely die before I even reached breakfast tomorrow. My joints ached at the very prospect of it.

"Nawr te, who do we have yur then?"

The woman's accent echoing down the corridor was thankfully much clearer than Lewis's. She almost sang the words as she appeared from under a white doorway right in front of us. The woman had a rosy face and the same tawny hair as the little girl, though hers was pulled back into a more practical style. She was older than Mum but younger than Granny, with a cooking apron tied over her broad, rounded figure. She had the kindest smile in the world as she approached, rubbing her coarse hands together excitedly.

"Oh aren't you just lovely, the pair of you!"

She dropped to her knees before us and pulled my shoulder forward for a hug. My chair gave me a little space at least from her lovingly iron grip, but Leighton had no such luck. He was pulled straight into her ample chest where he could hardly breathe from the warmth of her embrace. He emerged red-faced a moment later, stumbling backwards.

"Leighton, Catherine," Officer Lewis explained, "This is Mrs Gladys Price, your new guardian."

"Call me Mam if you like," she added, "Everyone does round yur."

Mam stayed at eye level with me, crouching on the floor with her warm hand on my knee. She smelled like cakes and biscuits and her voice had a soft melodic note, like there was music in every word she spoke.

"Thank you Mam," I said and Leighton repeated me. I was embarrassed at how stiff my voice sounded, but Mam didn't seem to notice.

"Well come in, come in!" she said, yanking herself up to her full height, "You must be starving after that journey!"

The mention of any kind of food had won Leighton over immediately. He bounced on his heels as Mam circled him to take the back of my chair. We said goodbye to Officer Lewis as he doffed his hat, then suddenly we were off at Mam's brisk pace down a dark corridor until we emerged into a massive kitchen. A huge oval table made of dark wood sat in the centre of the space, already laden with cakes, sandwiches and a big jug of fruit cordial. Leigh's jaw dropped to the ground.

"Oh sit down love, tuck in," Mam said to him as she wheeled me up to the near end of the table. I could already see the space where a chair had been moved away to accommodate me.

My little brother wasted no time in heeding her. He took off his cap as he dropped into a wooden chair near me and reached out for a sandwich the size of a doorstop, taking an impossibly large bite compared to the size of his mouth. Mam sat herself down just opposite me and the tiny little girl who had answered the door came running up to her. Scooping her up with warm, wide arms, Mam set the girl on her knee and caught my eye.

"Is this your daughter?" I asked, giving the little girl a grin. She shied away, but she was smiling too.

"Yeah," Mam nodded proudly, "this is Vanessa. We call her Ness Fach. My little miracle she is!" She cuddled Ness close before setting her down again.

"What do you mean?" asked Leighton with a mouthful of bread and cheese. I made a point of remembering to tell him off for bad manners later.

"Well yur's me with three grown up children, then suddenly Ness comes along out of the blue! I didn't even know I was pregnant for a while!"

Mam sat back with a happy sigh, watching Ness Fach, who was eyeing Leighton with interest. She put her nose up to the edge of the kitchen table and stood on tiptoe to look at him.

"Do you speak English?" Leighton asked her.

"Yeah," she said unsurely. I could see the fascination in her little face. Girls always liked the look of Leighton. It was going to be a problem when he got older, I knew. "How old are you?" Ness mumbled.

"Ten," Leigh replied, "What about you?"

"Three," she said more strongly.

"You're a tall girl for three," I observed with extra enthusiasm, and she turned and beamed at me. "This is Leighton, and I'm Catherine." Ness nodded her tiny tawny head. "And my friends call me Kit. If you like, we can be friends, then you can call me Kit as well."

Ness Fach took a moment to take in the proposition.

"Kit," she said shyly.

"That's right," I replied.

Ness suddenly scampered off again, disappearing

15

out of the kitchen door and back down the dark corridor. Mam watched her go, shaking her head.

"She'll be getting her Dolly to show you now," Mam explained, "Everyone has to meet Dolly. You haven't touched your food yet love."

I started to fill a small plate with food, feeling my heart settle like it was being laid on a fluffy pillow. The situation could have been so beastly for Leigh and me, but things were definitely on the up. I wanted to be as polite and likeable as possible for Mam, hoping that Leighton's evident delight in her cooking was enough to ingratiate him for the moment.

"You said you had three other children Mam?" I asked, taking a bite of a cucumber sandwich.

"Oh yes," she answered with great warmth in her tone, "My two eldest, the boys, they're with their father in the RAF, learning to fly at Porth Neigwl. It's a bit of a way from yur, too far to visit like, but it's nice to know they're still on Welsh soil, isn't it?"

"Do you suppose they'll be training for the war?" I asked, fascinated.

A softness came to Mam's eyes, her smile faded just slightly before she brushed off her apron. "Oh if they're as brave as their father, they'll be out there battering the Germans in no time," she exclaimed, "He was in the first war you know, my Clive." She smiled again proudly as I ate. "And," she continued, "I have a daughter, who is in the house somewhere. I don't know where she's got to, actually, I did tell her you were coming."

16

Even as she was saying the words there came a clattering sound and a voice answered her: "She's been all over the house, actually, because her mother gave her a million impossible things to do before lunchtime."

The young woman who entered the kitchen was carrying a large stack of washing which she dumped onto a counter with a huff. She was the most beautiful girl I had ever seen, with pale skin and blonde curls and sparkling blue eyes. I envied her instantly, most especially her strong, slender legs. I'd have bet any money in the world that she was good at dancing.

"Blodwyn, this is Catherine and Leighton Cavendish," Mam said in her sing song voice, "They're just arrived from London."

"Pleasure," said Blodwyn without smiling. Her voice didn't quite have the same melody as her mother's. "I'd be more welcoming, of course, if someone hadn't worn me out asking me to do every bloody chore in the house, whilst *she* set about making a ridiculously big lunch that the five of us couldn't possibly bloody eat."

"What's all this language, Blod?" Mam chided in a shrill tone. She seemed more amused by her daughter's moaning than annoyed. She turned to me with a knowing look. "I thought she'd grow out of this attitude when she stopped being a teenager, you know, but she turned twenty last month and there's been no change."

The beautiful girl gave a frustrated groan so loud that it startled Leighton, who spilt the cordial he was drinking on his shirt. He looked at the pink stain with a

17

frown.

"Oh dear!" Mam said kindly, "Let's get that cleaned up quick, come with me love."

Leighton obeyed, exiting the kitchen by the far door. I saw him take Mam's hand as they went and I smiled, content that he was going to be well looked after at Ty Gwyn. When they had gone I realised that Blodwyn was watching me. She was leaning her perfect frame against the sink with a thoughtful look clouding her eyes.

"I'd love to be twenty," I said awkwardly, "I bet you've got all kinds of freedom about the village."

"Not any more," Blod said, her rosy lips turning to a sneer, "Thanks to your arrival, I might add." She folded her arms sharply. "Now that you're here, Mam says I have to pick up the slack, because she's going to be busy seeing to *you* all the time."

I got the distinct impression that she didn't mean 'me and Leighton' when she said 'you'. She was looking at my wheelchair disdainfully and I felt like I wanted it to fold up and swallow me whole. Blod approached me suddenly, her blonde tresses flowing like some vicious goddess. Her blue eyes hardened as she looked down into my face.

"So don't go thinking we'll be like sisters, or friends, or anything like that," she snarled, "Because all you mean to me is more bloody work."

She stormed away after that, nearly knocking Ness off her feet as the little girl appeared in the doorway. She groaned that loud groan again in anger. "Out the way, pest!"

Ness stumbled around her so she could continue

K.C. Finn

to parade from the room in fury. The little girl blinked in surprise, but she didn't seem upset by her sister's remarks. Instead she caught sight of me and started to smile again, ambling up with her hands behind her back. She bit her lip, then brought her arms around to her front to reveal a little ragdoll with ginger-brown hair the same shade as mine.

"Dolly!" she said proudly.

I tried to smile for her, but it was suddenly difficult again.

CHAPTER THREE

Doctor's Orders

I needn't have worried about where I was going to sleep; it seemed Mam had thought of everything when it came to taking on an evacuee with an illness. She had turned her husband's sitting room at the back of the house into a bedroom for me so that I would never have the stairs to tackle. There was a fireplace, a wash basin and some basic ablutions to help me stay comfortable and plenty of space around the single bed for my chair to get around the room. I rather thought the bed had come from a hospital, but I didn't like to ask too many questions on the first day.

Mam left me to change for bed, which I could manage alone most of the time. I hauled myself out of my chair by leaning on the bed frame, then sat on the edge of the bed and shuffled out of my day clothes and into my nightie. My stockings were the hardest thing to get off; I realised sadly that Mum had always been the one to pull them off at the toes. But I managed eventually and I was rather proud of myself when Mam returned and found me wriggling in under the warm white covers.

I knew right away though, that she could see the

pain it had caused me to get about half a foot from the chair into the bed. I could feel my cheeks glowing red, my arms aching from putting all my weight on them, but I didn't like to think about the pain, much less to talk about it. Mam helped me with the last of the covers as I put my head on the pillow. She put a small glass of water and a biscuit on the bedside table.

"My bedroom's right above yur," she said softly, "so if you get into trouble you give me a shout."

"Thank you," I answered, stifling a yawn.

"You get a good rest love," she continued, "I had a telephone call tonight. They're sending a car for you tomorrow to go and meet your new doctor."

The news was not the kind that encouraged a good night's sleep. I thanked Mam politely and she put out the light, closing my door with a gentle hand. But when she had gone I shuffled my aching legs restlessly and rubbed my upper arms where they had taken on the strain. I didn't relish the idea of being prodded and poked by a new physician, it was bad enough being examined once a month by Doctor Baxendale in London and I'd known him since I was twelve when all the pain began. I wondered idly what the new doctor might be like, but the more I wondered, the more I worried, and I decided instead that my mind needed a different occupation tonight.

Aside from Leighton and my mother, I had never been able to use my secret gift to intentionally enter anyone else's head. I had always supposed it was familiarity that allowed me such easy access into their minds, but I also knew that my psychic ability sometimes had a farther reach. Most especially when I was sleeping, in fact. It had started to happen when I was around eight or nine, but of course for a long time I thought they were dreams. Dreams where I was in someone else's head, looking through their eyes, hearing them speak and feeling their innermost emotions like they were my own.

Now as I lay in my new bed of my new home, I closed my eyes, hoping that something interesting would come my way as I surrendered my mind to slumber.

Generally I didn't like looking through the eyes of men, and I knew this one was a man as soon as I saw the huge black boots crossed on the desk in front of me. He was clipping the end off of a cigar with two great hairy hands that looked rather old in a pale blue room with expensive-looking paintings on every wall. He lit the cigar and I felt the wave of satisfaction he got from the first long inhale he took. I was grateful at least that my powers did not extend to having to smell the smoke from the beastly thing, and I hoped that they never would.

The smoking man wasn't alone in his room for long. He turned my viewpoint to a set of doors painted in blue and gold as another man entered the room. My man leapt out of his seat so fast I felt sick from the transition; he was standing upright and saying something to the new chap in a language that I didn't understand. I saw the new arrival properly then, in his grey-green suit and trousers. No, not a suit. A uniform. His collar had two red rectangles sticking out under his fat chin, each covered in golden leaf patterns. A row of coloured medals adorned the man's chest and his hat bore the symbol of a bird of prey in flight, with a u-shaped golden laurel thing and what looked like a target in the middle. And under the bird of prey was a symbol I knew. A swastika.

"Generalfeldmarschall," said the man whose head I occupied. I felt him give some kind of salute; his heart was suddenly pounding in my ears.

Even as I dreamed, I knew I was seeing something I shouldn't be. I drifted in and out of consciousness as the men began their conversation in what I now knew had to be the German tongue. There was a trick to maintaining focus in my sleep that I had not quite mastered; it was hard to stay alert when I knew that I was actually already unconscious. I noticed that the man whose mind I held also had the grey-green sleeves of the military uniform on. The other more superior man had ordered him to clear his desk, after which he laid out a map for him, and me, to see.

I had never been any good at Geography, even when I was still healthy enough to attend school. The map was a funny looking coastline with all sorts of jagged bits that didn't make sense, as though someone had taken a knife to the country and cut long deep valleys of water into it, with other valleys jutting off to the sides. If it was a country I knew by name then it wasn't one I'd ever bothered to look up on a map, but through my man's eyes I was forced to study it closely and carefully. I could feel his nerves rising the more his superior talked at him, until the high ranking man slammed a strong, old finger down on the map at a space on the coast.

Oslo.

I knew the city's name, but the country was still lost on me. As I tried to pull the information from my conscious memory I felt the familiar cold shiver start to creep up my spine. I tried to resist, tried to stay with the mind I had found, but I knew really that it was too late. The connection was fading. I was falling into a proper sleep.

I awoke the next morning to the sound of birds outside the window, which alarmed me at first. The only birds to ever wake me in London were the pigeons, and whatever was outside in the farmland right now was much louder and less considerate than they were. As I lay flat looking up at the black beams of the ceiling my mind drifted back to the German viewpoint I had discovered the night before. It was such a fabulous possibility, to be able to see right into the war. I sighed heavily, knowing that it would be pure luck to ever get back to it again.

I jolted my spine as I heard my door starting to open, but I was relieved to find it was only Leighton stumbling in. The sight of him in his stripy red and white pyjamas made me ache for Mum and home suddenly. He had a sad look on his usually cheeky face that made me suspect he was feeling the same way. Leigh said nothing as he rounded my bed and clambered in, taking the biscuit Mam had left me the night before and starting to munch. He cuddled up next to me very slowly; he knew how difficult my morning stiffness was. It hurt to bring my arm down and put it around him, but I did it anyway.

"Is your bedroom nice?" I asked him as I felt his little jaw chewing against my side.

"It's bigger than at home," he answered with his mouth full, "But I had strange dreams."

"Don't blame the room for that," I soothed, rubbing his back, "That's just you stuffing your face with cheese all day."

Leighton giggled for a moment, but it faded away. "Do want help to sit up?" he asked.

I felt a pang inside. Mum had always been the one to hoist me up in the morning. I wasn't even sure that Leighton would be strong enough to pull me.

We had just about managed it between us when Mam arrived in the room, looking very smart in a pink dress that clung to her round shape. She thanked Leigh for helping and told him to dress before breakfast, which he found very odd indeed. At home he and Mum had always eaten jam on toast upstairs in my room whilst I tried to get my strength together for the day. The smell of cooked breakfast food wafted in as he stood there in doubt and I smiled as it tempted him away to find his clothes.

"Do have something smart to wear Kit?" Mam asked as she gently brought me nearer the edge of the bed.

I was about to ask what for until I remembered with dread. The German in my head had pushed out the appointment, but now I knew once again that I had a date with the doctor not long from now.

Leighton was invited to stop at home and explore Ty Gwyn whilst we went over the hill to meet the doctor. Though I didn't like the thought of Blod's version of looking after him, he seemed keen to have a wander round the out buildings in search of chickens and things, so I put my faith in Mam and let him stay. It wasn't fair really to drag him out to sit in a doctor's waiting room anyway, no matter how much I needed a familiar face with me. I knew Mam had sensed my nerves because she put her warm hand over mine all the way to the surgery in the car. Every time I looked at her rosy face she was smiling, which made me feel a tiny bit better when the lovely white car pulled up outside a little cottage.

It certainly wasn't the whitewashed, sterile office in Bethnal Green that I was used to. When Mam wheeled me inside I was fascinated by the photographs of happy miners and farmers on the walls and the cosy collection of various armchairs that had been donated to make up the waiting room. The secretary that took some information from me was a dear old lady who offered me sweets as she starting telling Mam all the latest news from the village itself. I tuned out of the conversation, settling into the place and enjoying the smell of fresh flowers and peppermints as I waited.

"Catherine Cavendish?"

"Oh hello Doctor Bickerstaff," Mam said, wheeling me round to the source of the voice.

My first thought was that he looked like Robert Taylor the film star, except that he was much more fair-haired. Mum had taken me to see *A Yank In Oxford* last year in Leicester Square for my birthday treat. Doctor Bickerstaff couldn't have been a day over 30. He was smartly dressed with big blue eyes that landed on Mam. He gave her a polite nod, and when he spoke again I realised that he was English.

"Ah Mrs Price, good day. I'd like to see Miss Cavendish alone for the initial assessment if you don't mind."

"No, no, whatever you think is best Doctor," Mam answered. It was clear that she revered the young professional a great deal.

Bickerstaff looked down at me, but he didn't move to take my chair. I didn't move either, of course, which left us in a strange, awkward staring contest for a moment. The fair doctor folded his arms.

"Well?" he demanded, "Can't you wheel yourself?"

There was something terribly harsh in his voice like a schoolmaster. I felt my nerves rising again.

"No of course not," I answered, half anxious and half annoyed. Couldn't he see how incapable I was?

Doctor Bickerstaff sneered, and suddenly he wasn't

so much like a film star.

"How disappointing," he observed.

He walked with disturbingly brisk strides to take my chair and wheeled me very quickly into his office. I had to hold on to my armrests so as not to slide out of the chair when he stopped short of his desk. Instead of sitting behind it he pulled up a chair opposite me and took a paper file from his desk, ignoring me for several uncomfortable minutes as he consulted it.

"Juvenile Arthritis," he concluded, snapping the file shut.

"Excuse me Doctor," I said quietly, "But Doctor Baxendale called it Still's Disease. Is that the same thing?"

"Your Doctor Baxendale's an idiot." Bickerstaff hardly looked at me when he spoke. "He doesn't know his ilium from his olecranon. Now, I want to see you stand. Get up."

He said it like it was an easy thing to do. The blonde sat back in his chair expectantly, making it quite clear that he wouldn't be giving me a pull to help me to my feet. I steeled myself, reaching both hands out to grip his desk ready to make the effort. When my feet found the ground I could already feel the pinch where the skin around my ankles was swollen, when I pressed a little weight onto them the sensation was like somebody inserting a screwdriver right into the joint and twisting it hard. I cried out at the first sharp moment of pain, looking at the doctor viciously.

"I can't," I said through gritted teeth, "I'm sorry Doctor, but I can't."

"Get up," he repeated.

I felt the hotness of water rising behind my eyes but I did my best to bite back the tears that wanted to come pouring out. I felt like his stern face might just break into a smile if I did. The only way to win the argument was to prove myself right. With an almighty force I hurled myself onto my feet as though I was shifting my weight onto a bed or another chair, but instead I used the desk to push all of my weight onto my legs. My knees buckled under me after just a few seconds and I felt myself dropping to the floor like a crumpled sack of vegetables.

And Doctor Bickerstaff let me fall.

He actually let my head hit the lino floor in his office before he even moved a muscle. After I had landed the impact sent a shockwave of pain through me so hot I'd have sworn I'd been set on fire. It was then that Bickerstaff got up to assist. He lifted my weak little frame with ease back into my wheelchair in seconds. I kept my head down, determined to show him no gratitude for the aid, since it was his fault I'd fallen in the first place.

"I told you I can't do it," I spat, seething as blood flushed into my cheeks.

"How interesting," he said.

Out of the corner of my eye I could see him offering me a tissue. I snatched it out of his hand like a child in my rage. Interesting? I'm sure he'd find it terribly interesting if he fell flat on his face and nobody gave him any sympathy. After I had dried my eyes I managed to look at him again, but he had his nose back in the file and he was writing something down. Then without even checking on me he got up and went to call Mam into the room. To my great relief she came in in a flurry as soon as she saw me red-faced and teary.

"What's this now?" she demanded as she pulled up the chair the doctor had been using and wrapped one matronly arm around my shoulders.

"Nothing to worry about Mrs Price," Bickerstaff said casually, "Catherine's had a bit of a strain from the physical test I gave her."

A bit of a strain? Rude as it was for a young lady, I wanted to slap him across the face. If I had had the strength, I might have. The young doctor took his place behind his desk and pulled open a noisy drawer, producing four large objects made of fabric and wood. There were two boards about the length and width of shoe boxes with fabric straps attached to them, followed by two more that were only about the length of a domino box. The smaller ones had two boards each on them with a strap going all the way around, as though they were designed to be wrapped around something.

"What are those?" I asked, my nose turning up against them.

"Your treatment," Bickerstaff replied in that same clinical voice. He turned his attention to Mam. "Catherine's condition is quite serious, I'm afraid, and her previous doctor has done very little to improve her chances in the last three years. We must resist the contractive fusing of her joints overnight before it becomes permanent." Mam was hooked on every word he said, nodding profusely. "Every night for the duration of the night, Catherine must wear these splints on her knees and elbows to keep the joints straight and prevent contraction."

"*Every night?*" I exclaimed, looking at the horrible hefty things with loathing.

"And I want her to practise propelling herself in the chair," Doctor Bickerstaff continued as though he hadn't heard me at all, "So give her some old gloves to handle the wheels and encourage her to move short distances alone. Don't be tempted to help her."

Don't help me. Had he really just said that?

CHAPTER FOUR

Idrys Pengelly

I told Leighton about the horrible Doctor Bickerstaff when we got back to Ty Gwyn and he called him some names that I didn't know were even in a ten year old's vocabulary. I should have told him off for them, but in truth it made me happy to see Leigh go for him. He promised me that when he grew big and strong he'd punch the nasty doctor on the nose, but as he mimicked the punches I noticed his hands were pink and pruney. I made him come closer so I could take a look.

"What have you been up to?" I asked him, looking at the crinkly skin on his little palms.

"Blod made me wash up the dinner service," he said with a scowl, "There were loads of dishes. She says someone special is coming to dinner."

"And I'll bet Mam asked *her* to do it, not you," I added with a frown.

We were in the kitchen having a drink when the culprit returned to the scene of the crime. Blod strode in wearing a flowing cotton dress and high heeled shoes. She had a sunhat on and a magazine and I knew exactly what she had been doing whilst Leighton was enslaved with her chores.

"Enjoy yourself catching the last bit of summer, did you Blod?" I asked.

She turned with a wicked grin, taking off her hat. "I'm trying to keep my legs a nice colour for the harvest dance," she explained, "Not your kind of concern, I suppose."

I had tried to reason that Blod might come around to our presence in time, but twenty four hours with the young woman had done nothing to support that idea. Blodwyn Price was a cow, and that was that.

"Listen you," I said, channelling all my rage from the Doctor Bickerstaff encounter into my voice, "You don't tell my brother what to do. Only Mam's in charge of us here. Not you and not anyone else."

"Oh really?" Blod answered, "And what are you going to do? Leap out of that chair and knock me down if I'm mean to you? I don't think so somehow."

I was all the more angry because she was right. If there was ever a time to learn to propel myself in this chair it was now. Perhaps if I got good enough I could run her over.

"No, but I'm sure Mam would have something to say about the state of Leighton's hands," I countered.

Blod's beautiful face faltered for just a moment. "Well, if you want me to get on with the chores so badly, then clear out the pair of you. Bampi's coming for dinner and he's not going to want to see you scruffy articles cluttering up the place."

The Mind's Eye

Leigh took the handles of my chair and pushed me out of the kitchen slowly. When we made it to the black and white hall I told him to stop and open my bedroom door. As he did so I reached down beside my leg and produced the old pair of leather driving gloves that Mam had fished out of her husband's old trunk. Leighton watched me from the door. I put on the tough gloves and gripped the wheels of my chair, starting to push.

But nothing happened. The pressure wasn't enough. I pushed harder, feeling my elbows start to strain. When they were stretched so far out that my shoulders started to tense I felt movement at last, but the pain was too much to push again. I had to stop for breath. I had wheeled half an inch, perhaps less, and already my bones were creaking. I dropped my arms, exhausted. I could feel my heart banging on my ribcage in protest at the effort.

"Honestly that Doctor's got no clue," I sighed, "How does he think this is even possible?"

Leighton made his punching motions again and I laughed, taking off the gloves.

"Shall I push you then?" he offered.

"Yes please," I replied, "You heard Evil Blod; we have to get scrubbed up for dinner with a Bampi, whatever that is."

It turned out that Bampi was the pet name for Blod and Ness's grandfather, Idrys Pengelly, who was the owner and operator of the farmlands around Ty Gwyn. He was Mam's father and he lived in a cottage on the far side of the pasture behind the house where the cows grazed, so

Ness Fach was the first to spot him coming when she was playing outside that evening. At her announcement that Bampi was walking through the field, Mam helped me into the sitting room so Leighton and I could be introduced.

The first thing we knew of him was his booming voice as he entered Ty Gwyn; I could hear him greeting Ness in the wide hallway. He came into the sitting room at Mam's call carrying her under his arm like a briefcase whilst she giggled. Idrys Pengelly was a tall old man with the same rosy face as his daughter. When he smiled he had several missing teeth at the sides of his mouth, which was surrounded by a reddish beard and moustache. The hair on his head was much more grey and nestled largely under a flat-cap, which he took off as he dropped Ness onto the sofa beside him.

"Well now," he said loudly, patting his knees with a thump, "Who do we have yur then?"

He spoke almost exactly like Mam save for the deep, echoing tone that threatened to shake the roof from its rafters. I instantly liked him with his warm smile and the fact that he had worn his bright blue farmer's overalls to dinner, he reminded me of my own Granddad, who had died when I was eight.

"I'm Catherine, Mr Pengelly, but people call me Kit."

"Short for Kitty, isit?" he asked. I nodded happily, then nudged my brother in the side.

"Oh! I'm Leighton," he said with a start.

"Are you indeed?" Idrys replied. "Well come yur and let me look at you."

Leigh gave me a nervous look but I pushed him in the back, grinning. He approached the old man very slowly until he was close enough for Idrys to take hold of his shoulders. He looked at him carefully with an approving smile.

"Ie, ie," the old man said, "you're a strapping boy all right. But what's this behind yur yur?"

"Behind my *what*?" Leighton asked, but Idrys had already put his hand up to my brother's ear. He pulled back his hand to reveal a shiny sixpence, grinning at Leigh.

"I think this must be yours mate," he supposed, "I wouldn't keep it back there, if I were you."

Leighton took the coin with a look of amusement on his face.

"Say thank you," I pressed and he did, but very shyly.

"Blod and I'll get the dinner on," Mam said from the doorway, "We'll call you when it's ready Da."

"Ta love," Idrys replied.

He settled back comfortably into the sofa and Ness crawled onto his knee and lay down, looking up at the ceiling. Idrys tickled her belly until she ran away to the corner with a huge grin.

"It's lovely to have young people in the house again," the old Bampi remarked, "Ness is too young to yur my stories, see?"

"What stories?" Leighton asked, learning forward eagerly in his armchair.

"Well I was in the first war, see, the Great War, but I must've told Blod a hundred times and well, she's grown

36

K.C. Finn

up now init? She's yurd it all."

"I'm sure we'd love to hear some stories before dinner, Mr Pengelly." It wasn't just that hearing about the war would be interesting; the mention of Blod made me feel the need to escape from the present moment for a little while.

"Well then," Idrys said happily, "D'you want to yur about the battles or the spies?"

"Ooh!" Leighton exclaimed, raising his hand like he was in a schoolroom, "The spies please!"

"In that case, I'll tell you something you'd *never* believe and you tell me if you think it could be true." Idrys leaned forward and steeped his fingers together, his loud voice becoming softer as he started his tale. "When I was in Dover waiting to be sent out to France, there was a spy billeted with us, sleeping in our barracks, like. It was his job to infiltrate the German forces and look at their top secret plans, but he did it all without ever leaving Dover."

Idrys paused for effect.

"What? How?" Leighton asked impatiently. I found myself eager for the answer too.

"Well, he was what you'd call a psychic," Idrys answered, "He said he could travel, in his mind's eye, to see things on other continents."

I felt my breath catch in my throat.

"But that's ridiculous!" Leighton exclaimed, slapping his leg, "That's like a fairy-tale thing!"

"Ah well," Idrys said, holding up a finger emphatically, "I thought that too, so did all the fellas, so we asked this psychic if he'd prove it to us."

"And what did he do?" I asked, finding that my voice was trembling. I had never met anyone who talked about things like this before, never heard anything even slightly similar to my secret gift outside of fiction.

"Well we locked him in the loo see, where it was pitch dark and he couldn't talk to no-one, then we sent our mate Billy into the billet. Billy went round taking things out of everyone's packs and cupboards and putting them in new places. Then we sent Billy away so he couldn't give no hints and brought this spy fella back to the billet. He stood at the door and he told us everything that had just happened. He told us exactly where to find every object that Billy had moved, he told us how Billy had swapped some things over and changed his mind, then swapped them back. He told us all sorts of things. And Billy came back and said it was all true. Well if you can tell me how that's possible, you're a better man than I am, Gunga Din!"

Leighton sat scratching his chin thoughtfully and Idrys gave us a satisfied look. I knew, of course, exactly how it was possible. If you locked me up somewhere and had me tell you what Leighton had been up to all day, I'd be able to rattle off every action as though they'd been my own. What fascinated me was not the demonstration, but the fact that someone else out there had what I had, knew what I knew.

"Suppose it's true that this friend of yours was psychic, Mr Pengelly," I began carefully, "Did he tell you how he did it? What was his process to travel with his mind?"

"Ah, you're a scientific one, are you?" Idrys said with what he thought was a knowing grin. Clearly he thought I didn't believe him. "Well Kit, he told me and the boys that all he had to do was close his eyes and think."

"Think about what?" I pressed.

"About where he wanted to go, or who he wanted to find," Idrys answered.

"And was it easier to reach people he knew, but harder to find strangers?"

Idrys quirked a grey eyebrow at me. "That's a funny question," he said with amusement, "Are you thinking of trying it sometime?"

It was hard not to be flustered by the accusation, so I tried to laugh it off.

"I'm just interested," I lied, "It'd be nice to think we have people who can spy in on the Germans now, in this war, wouldn't it?"

"I wish I could do it," Leighton said excitedly beside me, "I'd give all of Hitler's secret plans to the Prime Minister!" I wished I could tell him that it wasn't as simple as that.

Idrys moved on to his battle stories at the dinner table, which caused Blodwyn to groan regularly between bites of her roast. She only perked up when her Bampi told her how pretty she was looking. I was totally lost to my own thoughts as I chewed aimlessly on a piece of chicken at the far end of the table, wondering about the psychic spy of the Great War and his special skill. If it were true, then that meant other people out there could do what I could do. If it were false, then people who could pretend to be psychic were making a fool out of the military. But the military wanted them, needed them even, to gather their information.

It was silly to think that a girl like me could ever be of use in the grand scheme of the world war, but it was also quite possibly true. If I could hone my focus into people and places further away than just Leighton, there was a chance that I could actually be useful to someone. I thought back to the German man from my dream the night before and spoke without thinking, interrupting one of Blod's little rants.

"Where's Oslo?" I asked.

Blod shot me a stabbing look across the table. Idrys swallowed his mouthful of potatoes as he turned to look at me.

"Norway, love," he answered, "It's the capital city."

"Why'd you ask Kit?" Mam said, shifting more vegetables into the available space on my plate.

"I, um, I heard it in a dream," I answered, realising seconds later how stupid I sounded.

"That's funny," Mam remarked with a kind smile.

"Yeah, she's a funny girl, isn't she?" Blod added. She too was smiling, but not in the same way. The urge to slap people's faces was apparently quite a popular one for me today.

CHAPTER FIVE

Dedication

Leighton started school again in the village the week after our arrival, so I was left in peace in the sitting room most mornings in order to practice propelling myself in the chair as the rotten Doctor Bickerstaff had ordered. But with the luxury of time without supervision all I could think of was Idrys's tale of the psychic spy and the soldiers I had seen in my dream. If I was going to get back into the head of the German man talking about Oslo, I would have to stretch my mind a lot farther than it had ever deliberately travelled.

The first thing to practice was finding Mum. I had been able to do it with ease when we were at home, when she was in another room or even down the end of the street chin-wagging with the local gossip, but I had never attempted to reach her any farther afield than that. Now was the time to try. I raised my hands up for the heel of each palm to touch my forehead, my eyes slipping shut. Two big breaths. In and out and in and out. And I thought hard, thought of Mum and her short, curly hair the colour of autumn leaves, her eyes the same navy blue shade as mine, her smart brown hat with the pretty white bow that she wore to go out and about.

I opened my eyes to a familiar scene: Blackwell's Post Office in East London. I could see my mother's slim white hands holding a small stack of letters. She was waiting in a noisy little queue. I congratulated myself very quietly on a job well done. My gift had taken me all the way back to London, though it was still into a head that I already knew I could reach, it was something. Distance was possible.

"Hello Gail," said a woman behind my mother in the bustling queue. She turned and through her eyes I was overjoyed to see the familiar sight of Anne, my mother's childhood friend who lived not far from us.

"Oh Anne," Mum said, giving the woman a hug with one hand whilst she clasped her letters in the other, "How are you dear? Did Bobby and John get off okay?"

"Yes everything was smooth as you like," Anne replied with a smile, "They sent me a letter from Merthyr."

"I thought they were going to the Rhondda something-or-other?" my mother pressed.

Anne waved a casual hand. "Oh there was a terrible mix up, too many kids in one place and not enough homes to put them in!"

"How awful," Mum said. I thought the same thing.

"No harm done, the boys are all right with the new family. Have you heard from your two?"

As I felt a wave of disappointment wash over Mum, the crushing guilt grabbed me like those awful splints

Bickerstaff had given me, except this time the hard boards were cramping around my heart. I hadn't even thought to write to Mum yet, everything had been so busy here and I had set off on this new psychic mission without even thinking about her as more than a practice target. It made me feel a little sick.

Mum was trying to smile; I could feel the movement in her face. "I'm just sending them a letter now," she said, indicting her pile of mail as the queue shifted forwards, "So I'm sure they'll send me all their news then."

Too right we would. I would make a point of sending pageloads to tell her how much we missed her and make sure Leighton did the same.

"I have heard from her doctor though," Mum added, "He wrote as soon as he'd seen her the other day."

I froze, hating Doctor Bickerstaff all the more for pipping me to the post with my own mother, especially before I could give her my own impression of him.

Anne asked the question that was on my mind. "And what did he say?"

Mum had reached the front of the postal queue. I waited in anguish for her to pay for her letters and get her change. She took Anne by the arm and guided her out of the post office before she spoke, so I spent every moment trying not to project any of my worries too close to her thoughts. The last thing I wanted her to do was catch my voice in her head. It was all right with Leighton, he had no clue what was going on when I injected a thought here and there, but Mum, I felt, would not handle my voice in her mind in quite the same way. When they were out on the street Mum and Anne stood browsing the postcard stand away from everyone else, where finally my mother was willing to let slip the doctor's verdict on me.

"Well, you know he's a specialist don't you?" Mum began.

Anne nodded. "That was the point of sending her to middle of nowhere, wasn't it?"

Mum nodded too. "He's a forward thinker, this Steven Bickerstaff, very brisk and proper on the phone, you know?" I could already imagine his emotionless tone talking to Mum. She would no doubt be impressed by it, thinking it ever so professional. "And he said…"

I could feel a strange warmth rising in her chest. Her heart was quivering just a little when she spoke, and I recognised the hotness building under her eyes. Anne looked quite concerned and took my mother's arm.

"He said it might not be too late."

Now I was concerned. Had it been too late for me already at some point that I wasn't aware of? And too late *how* exactly? Too late for what? Was my nice old Doctor Baxendale really the idiot Bickerstaff claimed he was? Had he handed me a sentence that I didn't have to serve?

"Well that's wonderful!" Anne said, rubbing Mum's arm. "Gail, why are you so upset? Isn't this good news?"

"Of course it is," Mum answered, fishing a tissue from her bag to dab her eyes, "He said he's started her on a new treatment and this Mrs Price that's got her is going to make her to stick to it, but-" Her voice collapsed there and her sadness overwhelmed me. It was a heavy kind of sorrow, like her heart was tied to a brick. "But it should be me there helping her," she whispered, "I feel so helpless now I'm so far away."

It was my turn to feel sad again, because I couldn't tell her how close I really was. I contented myself that a speedy reply to her letter would have to suffice.

"But think of it this way," Anne soothed, her kind face framed with blonde strands, "The next time you see her, she could be... well, she could be a lot fitter."

"She could also be thirty the rate this war's going," Mum sobbed bitterly, "I wish they'd get on and clobber the Krauts so we can get back to normal."

"But the longer she's with that doctor, the better a chance she's got," Anne reminded her.

I didn't agree. So far all Bickerstaff's night splints had done were give me bruises behind the knees and inside the elbows that Mam had to cover up with make-up. If anything I was moving my joints even less than before. But my mother's high hopes for me were not unfounded, especially if there was a way to put my real talents to good use.

Anne soon changed the subject of conversation to shake my mother from her guilt, and though it pained me to have to leave her I let my mind slip back towards Ty Gwyn until the connection was broken. When my eyes flickered open I found I was crying. As I rifled in my pockets to fetch a tissue my head ached terribly as it often did when I'd been visiting Mum. Even though the little brown sitting room was much darker than the other rooms of the house, the light streaming in through the small windows was far too bright. I closed my eyes, hearing my pulse in my head as the door opened gently.

"Oh dear," Mam said as she rushed in from the door. She crouched in front of my chair and helped me dry my tears, rubbing my arms. She clearly thought I had been trying to propel myself in the chair. "Oh Kit, love, you mustn't strain yourself. Only do what you can manage, eh?"

I just nodded, feeling as though my head was about to explode. What I could manage just wasn't enough.

The whole Price family went to chapel in the village every Sunday, which was a strange experience for Leighton and me. We had both been christened Church of England, but Mum and Dad were never big chapelgoers except at Christmas and Easter. Mum always made us sit in front of the wireless and listen to something religious on a Sunday after breakfast, but that was a nice, peaceful affair. Sunday after breakfast at Ty Gwyn was something else entirely.

The routine started with Idrys arriving at eight o'clock in his best chapel attire and complaining that Mam was never ready when she said she would be. Mam was in her smart white chapel dress but she still had her apron on and half a dozen rollers curled into the back of her head. Every time she tried to go up to her room to finish getting ready, something would interrupt her, like Ness appearing with her socks on her hands instead of her feet, or Blodwyn storming through the house complaining that all of her stockings were laddered. Idrys watched the whole fiasco with amusement for about the first twenty minutes, until he realised that the family would actually be late for chapel if he didn't do something soon.

At that point he disappeared with Ness and reappeared about five minutes later with her properly dressed, then wheeled me out in front of the door and set the little girl on my knee where she was quite happy to sit and discuss dolls. He then marched back into the house and let his booming voice loose on the remaining populous; promising them that if they didn't assemble outside in five minutes flat, the preacher would condemn them all to Hell. The first time Idrys said it Leighton came running out of the huge door like a greyhound, standing next to me in his little powder blue waistcoat.

"I bet you don't remember what church is like, do you?" I asked, "You didn't even come with us last Easter."

"Of course I do," Leigh answered with a look of protest, "It's a bunch of old people and boring stories and all the singing's out of tune."

He was right on two counts out of the three, but I did rather enjoy the hymns for a change. Most of them were in Welsh, which I think made God and faith sound a little more uplifting, but that might have been because I didn't understand the words. The actual service itself was a dull one, but being in the little chapel did give me a chance to see the collected mass that was the rest of the village.

Judging by the sizeable crowd, it seemed that Bryn Eira Bach was the kind of place where absolutely everybody went to chapel, so I was glad to be part of the experience.

That was until we were outside the chapel gate afterwards, when the familiar frame of Doctor Bickerstaff started approaching us. I was stood with Mam as she adjusted her hat against the bright autumn sun, so I saw him coming first. He caught my eye with a familiar look of disdain, his gaze extending to my elbows, at which I immediately crossed my arms. I wouldn't give him the satisfaction of seeing the badly-disguised bruises his contraptions had caused.

"Good morning Mrs Price," he said as he stopped before her.

"Bore da, Doctor," Mam replied happily, "Lovely service today wasn't it?"

"Hmm," Bickerstaff answered thoughtfully, "the preacher speaks well on the progress of man indeed. I actually came to check on some progress of my own." His round blue eyes settled on me. "How are you doing with the new treatment, Catherine?"

Thankfully Mam's exuberance spared me from having to answer him.

"Well we've had the splints on every night and not a word of complaint," Mam began, "and she's had time every day to practice moving herself around."

Bickerstaff didn't look impressed in the least. "In that case I look forward to seeing your progress on Friday," he said.

"Friday?" I repeated.

"Your next appointment," the doctor replied.

In her attempts to make me sound good to the doctor, Mam had dropped me smack bang in the centre of an awkward situation. The mornings I should have spent trying to strengthen my arms to move the chair had been reserved for stepping in and out of Mum's head in London and Leighton's at the village schoolhouse. I was surprised that Mam hadn't noticed I was in exactly the same place where she'd put me every time she came back to the room. Or perhaps she had and she was just more sympathetic than the suited cretin now judging me at the chapel gate.

"Same time as before, isit?" Mam asked.

Bickerstaff nodded, which meant I had exactly 120 hours to learn how to move more than half an inch across the floor without having a heart attack. It was a much more daunting feat than learning to infiltrate war-torn Europe with my mind, that was for sure, but I would have to make a serious go of it now before the doctor caught me out.

"Are we going then or what?" said a balshy voice approaching us. I twisted my neck to see Blod ambling down the cobbled path in her heels.

"Don't be so rude in front of the doctor, Blodwyn," Mam chided, and this time it was a proper chide, one with no amusement in her tone.

"It's quite all right, I was just leaving." The words came rushing out of Bickerstaff's mouth faster than Leighton had moved when he thought he might be sent to Hell. He said good day to us all, put his head down and moved off at his usual brisk pace back towards his shiny white hospital car. I watched him go; already regretting that the next time I would see him was so close at hand.

"Honestly I can't take you anywhere," Mam grumbled at Blod, "Make yourself useful and push Kit back up to the house. It's not fair us letting your Bampi do it both ways."

Blod grumbled, contorting her pretty face into a dramatic frown. She gave me a nasty look and put her hands on her hips.

"What have you got a face on for?" she demanded.

I opted for honesty since I didn't actually care what Blod thought of me.

"I really hate that doctor," I answered bitterly.

The beauty queen cracked a little smile on her made-up lips. She came round me to grab the handles of my chair, letting out a little laugh.

"Well that's one thing we have in common," she observed.

I found myself a little happier too. We had bonded, if only for a moment. Nevertheless, Blod pushed me over every large or jagged cobble she could find as we made our way home.

CHAPTER SIX

Progress Indeed

It was Thursday night that I started to worry about the appointment. During the week I kept telling myself that if I practised with the chair I'd improve, but as Friday drew nearer and nearer I had managed only two inches of distance before it felt as though my shoulders had been ripped from my body like a ragdoll caught in a bulldog's teeth. I had to tell myself firmly that any distance was better than no distance and if that didn't impress Doctor Bickerstaff then he could lump it for all I cared. I wasn't sure if I'd be brave enough to tell him that to his face, but I supposed that when the time came to challenge him I'd find out.

That was how I came to be thinking about him at bedtime, most especially when Mam strapped my arms and legs into the torturous splints that were slowly turning my joints a regal shade of purple. I had gotten used to sleeping with them as the nights wore on; it was the pain in the morning that I'd begun to dread, especially that first agonising moment after taking them off. I tried not to think of it as Mam tucked me in with her kind, rosy face, leaving me the water and the biscuit that Leighton would come and steal in the morning. She put out my light and left me lying in the dark where I tried not to think about tomorrow.

I expected, as I always did, that I would probably visit somewhere interesting on my way to sleep, but I was most confused in my half-slumber to find myself staring directly at Doctor Bickerstaff's movie star face. It took me a while to realise that I was looking into a mirror, at which point the horror set in. I was in his head. Bickerstaff was looking at himself in the polished mirror of a very pokey little bathroom with grey tiled walls. His blue eyes were bloodshot in the harsh light from the unshaded bulb and his chin had a dark, stubbly shadow growing on it.

It was strange enough seeing him in his navy pyjamas, but as the doctor started to brush his teeth it was the strength of his emotions that disturbed me the most. He had a very peculiar feeling hanging about him; he kept stopping in his night time routine to stare at his face again in the mirror, like there was something about his look that troubled him deeply. It was like that feeling when someone takes the last cake off the plate just before you go to grab it, except that it consumed him completely. He was Leighton when he'd finished a particularly good dessert, staring at the empty bowl. He was me when I watched people dancing at a fete, feeling the cold metal of my chair against my useless legs.

Bickerstaff wound his way to a small, single bed with starchy sheets, into which he climbed with that awful feeling still weighing down his chest. He checked his watch before he flicked off the light, but in the darkness of his small bedroom he was just laid there staring at the ceiling. I had been to some depressing minds during my dreamtime visits, but there was something different about his. Perhaps it was just because I knew him that it was all so awkward. Perhaps someone somewhere was trying to teach me to hate him a little bit less.

But he didn't have to sleep with dirty great slabs of wood strapped to his limbs that bruised him all night as his joints resisted them. Aside from whatever thought was troubling his mind, his body lay healthily and comfortably in his crisp little bed. As my own sour thought overtook his deepening sadness, I felt a cold shiver travel through me. It seemed to travel through him as well, making him shift onto his side. Bickerstaff finally closed his eyes and soon we were both asleep.

I thought I could have done without the creepy and depressing experience of being inside Doctor Bickerstaff's head, but when I went to my appointment the next day I was surprised by how much less intimidating he seemed after my little excursion. When he wheeled me briskly to his room I cared nothing for his smug, sharp-suited façade; I rather thought he must have noticed because he even gave me a curious smile when he took his place opposite me next to the desk.

"You seem very relaxed Catherine," he observed.

"I really do prefer to be called Kit, if you think you can manage it," I answered. It seemed the sight of him, depressed and alone in his navy pyjamas, had done wonders for my confidence.

Bickerstaff almost laughed, haughty and oblivious to the source of my amusement.

"I do hope you'll be putting this newfound spirit of yours into your treatment," he said in his schoolmaster tone.

"We'll see," was my reply.

"I'd like you to try and stand again," he said.

Confidence, I learned then, is a very fragile thing. My sense of superiority flooded away as I remembered the embarrassing display from the last time the doctor had ordered me onto my feet. I thought about refusing to do it, but I had an idea that Bickerstaff was stubborn enough to just keep me there until I did as I was told.

"Do you enjoy seeing me fall over then?" I asked, gripping the arms of my chair as I forced my feet to find the lino floor.

"Not as much as you think I do," he answered. I was annoyed that it wasn't a clear 'No'.

To my surprise he stood up after that and crossed the small gap between us, waiting patiently for my upheaval. Dragging my torso up by the strength of my elbows was just as painful as the last time I had tried it; I felt the familiar burning of the strain as flames of pain seared up and down my arms. I persevered, shifting myself forward forcefully onto my unsteady legs as I had before.

For the briefest of moments, I thought I had done

it. I was standing. But it was just a few seconds of false hope, and this time as my knees gave way the doctor at least had the courtesy to catch me around the waist and drop me back into my chair. I felt the red flush of defeat in my cheeks, turning my face away from him and chiding myself for my own stupidity. I don't know why I thought I could win against him, because every time I fell back into that chair I had lost. And I would always fall back into the chair.

Bickerstaff was writing in his file when I dared to look again. At least I had stopped myself from crying this time. His pen raced across the page he was turned to.

"You're not practising moving around enough," he said without looking up from the page, "Your elbows ought to be stronger."

I bit my lip to resist answering him back. There were a lot of things about my body that I thought ought to be different; I didn't need him pointing them out one by one like they were easy things to fix. No matter how troubled the doctor was in private, at least he could hide it behind his smart suit and smug face. I was troubled for all to see and pity me for it, and so long as I was stuck in this chair that fact was not going to change.

The first few months of life at Ty Gwyn turned into a drab but comforting routine from there on in. I devoted about a quarter of my free time to Doctor Bickerstaff's rotten exercises and my mobility in the chair grew inch by inch until I could wheel from my bedroom door to the edge of the bed unaided. It was about three feet, which was not much use to me or anyone else, but it was enough to shut the rotten doctor up, which meant I had the other three quarters of my time left to train my other, far more important skill.

I went to school with Leighton many times, mentally of course, but his lessons in the winter term were simple things that I had learned years ago and I grew tired of sitting in his mind listening in. I tried to visit Mum's mind plenty more times as the weeks went on, but the psychic journey to London gave me unrelenting headaches for hours after a trip. The headaches did get less the more carefully I focused on the connection between us, but in all truth her growing sense of guilt for our welfare and fears about the war made it hard to stay in her mind for very long.

With my two usual avenues of practice fast becoming useless, I decided that a few other targets around me would be a better use of my time. I deliberately avoided Doctor Bickerstaff for fear that his depression might be catching, but if I could get into his head from over the hill then the inhabitants of Ty Gwyn's farmlands were surely within my grasp. Ness Fach was easy to find; one thought of her huge blue eyes and I was there with her rolling in the stiff winter grass and flinging Dolly across the mud. I was there when her Bampi picked her up by the ankle and told her it was too cold to play outside. I watched the upside down world full of her giggling joy as she was transported back into the house.

J.C. Finn

I tried Blodwyn a few times before I actually got her, my own eagerness to see what little miss perfect got up to in her spare time making me all the more determined. I wasn't surprised to find that she was just as shallow in private as she was in public. Blod spent most of her free time doing and re-doing her hair into different styles from her magazine, trying on clothes and practising dance steps to the radio in her bedroom. I also learned through these little trips that the young farm boys Idrys had taken on for the winter were throwing love letters into her window attached to little stones. She laughed at them all, the boys were only about my age, and wrote things back like 'No chance mochyn' and 'When you start to shave, we'll see'.

I'd be lying to say I didn't envy the attention; the farm boys treated me like a leper at worst and a statue at best, either way I was something to be avoided. But then what chance did I have with a newly-adult Celtic goddess flouncing about the place? The only thing that really surprised me about Blod was that she was, sometimes, actually nice to her sister. In the public parts of the house and when she was doing her chores, Ness was just constantly in Blod's way and consequently was always being shouted at. But when Blod was upstairs having a break Ness quite often wandered into her room uninvited. The first time it happened I expected to feel Blod hit the roof and order the little wanderer out forthwith. But despite the huge age gap between them, Blod was actually quite a good sister when she thought no-one could see. She let Ness put some of her make-up on and let her bounce on her bed to the radio tunes. Sometimes she even sat and talked to her.

When those moments happened I let her mind go, too jealous of the sisterly bond to stay and listen in. I had Leighton, of course, but it wasn't the same. And girl chat made me think of Mum too, for that matter. I had noticed a strange thing on that score whilst I was practising my visits. Out of any of the new minds that I had tried to reach in Bryn Eira Bach, none of them gave me the splitting headaches that I got from reaching Mum in London. I was tired certainly, after every encounter, but there was never so much pain as when I took my mind to hers. I pondered if it could be the distance between us that hurt so much, but the visits I made in half-sleep took me to all sorts of places much farther than London and I never woke up crying from those.

By the time the snow set in and Christmas loomed on the horizon, I felt I was ready for some serious new challenges. Mam had given me a few little chores to do in the house as my arms grew stronger, just polishing things or peeling vegetables before dinner, but I still had more time alone in December than I knew what to do with. Once Leighton was off school things were better and there were no shortage of preparations to be made for a Price family Christmas. Things went especially mad on the 22nd when Mam received a telegram delivered from the village post office.

"Clive and the boys are coming home for Christmas dinner!"

I was most keen to meet RAF Flight Sergeant Clive Price, so when they arrived on the morning of Christmas Eve I gave it my best effort to wheel myself out into the hall before anyone had to fetch me. I was so successful that Mam tripped over me when she came out to wait by the door herself, but she was good natured enough to congratulate me on the effort all the same.

"Oh Doctor Bickerstaff will be pleased with you," she observed.

I didn't care a fig for how the rotten doctor felt; I was just interested in keeping him from causing me trouble.

The door of Ty Gwyn burst open, bringing a flurry of cold, snowy air into the hall that made me shiver all over. The blast let in three tall, strapping figures in smart blue uniforms, the tallest of which slammed the door behind him. Clive's smiling face was red with the morning frost as he took off his blue officer's hat and hung up a huge overcoat that he had been carrying. It was clear that he and his sons hadn't wanted the sight of their uniforms to be obscured as they made their way here. Mam rushed to Clive with an explosion of pride and relief, hugging him repeatedly before it was the turn of her sons to have their bones crushed.

I knew that Thomas was the blonde one and also the eldest child. He had a handsome face with a lot of Blodwyn's features and the same pale blue eyes that ran through the whole family. The other son, two years younger at twenty-two, was Ieuan, which I had learned to say as Yai-yan in the run up to meeting him. He had Idrys's gingery look, but with Clive's long nose and square jaw.

"You must be Kit," Ieuan said when Mam had released him. He shook my hand very gently. "Mam must've written a hundred letters about you and your brother being yur. I feel like I know you already."

"Pleased to meet you Ieuan," I replied with a smile.

There was a lot of bustling as Idrys, Ness and Blod each got their hugs whilst Leighton and I were introduced to the boys. It was a long time before everyone had spoken to everyone and we were all stood frozen in the black and white hall by the time they were all settled again. Clive and the boys were exhausted from their overnight journey across North Wales in the back of a truck, so Mam packed them off to bed each with a cup of tea and a biscuit and set about making a huge welcome home dinner. Idrys tried to put her off since we'd already be having a huge lunch the next day, but she wouldn't be deterred.

I had gotten used to a full table of food at Ty Gwyn, but now that her boys were home I finally understood Mam's tendency to overprovide. Clive, Thomas and Ieuan ate like they had been starving in the desert for weeks on end, consuming everything in their immediate vicinity and then asking for more, which Mam dutifully provided. Leighton seemed very glad to be at my end of the table where his share was safe from them, but as he gave me one of his cheeky looks, his eyes fell to my hands and he frowned.

"What's happened to your skin?" he asked in a whisper.

I looked down, horrified to see a peculiar salmon-coloured rash spreading in blotches over my left hand. I pulled up the sleeve of my jumper to find it was travelling there too. It had happened before, now and then, just small patches, on my leg or on my tummy, but never anywhere that anyone could see, and certainly not on such a scale. Doctor Baxendale had told me it was just something some people got. I shoved my hand under the table, eating with only my fork.

"It's fine," I told Leighton, "Get on with your dinner."

But it wasn't fine, it was hideous. And, worse than that, I was starting to feel very hot in my jumper. Clammy beads of sweat formed under my hair at the nape of my neck, but if I took off the jumper now then someone besides Leighton was sure to notice the rash and make a fuss. It would most likely fade like it had in times gone by, so the last thing I wanted to do was make a spectacle of myself, especially with new people at the table. It had taken the last four months to get used to the first half of the Price family, I didn't want to make an odd impression on the rest.

But the heat grew as dinner went on; I was starting to think it wasn't just the jumper. I could feel sweat behind my knees under the table, even my feet were clammy in my shoes. When I checked under the table, the blotchy pink rash was also on my legs and in the space of fifteen minutes at the table it was suddenly on my right hand too. Mam was so thrilled to have her boys back that she hardly looked at anyone else, that was until I dropped my fork and it went clattering onto the plate loudly.

"Sorry," I said clumsily, my eyes shifting in and out of focus as I tried to find her at the busy table, "Excuse me."

I reached forward for the fork, but when I went to grab it my blotchy hand didn't seem to find the right place.

"What on earth's wrong with her?" Blod demanded. Her voice echoed in my head.

The room was suddenly darker. I wanted to ask who had switched off the lights.

"Oh my God," said Mam somewhere very far away, "Somebody phone the doctor!"

CHAPTER SEVEN

The Jackboots' Echo

The next thing I was aware of was the sight of the black beams of the ceiling in my downstairs bedroom. My eyes flickered open six or seven times before I could get them to actually stay open, so when they did I let them focus on the ceiling for a while as I tried to remember what had happened. I noticed as I lay in the bed that I wasn't wearing my splints, so I shifted my weight around to see if any damage had been done when I presumably collapsed out of my chair at the dinner table. I was still horribly sweaty all over, my limbs were weak and though I could move them it was a terrible strain.

"Ah, good afternoon," said a voice I recognised beside me.

I turned my head too quickly, feeling dizzy and sick. Doctor Bickerstaff. He wasn't wearing his usual doctor's attire, just a woolly jumper and a pair of corduroy trousers. He had a book on his lap and his face was terribly haggard. He looked as tired as I felt and a thick layer of blonde stubble covered his jaw.

Good afternoon, he had said. If I had collapsed on

Christmas Eve, then that could mean only one thing.

"I've ruined their Christmas," I said, my voice tiny and weak. It was too exhausting to be sad; the words came out flat and dry.

"No, they're fine," Bickerstaff said in his proper tone, "They're all downstairs around the wireless waiting for the King's Christmas message. You've only ruined *my* Christmas, and I daresay you'll feel a lot less guilty about that."

"Sorry," I whispered. He was right, but I did feel a little bad for him in spite of everything.

"Don't worry, it wasn't much of one to ruin."

There was no invitation to press the topic any further, but of course I knew that he lived alone without him having to tell me. Bickerstaff put the back of his hand across my forehead and I could feel my damp skin sticking to him.

"Do you feel hot or cold right now?" he asked.

"Cold," I replied, "What's happened to me?"

"Fevers and rashes are not uncommon symptoms for people with your condition," he replied clinically. There was no trace of empathy in his face whatsoever.

"I used to get fevers when I first got sick," I replied. He just nodded. I didn't feel feverish now, just sticky and horrid.

The door to the bedroom opened and Ness Fach ambled in wearing what looked like a new dress. Doctor Bickerstaff turned in his chair to see her. She watched him carefully for a moment, sucking on the hand of her Dolly.

"Hello little one," he said in what he must have thought was a warmer tone. It didn't sound much different to his usual one.

Ness ran away without a word. Bickerstaff's mouth twitched awkwardly a little, and he was about to speak to me again when yet another visitor appeared in the wide doorway.

"Oh she's awake then," Blod said, her look was not relieved in the least, "Mam sent me to see if you wanted another cuppa."

Doctor Bickerstaff stood up and brushed off his jumper, forgetting the book on his lap which dropped to the floor with a thud. His mouth twitched again as he looked at Blod.

"No, no," he stammered. Was he nervous of something? "I daresay Kit'll be up and about by this evening. Her fever's broken, so I'll be going once I've spoken to your mother."

Blod eyed him with the kind of contempt she usually reserved for me, which was a nice change, I'll admit.

"All right then," she said, quickly turning on her perfect heels to sweep away.

Bickerstaff looked at the space where she'd been standing for a moment before he turned back to me. I knew I was giving him what must have been a rather rude, quizzical look, but he chose not to challenge it.

"I'm curious as to what brought this fever on, Kit," he said, his face falling back into its relaxed emotionless template, "Your physical progress isn't good enough to suggest overexertion. Have you strained yourself in any other way?"

"Peeling a potato is a strain in my world, doctor," I answered, "You're going to have to be more specific."

"Well what about mental strain?" he pressed, a glimmer of annoyance hanging on his lip. He wanted to sneer, I was sure of it, but for some reason he was holding it back. "Have you been reading a lot or doing something else that uses your concentration?"

"I have been reading a lot," I lied quickly, "There's not much else to do here." Of course I knew the real answer to his question.

"Well that could be bringing it on," he explained, "A relaxed mind does wonders for one's health, see that you remember that."

I would, if it meant stopping him from invading Ty Gwyn ever again. I watched him pick up his things and go, already formulating a new way to balance my mental training and keep my brain strain-free the rest of the time. The fever had been awful, but now that it was over there was a lesson to be learned and more practice to be done. But first, I remembered, there were a few hours left of my first Welsh Christmas to enjoy.

The New Year brought plenty of nasty shocks with it, including the introduction of rationing, which sat about as well with Mam as the idea of birth control did with the

K.C. Finn

Pope. Mam said that she was terribly grateful that Clive and the boys had been home at the right time before the government had taken control of how much food each household could have, but she couldn't imagine what she would feed them the next time they came for a visit. I felt sad that I had only spent a few hours with them before their scheduled return on Boxing Day, but she assured me they would come again when they could. Leighton was hit almost as hard as Mam by the news that he could no longer have a snack at every hour of the day and night.

"But this is farm isn't it?" he protested, "What you grow and make here should belong to you, not the Prime Minister!"

Idrys fielded the question until Leighton understood the problem of feeding all the soldiers defending us whilst also compensating for the supply chains that had been cut off from some parts of Europe. "This is how we do our part for the war!" he explained proudly, and Leighton seemed happy with that, even if his stomach disagreed.

In the time it took for winter to change into spring I had once again honed my mind-hopping skills to overcome the new obstacles in my path. By staying away from Mum and the painful connection to London I had reduced my raging fevers to nothing but mild sweats, which kept Doctor Bickerstaff away from the house right up until the start of April, when he turned up out of the blue and spent a very long time talking to Mam in the kitchen. I resisted the urge to step into his head and listen to what he was telling her, and I was sincerely glad I had when Mam told me later that I wasn't making enough physical progress and the doctor asked 'could I please try a bit harder when I had the time'. I was certain Doctor Bickerstaff hadn't been that kind in the phrasing of his request.

I could have been annoyed, but the doctor didn't matter to me that day; I had bigger fish to fry. Leighton was at school and the family were going out shopping for a new dress for Blodwyn's birthday. The house was mine for three solid hours uninterrupted. And I was going to try to reach the German soldier at last.

I had been very nervous of trying to reach Germany in my head in case it brought on a fever, but April the 9th had a feeling about it, like the time was right. I felt unusually healthy as I settled myself in the sitting room, pushing the door shut behind me. I could wheel myself much better than what I had shown the doctor, or anyone else, so I put my chair in the centre of the room and turned away from the bright afternoon light in the windows to prepare for the usual routine.

Palms up. Eyes shut. In and out and in and out.

I tried to remember the German's great hairy hands, the billows of smoke from his cigar, the nerves he felt when his commanding officer pointed to the map. Pointed to that jagged coast, that little red dot marked Oslo.

It was a grey day, wherever I was. Great silver clouds hung low in the sky as I looked out into a city through someone else's eyes. It wasn't England; I knew that by the grand old buildings in red brick or cream coloured stone. They were not the slate grey spires of London; there was something much more traditional to their style. The eyes I was looking through belonged to someone standing at a second floor window looking down into a wide boulevard lined with huge green trees.

I had a feeling I had not found the hairy handed German I was in search of, the emotions running through this body were far easier for me to interpret than his had been. The body was quivering against the cold air streaming in from the half-open window, a steady but quickened pulse racing in its veins. One look down revealed a pair of hands wringing together nervously. They were smooth and a little tanned with the lightest dusting of brown hair starting at the wrists, climbing up to two strong arms. A male, for certain, and quite young judging by the lack of blemishes on his skin.

The fearful young man gazed out into the grey street again where I noticed there were very few people out and about. One small clump of pedestrians gathered under the leafy trees, looking expectantly out into the road, which was totally devoid of traffic. They were waiting for something. Somebody spoke in the room I was in and the boy turned his head to glance at the speaker. The room looked like a store room for fabrics and such; it contained a crowd of some two-dozen people who were all craning to see out of the window into the silent street. They muttered nervously in a guttural sounding tongue that I didn't understand. Not German, I decided; my attempt to focus on the specific target had failed.

But I wanted to stay all the same; I had to know

what this foreign mass was waiting for. What did they expect to come down their beautiful boulevard? And why did they await it behind bricks and glass? The boy I inhabited grew more nervous by the minute; I could feel him rubbing his palms together, his keen eyes expanding as he spotted a disturbance at the far end of the street. He pointed, shouting something foreign in a rich, smooth voice. Everyone crowded closer to the tall glass windows for a better view.

A procession of vehicles was traveling slowly down the boulevard from the far left of my field of vision. The first few cars were beautiful creations in glinting silver, open-topped to display a series of military personnel in their full regalia. I recognised the grey-green shade of their dress and the flashes of red on some of their collars. My boy's mind grew suddenly angry. He clenched his fists.

The grand vehicles came to a halt right in the centre of the road almost directly below the building we were in. The remainder of the convoy was made up of covered canvas trucks in varying shades of green that spread out into different positions, including some on the wrong side of the road. Someone in the crowded store room said something that sounded an awful lot like the word 'Nazi'. Other people muttered their anxious replies. My boy nodded his head silently as the canvas trucks began to open one by one.

I saw their shiny black boots first as the soldiers hit the empty pavement pair by pair. They all wore spherical helmets obscuring their heads, making them look like one never-ending line of identical toy soldiers during the disembarkation. They formed precise, tight ranks at once as their commanding officers came to appraise them; they had alighted from their more stylish transports. Where minutes before the grand boulevard had been almost empty, now at least a hundred soldiers convened on its empty roads. The grey-green mass saluted without a word, followed almost instantly by the clicking of a hundred pairs of polished black boot heels. The sound was eerie on the deadly silent street.

Then out of nowhere bursts of colour exploded through the grey. In the middle of every neatly-ordered pack of soldiers came a flash of red fabric, revealed moments later as the standard of the leader under which they marched. The red, white and black of the Nazi flag was raised above every unit as some inhabitants from the very first car fired single shots into the air. They had arrived in this place, perhaps for the first time, and they were keen to make it known. The boy who I occupied let his strong stance deflate, his anger and fear fading off to give way to sorrow. He raised one smooth hand to his temple, rubbing the space above his ear.

"Min elskede Oslo," he whispered.

Oslo! So something had gone right in my practice after all.

"Hvem sa det?" the boy said, looking around him frantically. The rest of the crowd gave him funny looks, some shook their heads. I felt his eyes narrowing in suspicion, his ears pricking as he continued to look around. Had he *heard* me? I focused hard on him and what he was doing. It felt like deep concentration, like listening. He closed his eyes, turning my viewpoint black.

Oslo, I thought again.

He jumped, startled. His eyes flew open and once again he looked around for the source of the voice, but the females in this room were older women who were all staring out at the display on the street. My boy pushed his way through the crowd and out of the room, into a poorly lit corridor with a buzzing electric bulb. I didn't know what to do, but I felt I owed him some kind of explanation. I thought of what my mother would do if she were addressing someone from foreign parts.

Hello, I thought, *Do you speak English?*

The boy let out an audible cry as he scanned the corridor around him. It was totally empty. So now he knew my voice had no body. I didn't know if that was a good or bad thing.

"Some English, yes," he answered. He was more nervous now than when the Nazis had arrived. "Please miss, where are you speaking from?"

That was a loaded question, but I decided on honesty.

Great Britain, I replied.

"But that is impossible," he whispered. I liked his accent, the way he pushed his vowels out of his mouth with stress.

Yes, but it's true.

"Why can the others not hear you?" he asked, his nerves abating a little once more.

I'm afraid I have used your mind to see what's happening in Oslo. It was true enough; he didn't need to know it had happened accidentally.

"You have powers," he began uncertainly, "Synsk... I do not know the English word. But this is very, very impossible."

He understood it better than I thought he would, which told me he had enough sense about him not to think himself mad for hearing voices. He believed that people like me existed, however afraid he might be of the idea. I was about to speak again when that familiar cold shiver started to creep up my spine, the dark little corridor was fading in and out. I panicked, focusing hard to maintain for a few seconds more.

Your name, I demanded, *Please, I have to go, but give me your name. I can find you again with your name.* I clung desperately to Oslo, hoping what I'd just said was true. And then I realised that perhaps he wouldn't want me to find him again. I started to sink away despite my efforts; almost everything in the corridor was gone when one last sound reached my ears.

"Henri."

CHAPTER EIGHT

Henri Haugen

I was too exhausted from the length of the visit to focus on finding Henri again right away. I went to bed that night hoping my mind might take me there anyway, but had no such luck, and the next day there was no peace to be found at all at Ty Gwyn. Mam was intent on mending the impenetrable rift that had built up between Blod and I during my eight months thus far in North Wales; she thought a nice trip to the cinema was the solution. Blod only agreed because my wheelchair meant that she would most likely get a seat right at the front of the picture house.

Unfortunately Mam also made the insane decision to break a piece of bad news to Blod on the way to the cinema, namely that she couldn't have the dress she wanted for her 21st birthday. Blod hit the roof shamelessly as we went down the uneven streets of Bryn Eira Bach, but for all her complaints there simply wasn't enough money in the family to give her what she wanted. Fabric was in short supply and necessary for the war effort, so the few new dresses that remained in Evans the Tailor's window had more than tripled in price since the start of the year. By the time we reached the ticket booth Blod had a face that could summon stormclouds and though we did get our seat at the front of the tiny screening room, she slumped back into her chair, crossed her arms and stared at the screen determinedly even before the reel started to run.

The first thing that popped into life on the screen was a news reel detailing the current state of the war. At first there were some flickering images of our boys in ranks, saluting and waving their sweethearts goodbye. People in the picture house cheered all around me. But the atmosphere dropped into a sombre one as the great black and white screen was overtaken by the Nazi swastika flying high. The narrator of the bulletin erupted into a deeper, darker tone.

"But out in Greater Europe our allies are falling to the great German threat."

Still photographs appeared of people being flung out of their houses by German troops, children crying in the streets and properties smashed and destroyed. Until one image flickered into focus, an image that made me gasp aloud. Oslo. The boulevard that I had been looking down on with its leafy green trees and the lines of soldiers in their big black boots next to the open canvas trucks. Except that now those soldiers were dragging people away, and part of the street in the forefront of the image was smeared with something dark. Blood.

"The occupation of Norway began this week seeing hundreds of innocent residents in the capital city of Oslo taken away. These propaganda photographs released to the European newspapers claim that the Nazis are hounding out traitors and resistors to their cause. The Norwegian government has been overthrown and replaced by…"

I couldn't bear it anymore. I closed my eyes and my mind to the cinema screen. Henri was there in that awful place. He'd have seen the blood on the streets; he might even have been taken away. I had met with him for less than half an hour, but I knew he was a good young man. I considered my state carefully, deciding that I was no longer as tired as I had been in the morning. Perhaps I had rested enough to reach him. Blod was still sulking to my left and Mam was in the chair on the other side of her, engrossed in the newsreel still. I sank back into my wheelchair slowly, putting my head out of their field of vision.

My arms and hands took their usual position as I nervously began to shut out the sounds and sights of the screening. Perhaps if they saw me, they would just think I had a headache, or even that I'd nodded off to sleep. With a nervous, thumping pulse building behind my ears, I took my two deep breaths, thinking hard on the scenes I had just witnessed, the young smooth hands of the boy in the store room. His voice and his name. Henri.

When I opened my eyes I was at a table sewing on a button. Or more precisely Henri was. I recognised the trickle of the nerves down his spine as he tried to concentrate, the sight of his hands filled me with glee. If I had had the physical strength to leap for joy this would have been the moment to do it. I had the found the right mind at the right time for once. I watched him for a few seconds as he continued to attach the button to a man's

76

brown suit, but I couldn't resist the urge to make contact for long.

Hello Henri, I thought.

The young man stabbed himself with the needle as he jumped half out of his skin. He looked up into the same store room he had been in when I saw him last. There were a few other stations for tailoring among the swathes of cloth, but he was alone.

"Hello?" he said aloud, sucking on his now-sore finger.

I'm so sorry, I answered, *I didn't mean to startle you.*

"No harm done," he answered with his finger still at his lips, "I had begun to think you were something in my imagination."

I had to rest my mind before I could come back, I explained, *but they're reporting on the occupation here, I wanted to make sure you were all right.*

"You did?"

Henri felt sort of warm suddenly. I was grateful that he wasn't able to see the blush that might have crept into my cheeks at his words.

I don't know how long we have to speak, I thought, avoiding his question.

"Then tell me your name," Henri prodded, setting down his tailor's tools.

Kit, Kit Cavendish.

"Kit," he repeated in his rich voice.

How old are you? I asked.

"Seventeen," he answered, "And you?"

An awkward moment settled on me. *Well, I'll be sixteen in June.*

"So you're fifteen," he corrected with a laugh hitched in his throat. I could feel his merriment rising slowly.

Where are you? Are you a tailor?

"Something like that," Henri replied. He looked up around the room again to make sure no-one had come in. "I was an apprentice, but all the older men fled north to escape before the invasion, so now I am the only boy left. This is Mr Hoffman's building, the clothing shop is downstairs." He paused a moment, scratching his chin. "Can you see everything I see?"

Yes, I answered, *whatever you look at, I can see it too.*

Everything suddenly went black.

"What can you see now?" Henri asked. I could feel a smile growing on his face.

You've closed your eyes, haven't you? I answered.

He laughed, opening them again. Then he held up his hand in front of his face, still chuckling.

"How many fingers?" he demanded.

Five, four, none, two. I followed his movements and answered as quickly as he made them.

"This is amazing," he remarked, shaking his head. He looked down at himself, revealing a brown waistcoat over a black shirt. "So what am I wearing?" he tested again.

I was about to answer when a sharp banging sound alerted us both. Henri snapped his gaze to the door where we both saw the horrific sight of big black boots kicking it open and marching into the room. A tall man with curly black hair stepped in wearing the German uniform. He had a thick moustache that emphasized his sneering lip as he approached Henri in the centre of the room. A half dozen more soldiers in their circular helmets followed him inside, gathering around the great dark man like a pack of wolves. Henri got to his feet as the German approached; all his merriment from a moment since was gone.

"You speak English, boy?" demanded the German. He was carrying some kind of officer's hat under his arm.

"Yes sir," Henri answered, his usually deep voice quivering a little, "I have a teacher. I am a student of Mr Bavistock."

The sneer turned into a horrid yellow grin under that huge ugly moustache. "Ah yes. He is an Englishman, no?" the German asked. Henri didn't reply; I could feel his muscles tensing. "We are... *talking* with him, at the moment."

I had a pretty good idea of what he meant having seen the awful newsreel. That poor teacher would be one of the people dragged out of their lives by the grey-green uniformed mass of invaders. Henri stood firm, his face reactionless. The German's dark eyes scanned the empty room.

"Who were you talking to just now?" he demanded.

"Nobody sir," Henri stammered, his stoicism starting to fail, "I was practising my English. I always practice out loud when I am alone. It is good for pronunciation." All the words came tumbling out in a nervous mess; I could feel his heart starting to thump in his ears, his blood rushing in anxious circuits to flush into his face. He felt hot suddenly, his breath was sharp.

The officer barked something in German at his men, who then descended on the room, overturning huge piles of fabric, clothes, patterns, even machinery. They hurricaned through the large, empty room in pairs, uprooting everything in sight. Henri spun on the spot as he watched them until his focus came back to their superior. It was then that I noticed the officer's great hairy hands folded in front of him and the clipped cigar perched in his pocket ready to be lit. I recognised them all too well, horrified to look into the ugly, dark face and realise I had been inside the mind attached to it.

"Just a little inspection," the officer explained with a horrible smile, "it is within the law."

"Whose law?" Henri asked. He seemed shocked with himself for even asking it.

"Your law, by next week," the officer answered, "things are about to change around here, Herr...?"

"Haugen," Henri answered, "Henri Haugen."

The officer approached with definite strides of his huge boots. He was at least half a foot taller than Henri, his dark eyes boring down on him. He took Henri's chin in his hairy hand roughly; I felt the force as though he'd grabbed me too. The German's yellow teeth were bared in another wicked grin.

"We could use some boys like you who know their English well," he mused cruelly.

Henri was shaking, but the fire of his anger and

injustice had returned. He took the German's hand away from his face by force, stepping out of his reach and back behind his table.

"I will not help the Nazi swine," he spat.

"You insolent little cur!" The German was instantly enraged, his hairy hands balling into fists as though he might swing for Henri any moment. I feared him, though Henri was now more angry than frightened, but a thought occurred to me as I recalled my previous encounter with the pig-headed officer. He was afraid of someone too.

Quick Henri, say what I say exactly.

"Officer," Henri began as I fed him the words, "I hope you will not consider doing anything outside of your orders here today. I'm sure you weren't ordered to harm civilians. The Generalfeldmarschall might hear of it if you do."

The dark German stopped in his tracks, a flicker of hesitation crossing his furious dark eyes. I knew the man's fear of his general, I had felt his heart thump in his chest just like Henri's and mine did right now.

"Watch your tongue in future, Herr Haugen."

The officer barked at his soldiers again and they stopped their rampage of the store room, leaving everything in a mess as they followed their commander swiftly from the scene. Henri waited several long moments as we listened to them descending the stairs. He went to the window, watching until the little troop of jackboots had marched off into the street, then let out a huge relieved sigh.

"You saved me there," he told me in the empty,

wrecked room, "Sometimes I do not think before I speak."

What you said was very brave, I replied. I felt the heat of pride building in Henri's chest. *But he might have given you a beating for it.*

"Yes," he agreed, "I'll have to learn how to manage with these dogs in command." Henri walked to the smallest of the piles of upturned fabric and began to right them. "I expect Mr Hoffman will be up in a moment to inspect the damage."

I'll go then, I began, feeling the store room start to blur even as I said it.

"But you'll come back?" Henri asked. His voice was level, but there was something much more hopeful in the way he hitched his breath, awaiting my answer.

Of course, I replied. He let out the air he was holding in.

"Good," he answered, smiling, "I might need you to save me again."

I expect you will. The room started to flicker in and out of view. I could feel myself smiling too.

"I'm alone at this time almost every day," Henri offered.

The cold shiver in my back caught my attention and I focused hard for one last moment to feel that smile on his face.

We'll speak soon then, I promised. And suddenly Norway was gone.

"What's wrong with you?" Blod demanded in a whisper as my hands dropped away from my face. She nudged me hard in my shoulder until my eyes refocused and I remembered where I was and what I was supposed to be doing.

"Oh, I had a headache," I answered all too loudly. Someone behind shushed me.

"Oh shut your face," Blod snapped at the disgruntled person before turning back to me, "You've missed half the film. Look don't let Mam see you feeling ill. I'm enjoying this film and I don't want to have to go home 'cause of you."

"Right, sorry," I answered quietly.

Blod went back to looking at the screen, placated. I too turned my attention to it for the first time. It was a war film, something about heroes and romance. A handsome blonde-haired chap in a pilot's uniform was wrapping some girl up in his arms, promising her that he'd return someday. The girl had dark ringlets blowing in the wind. She looked up at him with a loving smile and answered: "Til we meet again".

Somewhere, in the back of my mind, I had a tiny thought that that would have been a good thing to say to Henri.

CHAPTER NINE

The Secret

"Miss Cavendish, please," Doctor Bickerstaff said from the door of his office.

I looked up from the warm little waiting room, noticing immediately that he wasn't coming over to wheel me in. I looked down at my gloved hands and grimaced. This was yet another of his little tests, I knew. I pulled hard on the wheels of my chair until I made it to his door, but there was a bump where the carpet met the lino that I couldn't get over. I struggled determinedly until my skinny biceps burned and tears came unbidden to the corners of my eyes, at which point Bickerstaff rolled his big blue eyes and pushed me over the threshold and up to his desk in a snap.

"Poor progress," he sighed as he came to stand in front of me, "Let's see if your legs are any better than your arms."

He had been checking on me every couple of weeks for improvements and I knew the drill well enough by now. I could set my feet down with a lot more purpose than when I first met the cold, clinical physician, but the part where I had to actually stand on them always ended the same way. I resented the fact that he always had to help me back into my chair when my knees collapsed under the strain. This time I hauled myself up more slowly than before, trying to lock the joints into a stronger position. It was a good idea in theory, except that as soon as I was standing I felt as though my knee caps had been replaced by two nervous jellyfish.

Bickerstaff held out his hands, palms up. "Lean some weight on me," he instructed.

This was new. I took his too-clean hands, happy that he'd have to hold onto the dirty palms of my gloves, and pressed into them.

"Too much," he said immediately, "Take some weight back and try to balance. Don't depend on me."

"I wouldn't," I answered. It took me a moment to realise I'd said it out loud, but Bickerstaff didn't look offended, in fact he was far too preoccupied in looking at my feet to even hear me.

I was still standing. It had been perhaps thirty seconds, which I thought was longer than any of my other attempts, and my feet were planted firm. The jellyfish sensation in my knees was definitely present, but the more pressure I put into Bickerstaff's grip the less I felt the nervous twinge. It didn't feel like they were going to give way for quite some time. I smiled in spite of the vile company and it was just my luck that the doctor chose that moment to look up at my face. He gave me a smug look.

"Shall we try taking a step?" he asked.

I hated his self-satisfied face, but the prospect of

actually walking was too exciting to hide. I swallowed my pride and nodded eagerly, looking down at my own feet. It was a strange perspective to see myself standing upright like that; I was so used to looking at my knees that it was funny to have them out of sight under the flowing pleats of my skirt. Under Bickerstaff's instruction I gently loaded more weight onto one leg than the other, eventually letting one foot come off the ground completely. But before I could use it to step forward the jellyfish feeling in the knee with the weight on it vanished, leaving only the crushing agony of bone hitting bone as it jarred.

I collapsed in an awkward swinging motion, my lifted foot finding nowhere good to land, and suddenly I felt the familiar wave of defeat as the doctor's arms swept around my torso and put me back into the seat of the chair with a little heave. I tried to tell myself that I had made a great stride, that this was serious progress, even if it had still ended with me flailing and landing back in the chair. A dark little voice also told me it was Bickerstaff's fault. He always pushed me too far. He had his nose in his file again immediately, one blonde strand of his hair falling down over his eyes. He pushed it back sharply without looking up from his notes.

"I want you to try standing like that for a few minutes at a time," he instructed. No praise for my progress, as usual. "Lean on a person or a mantelpiece or something."

I didn't bother to say 'Yes, Doctor' because it was quite clear he wasn't listening. Bickerstaff wrote a few things down and then snapped my file shut, checking his appointment list like he always did, ready to call in the next patient whilst I struggled to get my chair out of the way. When he saw the list his brow came down hard over his eyes and to my surprise he actually looked at me.

"Why am I seeing Vanessa?" he asked. It took me a moment to realise he meant Ness Fach. I hadn't heard her full name in months.

"She's bumped her head," I explained, "Mam thought you'd better see it."

Bickerstaff rose from his seat sharply and actually took hold of my chair to wheel me out. He did everything too quickly, like he couldn't wait to get rid of me, swinging his door open and pushing me back out into the waiting room where Blod sat with Ness curled up on her knee.

"Vanessa Price," he said quickly, abandoning me as he waited for Blod to scoop up her sister and follow him into the room.

She went in after him her usual haughty, high-heeled way. His behaviour was too strange to resist. There was no-one else gathered on the second hand chairs of the waiting room and the nice old receptionist was nowhere to be seen, so I closed my eyes and let my hands slowly rise to my face.

I got Bickerstaff immediately, which was both pleasing and awful as I remembered that horrid heavy feeling of being in his mind. I had steered well clear of connecting with him up until now, but as he shut the door of his office there was something new in the mix of depressing sensations in the doctor's head. Fear. He focused on Ness immediately and crouched beside where she sat on Blod's lap, pulling back her tawny strands to see the reddish-purple welt about the size of a shilling on her head.

"When did this happen?" he asked in a breathless tone. I could feel his whole face frowning as Ness tried desperately to wriggle away from his touch. Something sad hit him square in the chest when she turned her head out of his reach.

"Oh yesterday sometime," Blod said without a care, "She's fine, it's just a bloody bump."

"Where were you?" Bickerstaff demanded.

"Doing things," Blod retorted. Bickerstaff was watching her face now as she rolled her eyes at him. I wished I had the courage she did to be so rude to the unpleasant man.

"You should take more responsibility," he ordered.

Blod gave a short laugh. "Ha! You're one to talk."

"I would have," he answered sharply. I could feel him getting hot under his collar, tense and angry in an instant. "If you'd let me."

I was lost suddenly. They were talking about something that they knew about and I didn't.

"Shush!" Blod said quickly, looking down at Ness, who had once again curled into a hedgehog-like ball. "Don't say nothin'. She's repeating everything at the moment like a bloody parrot."

"Bloody," mumbled Ness.

"Especially that," Blod sighed.

I couldn't be sure at first, he was awfully hard to

interpret, but I rather thought Bickerstaff might be smiling a little. His focus went from Blod's beautiful, irritated face back to the little girl.

"I'll get her a plaster and a lolly," he said with a sigh.

"Lolly!"

Ness exclaimed the word suddenly, uncurling to look for the person who had promised her something sweet. And now I knew Bickerstaff was definitely smiling. A tiny spark of some nice feeling cut into his heavy chest, but it seemed like agony for it to stay there, like it was struggling against the crushing weight of sadness that consumed the rest of him. The young doctor went to his desk and retrieved a little yellow lolly and a sticking plaster. He unwrapped both but gave Ness the lolly first, using the time to attach the plaster to the welt on her head before she noticed what he was doing. As she slurped away happily his gaze fell on Blod again, who was looking right at him. Her mean face had fallen away, leaving just her pretty features and a blank, thoughtful look.

"Your hair needs cutting," she said softly. It wasn't a criticism. It wasn't an order. I didn't really know what it was; I had never heard her use that tone of voice before.

Bickerstaff sighed and settled into the chair opposite her. That blonde strand in his face had returned and he pushed it back again slowly. "No time to do it. I've started volunteering at the rationing office," he explained, "But I wish I hadn't now, it's too much bloody work."

"Bloody," Ness said again around her lolly.

"Stop it!" Blod slapped her hand gently, but then she

started to laugh.

The little glimpse of warmth in Bickerstaff's chest spread all over his face. "Do you need anything else for her?" he asked Blod.

Her lovely face stiffened again at that. "I don't need anything from you," she said proudly.

And suddenly the doctor's warmth was gone; it drained off like his very life was leaving his body. He was cold again with an empty chest. Bickerstaff rose so sharply that my head went fuzzy. He brushed himself off and cleared his throat which Blod seemed to take as her cue to leave too. She pushed Ness off her lap briskly.

"Go on, go and find Kit," Blod said, giving her a push.

Bickerstaff was looking at her again, his eyes wide with anticipation. Blod was about to speak, but I knew now that the office's door was opening and Ness would be headed straight for me. I wanted so desperately to hear what Blod was about to say, but as her lips parted I felt an icy shiver hit my spine and I was instantly another ten feet away outside in the waiting room. Ness was already ambling towards me with what was left of her yellow lolly to show me.

I watched her coming closer with her huge blue eyes, looking for the first time at their oval shape. Blod's were more like almonds, just like her mother's, and Clive's eyes were narrow and brown. The only other person I had ever seen with eyes like Ness's was Steven Bickerstaff. Blod emerged from the doctor's office a moment later with a face like fury, and Bickerstaff followed her out to see if his next patient had arrived. I took one last look at him before Blod grabbed my chair angrily and turned me around. I was right. He had Ness's eyes. Or more accurately, she had his.

It was an awful thing to have suspicions running around in my mind. I had half a story, an inkling of what might be going on, but no-one to talk it out with who could confirm or deny what I was thinking. No-one *here*, at least.

When the time came that I was left alone in the sitting room to practice my new physical task I checked my watch, delighted to find it was about the same time Henri had said he would be free. Learning to stand up could wait, my burning questions about Bickerstaff and Ness couldn't. I calmed myself enough to perform the usual movements, searching hard for Henri in the blank, black space between my closed eyes.

Aha!

"Hello Kit," Henri said in what he thought was a casual tone.

Hi Henri.

He was trying to hide the fact that I had startled him again, but of course he didn't know that I could feel what he felt as well as use his eyes. His heart was humming with nerves for a few moments as he set down the suit he was working on.

"So, what's new in England?" he asked in his lovely

rich voice.

I'm actually in Wales, I corrected, *We used to live in London, so we were moved away from danger.*

"We?" he pressed, "Are you with your family?"

With my brother, I answered, *And with a new family who are looking after us.*

"I see," Henri answered. I felt him rubbing his chin, there was a sound like scraping sandpaper and I wondered with a smile if he had stubble. "I am looked after too," he continued, "Mr Hoffman lets me live here on the top floor."

Don't you have family nearby? I asked.

I felt his chest deflate. "No," he said simply, "My parents died some time ago."

I'm so sorry.

"Don't be, it's all right." But it wasn't all right. I knew he was lying by the heavy weight on his heart and the flush I felt creeping into his cheek. "My mother was born in England, you know," he said as if he was still happy with the conversation topic.

Is that why your English is so good? I asked, trying to shift the subject.

"I suppose so," he said in a brighter tone, "but I have my English teacher too."

Bavistock, was it? Henri nodded. I remembered the mention of him in front of the German officer. *What will happen to him?*

Henri's sadness grew again. "I don't know," he replied, "I've hardly been out of the shop since the Nazis arrived. Oslo is not a safe place now."

Let's not think about it, I suggested, *How about you help me with something instead?*

"Oh?" Henri said. I felt one strong eyebrow going up on his face. "What could I possibly help you with?"

I told him everything I had heard in Bickerstaff's head, but then realised that I had to go back and fill in some things about Blod and Mam and our situation. I left out the part about how sad the doctor always felt so that Henri wouldn't know I could sense emotions and I also managed to steer away from any mention of why I myself was acquainted with the good doctor. Whatever mental image Henri had of me, I was pretty certain it wouldn't involve a wheelchair and jellyfish knees and night splints, so I wanted to let him have his own idea. It was surely be better than the truth.

"How old is this doctor?" Henri asked when I had finished my tale.

Late twenties, I think.

"But the little girl's mother, this Mam, she is much older than that, isn't she?"

Exactly, I answered, *and that's why I don't think she's Ness's real mother. I've heard of it before when my mum used to chat with the gossip on our street, some young girl having a baby with no husband and then the mother pretends it's hers instead.*

"It's a big suspicion," Henri mused, rubbing his stubbly chin again, "But you might be right. How can you find out for sure?"

Well, I can hardly ask them, can I? I responded. *Good*

morning Doctor, I say is this your illegitimate daughter? Hi Blod, had any secret pregnancies lately?

Henri burst into laughter at that, wiping at his eyes. "You're very funny Kit," he sighed, "I suppose you'll have to keep your eyes open for more evidence."

I sighed too, though I didn't know if he could hear me.

Look, I think I'll have to go, I must have been here ages telling you all this.

Henri checked his watch, a lovely brass coloured dial that looked very old and expensive.

"Thirty minutes!" he exclaimed, "I'm supposed to have this suit finished by now."

Oops, I said. He laughed again. *Sorry to bore you with all this, by the way.*

"It's not boring," he protested immediately, "Your voice is wonderful."

I was once again grateful that the hundreds of miles between us meant he couldn't see me blush.

I think next time, you can do the talking, I suggested.

"I promise I will," he replied.

CHAPTER TEN

The Painted Star

Clive, Thomas and Ieuan arrived on the back of a lorry during breakfast on Blodwyn's 21st birthday, which sent the young goddess into a flurry of delight. The RAF Flight Sergeant swelled with pride as he hugged his daughter before Mam attacked him with an embrace that covered his uniform in flour and bacon grease. The boys managed to avoid the same scenario by quickly sitting down with the rest of us at the breakfast table. Thomas slipped a brown paper packet out of his top pocket and handed it to Blod, who ripped it open and screamed the place down in delight.

"Chocolate!" she cried like a child. "Oh I haven't had chocolate in forever! Thanks Tom!"

"We brought some for everyone," Ieuan whispered to me with a glimmer in his eye, "But don't tell her yet or she'll sulk."

I just nodded and mouthed a quiet 'thank you'. Mam set about making a whole new round of breakfast out of the meagre rations we had left to support her boys. As Blod went off into excited chatter with Thomas about all her plans for her birthday weekend, Clive sat himself down between Leighton and I at the opposite end of the table. He ruffled Leigh's hair with a big, warm smile.

"And how are you, young man?" he asked in a deep voice.

"The school here's not as boring as the one in London," Leighton explained with a grin.

"Is that so?" Clive asked.

My brother nodded, shuffling right to the edge of his seat to be close to Clive. I realised with a pang that perhaps he was missing Dad, but then we'd both been missing Dad since before the war had even begun. Clive clapped a warm arm around Leigh as he turned to me.

"And you Kit? Mam says that doctor's doing wonders for you, isn't he?"

"Well," I began uncertainly, "He's trying to get me to walk, actually."

"Isn't that wonderful?" Clive said to Leighton, who nodded happily under his arm. The warm Welshman creased his dark eyes with the width of his smile. "I bet you'll be off like a shot by the time I see you next!"

"Do you know when it'll be?" Leighton asked.

Clive shook his head. "No, we're all being sent down London way from next week, training for some big manoeuver." He tapped his free palm on the knee of his navy uniform excitedly. "Us Welsh might finally get to go head on with Jerry at last!"

"Here's hoping," Ieuan added as he began the familiar process of shovelling a truckload of food into his mouth.

Blod's actual birthday was the Friday, so after breakfast Leighton had been carted off to school with a miserable sulk on his face and Blod was released from her chores to go out and about with her father and brothers. There was to be a much bigger celebration for her on the Saturday afternoon when Bampi Idrys would also be able to come, which meant I had to pick up as much of Blod's slack as I could to help Mam get ready for it. Which meant no time alone, no Oslo and no Henri. I went to bed that night doubly miserable, not just because I had spent the day peeling vegetables and mixing batter until my arms burned for the sake of the most ungrateful young woman on the planet, but also because I was worried that Henri might think I wasn't coming back.

I woke unusually early on Saturday morning and lay looking at the ceiling, waiting for either Mam or Leighton to help me up as usual. A glance at the clock told me they were nearly half an hour away from either of them expecting me to wake. For a brief moment I smiled as I considered finding Henri, but it wasn't our arrangement for me to catch him in his pyjamas, however much I'd have liked to know whether Norwegian boys wore striped shirts to bed or not. Instead I raised one arm stiffly to try and wipe my eyes, only to realise I had to combat the wooden splint forcing my elbow straight.

That was the moment I decided to change my

morning ritual for good. I clonked one splinted arm over my waist to reach the other, fumbling blindly until I could unfasten the fabric strap, then released my other arm from the same diabolical contraption. The splints fell with a dull thud to the carpeted floor of my makeshift bedroom. So far, so good, but the harder part was coming next. Digging the heels of my hands down under my back, I pushed with everything I had to sit up. I bit my lip with the strain of it. Bickerstaff was right, my arms weren't strong enough. But the thought of him and his awful smug face spurred something new in me and I withstood the pressure a little longer, giving one final push.

I was up. I scrabbled to grab at my legs in order to stay sitting up, shuffling until I had a little balance. It was strange to be sitting up in bed alone, but I didn't have time to dwell on such a tiny victory. Instead I went straight for the larger, heavier splints flattening my knees out, pulling off the straps that always left little red lines across my legs where they were tight against them. After several months of the hellish treatment my skin had become hardened against the pressure, so it only glowed pink for a short time now in the mornings, gone were the ugly purple bruises of the early days. With some agonising shuffles I got away from the splints and left them lying on the bed, swinging my legs around until they hung off the edge.

The bed was quite a low one and my toes grazed against the thin carpet of the converted sitting room. I pushed my feet out to trace a little line along a frayed part of the material with my toe, considering my next move. My wheelchair was parked below the window some three feet away with just clear space between me and it; there was nothing to take hold of or anything to help me get there, and I didn't fancy crawling on my belly to perhaps only get halfway and be found flailing like a fish by Mam in twenty minutes' time. I slumped, a little defeated, taking a sip of the water she always left at my bedside.

There was a dark, wooden wainscoting running the whole length of the room that came up to nearly the height of my chest and jutted out three or four inches like a little mantelpiece. On the far side of the room, above the fireplace, Mam had propped a few family photographs up on it which she always made Blod come and dust after chapel on Sundays, but on my side it was clear all the way to the wash basin in the corner. I put down my water and stretched to grip it, testing how good a purchase my fingers could get on it. It had a little lip that curled up at the end which seemed very steady to grip. I put both hands on it to test it a little more.

Bickerstaff had wanted me to find something to lean on to practise standing, had he not? I put my feet into the best position I could get and pulled hard on the wainscoting. For a moment I panicked in case it came away in my hand, but the old house was stronger than I was and it took my weight until I was up. I leaned hard on the wall, shuffling my feet like a penguin until they were straight enough to take more bulk. My knees quivered a bit, but they held. This was as far as I'd ever gotten without falling flat on my face and I was actually a bit sad that no-one was in here to see it. I stood there in my nightie leaning on the wall for a few more moments, pondering if the stiffness of my legs in the morning was actually helping me to stay on my feet. Whatever the contributing factor, I was grateful.

The next step was quite literally waiting to be taken. It wasn't that far to the corner really, perhaps about three or four paces for a normal person, surely it wouldn't be too much to bear if I leant on the wall as much as possible? I took a very deep breath and pushed one bare foot sideways a few inches on the thin carpet. I crossed one hand over the other, then brought the remaining hand and foot up to meet them. The ache was considerable, especially in my arms, but the fluttering elation that settled on my chest outweighed it plenty. I had moved on my own, if you didn't count wall, which I wouldn't of course.

I shuffled like a crab closer and closer to the basin, but it was such a slow pace that I began to feel really sorry for snails and tortoises and all the other disastrously slow things that I was currently on par with. By the time I made it to the basin and transferred to leaning on the stand, sweat beads clung to my head and my legs were shaking. I realised how long it must have taken me to get there when I heard the door opening behind me, followed by a sudden joyous whooping that could only mean it was Mam coming in.

"Kit! You're walking love!"

She rushed over to me and put an arm under my torso to keep my back straight; it was only with her warm, solid frame next to me that I realised how much I was shuddering. I turned to her delighted face and let out a sighing smile.

"Well I was awake," I mumbled, "So I thought I'd just sort of… have a go."

She couldn't have missed the quivering wreck I was from the effort, but Mam was wonderful at ignoring things like that. She gave me a little squeeze and then delicately put my chair behind me, settling me back into it with a smile.

"Well you sit yur a minute and I'll fetch some water for you to wash," she said, patting me on the shoulder, "I'll have to watch out eh? You'll be wandering all over the house in no time!"

I sat breathing heavily as she bustled away, my smile so wide it threatened to split my face in half forever.

The news of my independent perambulation spread fast through the contents of Ty Gwyn, which had the unfortunate side effect of totally overshadowing Blod's second day of celebrations. Though Mam was still frantically preparing cake and afternoon snacks for her party, she kept stopping to question me about what we should report to Doctor Bickerstaff and would I need a walking stick and should we get me some new shoes if I was going to be using them properly at last. The mention of brand new shoes sent Blod over the edge; she stampeded upstairs and her radio could be heard blaring down and filling the hall with jangling notes for the duration of the morning.

"Don't mind her," Clive told me with a patient smile, "She'd be more understanding if she had your problems."

My eyes flicked to Ness Fach, who sat on the kitchen floor giggling and playing pat-a-cake with a very patient Leighton. If my suspicions were anywhere near correct, then Blod had enough problems of her own.

I was granted the sanctuary of a free hour in the little sitting room at the front of the house to rest after my big exertion that morning. Mam promised that I could read or do whatever I wanted in peace until Bampi Idrys arrived for Blod's party lunch at two o'clock. 'Whatever I wanted' sounded extremely appealing. As soon as the door was closed I prepared myself for my usual ritual and though my arms were aching I raised them eagerly up to my forehead.

I was confused when I first found Henri, until I realised he had his hands over his face. His vision was blurry and his shoulders were heaving, stunted breaths were hot and ragged where they raged against his fingers. Wherever he was, it was dark and empty. And he was crying.

Henri, what's happened?

For once he wasn't surprised to hear my voice in his head; he had far too many emotions going on inside him for that. He wiped his tears away hurriedly until I could see his vision clearing, uncurling himself from his cramped position. He was in what seemed like a tiny little attic room where everything was brown and grey. The windowless space was lit by a dim lantern sitting on a little box beside the bed he was settled on. Henri sucked in his last sob, wiping his face on an old handkerchief before he replied.

"I'm sorry Kit, I wouldn't have intended for you to see me like this."

Don't be silly, I answered, *We all cry sometimes. I cried yesterday, just because I was sick of peeling vegetables.*

Henri laughed but it was hollow and sad. I could feel him rubbing his palms against his legs; a vein in his neck was throbbing too. He must have been upset for quite some time before I found him.

Whatever's the matter? I pressed.

"I will show you," he answered, shaking out his final tears before dabbing his eyes dry.

Henri rose from the bed and brushed himself down; through his eyes I saw his brown trousers were scuffed and dirty, his shirt un-tucked, his shoes covered in scratches. He walked slowly out of the dark room into the rest of the roof space where a dirty white door was ajar. He pushed it open with the swing of one smooth hand, revealing a dark little wash room with a grey sink.

"I shan't turn on the light," Henri continued, "You'll see me well enough."

Above the worn old sink was a small mirror and, a moment later, there was Henri's reflection. I'd be lying if I said I hadn't been imagining what he might look like, running hundreds of debonair faces through my mind, all foreign and interesting and all terribly handsome. Henri would have been handsome, if not for the huge purple bruises all over his face. Cocoa brown eyes stared out of his damaged face, sad eyes with red rings enclosing them from his crying fit. He had dark hair, almost black, that fell about his face like it was due for a cut, under his fringe on one side was a huge gash that had only recently finished bleeding. It had two poorly-done stitches in it; I shuddered to think he might have done them himself.

"Well? Do you see me?"

Gods Henri, who did this to you?

He laughed that empty, humourless chuckle again.

"Who do you think Kit?" he answered.

Of course I knew who. *But why?* I felt a surge of guilt. *Was it because you threatened that officer?*

Thankfully Henri shook his head, looking straight at himself with a stare so intense I almost forgot he couldn't see me. He had high, arching cheekbones that were almost black in the worst parts of the bruising and his face would have been sharply triangular if not for one part of his jaw that jutted out with swelling.

"His name is Kluger," Henri explained, spitting out the title with such a strong sneer that it hurt his face to pull it, "He's what you would call a captain, I think. But he was never really here for me." He hung his head suddenly and I found myself looking into the old sink and its watermarked rings. "It was Mr Hoffman he was looking for."

The shop owner? I pressed, confused. *Why do the Germans want him?*

Henri let his face rise back into the mirror's path, giving me a sad look with his lovely eyes.

"Can you stay a while?" he asked.

I think so, I replied.

Without another word Henri left the wash room

and made for a little staircase at the end of the dark upstairs corridor. He was indeed in the attic of the large building; his feet found two flights of stairs before I recognised the corridor near the store room where we had had our first conversation. Henri carried on beyond that space, passing some sad looking women who were smoking. They shook their heads when they saw him; I felt one pat him on the shoulder as he passed without acknowledging them, but he didn't stop. Henri didn't stop until he was down in the shop front itself where, like the store room, everything had been overturned.

He surveyed the destruction for the briefest of moments; I had enough time to take in the finest fashions ripped to shreds all over the floor. I saw the brown suit Henri had been finishing; it had been ripped off a model near the till so only half the jacket remained, the other sleeve and lapel lay in torn pieces not too far from it. I could remember so clearly the precision and the concentration Henri felt when he was working on that suit. I was livid at the cruelty of it all, but Henri's awful emptiness swallowed up my rage. He walked quietly through the destroyed shop and out into the street.

I felt his sore face start to sting in the light spring rain that was failing. Henri pushed his unruly hair back against his head, walking the deserted pavement until he turned to face the shop window. The title of the tailor's was in Norwegian, but the name Hoffman was clear enough within the words. Below the title someone had taken a tin of white paint and created a huge six point star. The Star of David. I had seen it a few times in London when we travelled through the posher bits. Another message was daubed underneath it.

Henri, what does that painted bit say?

"Protect yourself; don't buy from Jews," he whispered, "It appeared yesterday morning, then last night they came to take Mr Hoffman for questioning, just like Mr Bavistock."

Your English teacher, I mused, *What became of him, after the questioning?*

"Nobody has seen him since," Henri answered, "The people who go to be questioned... None of them have come back."

I'm so sorry. I felt helpless, totally useless and unbelievably guilty. Here I was, sitting in my cosy little room in North Wales looking forward to cake and party food, whilst people like Henri would be all over Europe mourning the loss of friends they'd known. I couldn't think of anything else to say except to repeat my regret. *Henri, I'm so, so sorry. I just wish I could help.*

"You're here with me," he murmured, "That's something."

And they can't take me away, I added.

Henri pressed his fingers deep into his palms as he stood staring at the painted star. As his vision refocused I saw his full frame, a blurred reflection in the dark window. He was dishevelled, his shoulders hunched and deflated, but he was a broad boy with long arms and legs. His face was too obscured in the window to see his bruises; there was just an outline of his jaw and his ears sticking out a

106

little against his messy hair. I wanted to hold his hand, to tell him that things would be right when England won the war, but I wasn't sure I even knew that to be true.

"When they came to take him today, I fought against them," Henri said softly, "My face is a warning to everyone against supporting a Jew. Hoffman was a charitable person, but his widow is not. I think she will turn me out soon."

Despicable, I seethed, *and after you defended him.*

He shrugged. "I think it's practical. I have made myself an enemy to Kluger now. I would cause her too much trouble if she let me stay."

So what will you do?

"I don't know yet," he replied with a sigh.

I'll come back, Henri. I'll come back every day that I can. It wasn't much to offer, but it was all I had.

"I hope so Kit," he whispered, "I could use a friend right now."

And that's exactly what you've got, I replied.

Henri took us back to his room and I stayed until his clock ran out my hour, letting him run his gambit of abuse about the Germans and the occupation. When he swore he did it in Norwegian for what he called 'gentlemanly reasons', but I agreed with every slur even though I could only guess their meaning. By the end of the time it hurt to let him go, but as I went I felt his aching face break into a smile.

CHAPTER ELEVEN

Caught

The end of Blod's birthday weekend meant saying goodbye to Clive, Thomas and Ieuan, which was a tearful affair for Mam, especially since this time they were actually going to England instead of back to the Welsh coast. With Leighton's help I managed to stand up from my chair to wave them goodbye, watching their tall navy blue figures cut a dash through the muggy spring afternoon as they started the walk to the village. Clive put his arms around his boys' shoulders as they disappeared down the grassy path and Mam turned away with a hanky to her nose. I watched Clive's smart RAF hat until it was totally out of view, hoping with pride that he and the boys would be there to bash the Germans and end this war all the quicker.

I was eager to get back to Henri, but my plans were scuppered when Mam received a telephone call from Doctor Bickerstaff saying he had an appointment free that day. She had sent him a message on Friday about my great excursion to the wash basin and now the rotten doctor wanted to interrupt my life to see it for himself. As much as I was happy to have taken a few steps, there were far more running one hand through his hair that messed up its slick, smart look.

"I suppose Blod told you?" he asked, looking at his desk.

"Of course not," I scoffed, red hot anger making sweat pool at the back of my neck, "She hates me."

Bickerstaff snapped his head up again at that, his brows crashing down to hood his eyes. "Then how do you know?" he pressed.

"That's my business," I said, borrowing the smug smile he usually wore.

The doctor pointed at me wordlessly for a moment then slammed a fist down on his desk that made his pencils rattle off the table. I flinched; my breath was hot and furious still.

"You kids," Bickerstaff spat venomously, "you think you know everything at fifteen, don't you? Think you can control the world around you. Well this kind of behaviour gets people hurt, young lady, I hope you mark that."

I wanted to shout at him, to answer him back with the same poisonous tone he was using, but the heat and the sweat and the pain from leaning on the crutches was suddenly too much. I had been standing for minutes, too many minutes taking all the strain of my tired limbs. I looked down to my aching arms, feeling my face turn clammy with a sheen of hot sweat. My eyes widened in horror at the salmon coloured rash all over my forearm, creeping up under the sleeve of my blouse. I looked down at my unstockinged legs, seeing the same hideous orange-pink blotches breaking out on my feet and ankles.

Bickerstaff was out of his chair and saying something about my face. I felt his arm close around me and heard the heavy wooden crutches fall away, but my vision was turning slowly black. I could smell the clean, soapy scent of the doctor's hands as one came up to feel my head, slipping all over it because I was caked in the salty water rapidly seeping from my skin. I knew for just one moment that the fever had returned before everything went black.

I had a horrible feeling that Doctor Bickerstaff might be sitting at my bedside when I was next conscious, so I was both surprised and relieved to find Bampi Idrys asleep in a chair when I managed to turn over in my bed at Ty Gwyn. The clock face told me it was six, but the light outside would not give way to it being either morning or evening and I had no way of telling what day it was either. The only solution to that would be to wake Idrys, which felt too cruel as I watched the gingery-grey farmer blow a bubble on his sleepy lip. Instead, I shuffled onto my back again and assessed my aching body. My mind felt clear, and though I knew it wasn't a good idea given the fever, I shut my eyes and raised my palms up over my face.

Henri?

Everything was black for a moment before Henri's eyes opened. He was staring up at a cloudy morning sky, the shadow of a pinky-blue hue lurking behind the heavy important things I could be doing, things that I couldn't justify to anyone, unfortunately. We trundled up over the big hill in the doctor's nice white car but all the while I could only think of how pleasant and safe things were in the damp spring climate of Bryn Eira Bach compared to Oslo, where perhaps at this very moment Henri would be walking the streets with his battered face looking for somewhere new to live and work. Alone.

Seething frustration filled me up like a kettle ready to boil by the time I was in Bickerstaff's waiting room. It was always crowded on a Monday with people who had gotten poorly over the weekend and he was late seeing me. Mam didn't ask about my livid expression, I supposed she was used to that kind of drama having raised Blod; she just read her magazine patiently and occasionally showed me what she thought was an interesting photo. I nodded sometimes, biting my lip, until she got into a very animated conversation with another mother figure that had just walked in and finally left me in peace. When Bickerstaff called me in, Mam was still chatting to her friend, but she gave the doctor a respectful nod.

"I'll come in when you're ready, Doctor," she offered.

He nodded curtly like he always did and waited for me to wheel myself into his room. I came at him so fast that the wheels of my chair flew over the bump between the flooring with ease and he had to jolt out of my way unexpectedly. I pulled up to his desk without so much as looking at him.

"I see you're feeling stronger, Kit," he observed flatly.

I didn't answer, since he was never really listening anyway, and I was proved right when he carried on talking. "I have some walking aids that you're going to try and use."

He was off to fetch them without awaiting a response, because there wasn't even a question about having to do as I was told. It was one of the things I resented most of all about my illness, above any of the pain and the inconvenience it brought, the fact that I had to just sit there and put up with the people around me. If there was ever a motivation to learn to walk, it would be that walking was the first step in learning to run away. If I could run away now, I could hide somewhere and find Henri, but instead I was stuck with Bickerstaff and his constantly disappointed expression.

The doctor returned with two tall wooden structures that had grips about a third of the way down and padded rests at the very top of them. They were long, triangular things that ended in a point where they met the floor. Bickerstaff leant them against his desk then offered me his hands.

"Up you get then, chop-chop," he said in that expectant way.

I wished I could have jerked myself up to show him how annoyed I was, but my attempt at a haughty leap only resulted in me failing the first attempt to rise. The second time I took it slower, standing and locking my knees as best I could. I looked down at the floor, colour creeping into my face. I had someone who needed me to be there for him, and here I was performing like a circus monkey instead for the beastliest ringmaster in Christendom.

"This soft part of the crutch rests under your arm," Bickerstaff said, shifting one of the walking aids under my left arm, "Lean on it whilst I get the other."

Soon I had one crutch under each arm propping me up where I stood. I felt like a heavy washing line drooping between the two. Bickerstaff put my gloved hands on the grips where I took hold of them with a vicious tightness; he nodded approval more to himself than to me, standing back and making some space between us.

"Let's see you walk then," he urged, "Use the aids one at a time to help you get your feet forward."

My feet, it turned out, were not the problem. The huge wooden structures were wickedly heavy, heavier even than the splints that bound my limbs at night. I struggled to get the first one forward even a few inches before I brought my foot to meet it, then the other crutch snagged on the lino for ages before I was able to haul it up level. I managed about four of these awkward movements before the pressure under my arms was too much to stand. I felt bolts of electricity shooting down from my shoulder to where my fingers gripped the handles of the wood, my eyes burning with tears from the strain.

"Your arms are still shocking," Bickerstaff snapped, "This really isn't good enough Kit, you'll never strengthen your legs without your arms for support."

He reached for his file like he was just going to leave me standing there in agony. I swallowed the heavy lump in my throat, bit back my tears and let my frustration get the better of me.

"I think you ought to start being a bit nicer to me, Doctor," I began, my breathing sharp.

He laughed at me without looking up. "Oh? Does that mean you're going to start making better progress for me?"

"I know about you," I said, narrowing my eyes on the top of his blonde head.

"Know what exactly?" he asked, still not looking.

"About you and Blod... and Ness."

It was a slow, surreal process when Doctor Bickerstaff next let his big blue eyes meet mine. His face was much younger when he wasn't scowling; his mouth was limp and open slightly as he studied my face. I hoped that the pain of leaning on my crutches was showing, adding to the anger in my burning eyes and gritted teeth. He didn't bother to deny anything, so I knew my suspicions were close enough to the truth.

"You dare to threaten me?" he demanded, leaning his hands hard into the wood of his desk. His mouth contorted back into its usual sneer, but his eyes were too shocked to comply.

"Yes I do," I spat angrily, "because you're a cold, nasty man who's horrible to me. Perhaps this will help you to change." It was satisfying to be the disapproving one in the conversation for once.

Bickerstaff's chest rose and fell a few times as he huffed. He looked at me, then away again, and then back again until eventually he dropped himself into his chair,

running one hand through his hair that messed up its slick, smart look.

"I suppose Blod told you?" he asked, looking at his desk.

"Of course not," I scoffed, red hot anger making sweat pool at the back of my neck, "She hates me."

Bickerstaff snapped his head up again at that, his brows crashing down to hood his eyes. "Then how do you know?" he pressed.

"That's my business," I said, borrowing the smug smile he usually wore.

The doctor pointed at me wordlessly for a moment then slammed a fist down on his desk that made his pencils rattle off the table. I flinched; my breath was hot and furious still.

"You kids," Bickerstaff spat venomously, "you think you know everything at fifteen, don't you? Think you can control the world around you. Well this kind of behaviour gets people hurt, young lady, I hope you mark that."

I wanted to shout at him, to answer him back with the same poisonous tone he was using, but the heat and the sweat and the pain from leaning on the crutches was suddenly too much. I had been standing for minutes, too many minutes taking all the strain of my tired limbs. I looked down to my aching arms, feeling my face turn clammy with a sheen of hot sweat. My eyes widened in horror at the salmon coloured rash all over my forearm, creeping up under the sleeve of my blouse. I looked down at my unstockinged legs, seeing the same hideous orange-

pink blotches breaking out on my feet and ankles.

Bickerstaff was out of his chair and saying something about my face. I felt his arm close around me and heard the heavy wooden crutches fall away, but my vision was turning slowly black. I could smell the clean, soapy scent of the doctor's hands as one came up to feel my head, slipping all over it because I was caked in the salty water rapidly seeping from my skin. I knew for just one moment that the fever had returned before everything went black.

I had a horrible feeling that Doctor Bickerstaff might be sitting at my bedside when I was next conscious, so I was both surprised and relieved to find Bampi Idrys asleep in a chair when I managed to turn over in my bed at Ty Gwyn. The clock face told me it was six, but the light outside would not give way to it being either morning or evening and I had no way of telling what day it was either. The only solution to that would be to wake Idrys, which felt too cruel as I watched the gingery-grey farmer blow a bubble on his sleepy lip. Instead, I shuffled onto my back again and assessed my aching body. My mind felt clear, and though I knew it wasn't a good idea given the fever, I shut my eyes and raised my palms up over my face.

Henri?

Everything was black for a moment before Henri's eyes opened. He was staring up at a cloudy morning sky, the shadow of a pinky-blue hue lurking behind the heavy

K.C. Finn

clouds. He groaned loudly, rubbing his face.

"Kit? Did I hear you?" he whispered.

You were asleep, I said guiltily.

"Of course I was," Henri added, clearing his throat, "It's seven in the morning, and I have no job."

And no home by the looks of it, I observed, *Where on earth are you?*

Henri answered my question as he sat up, showing me a series of great leafy trees, stone paths and benches. He was in a cold, empty park, lying on a hard wooden bench. Henri shivered against the morning breeze as he pulled a big overcoat out from under him and wrapped himself up.

"Thank God it's nearly summertime," he breathed.

What day is it? I asked him.

"Wednesday," he replied, "Do you not know?"

I've been... ill. I've been asleep a lot.

"Are you all right now?" I appreciated the concern in his lovely deep voice.

I'm over the worst of it, I answered, hoping that was true. I still couldn't decide if it was the strain of the crutches or the argument with Bickerstaff that had set me off. Either way I intended to avoid both for as long as possible now. *That suspicion I had about the doctor and Blod and the baby? It was true, by the way. The doctor knows that I know; he's furious about it.*

"You spend a lot of time with this doctor," Henri observed, "I think there's something you're not telling me."

He got up and walked in his scuffed shoes along the stone path, looking out into the park that was slowly filling

115

with people; some of them were soldiers passing through. I thought for a while about what I ought to tell Henri. It felt wrong to keep things from him when I could just invade his head whenever I felt like it. He passed a few people then ducked off the path down to a lovely little pond covered in algae. Henri sat down alone in the reeds, plucking one off and running it between his smooth fingers several times.

All right then, I began, *here's some things you don't know about me. I have reddish-brown hair, blue eyes and very white skin because I'm hardly ever out in the sun. I can't walk. Well, I can walk a tiny bit, but not enough to go out alone. I have to push myself around in a wheelchair.*

"That makes sense," Henri said, surprising me with his casual tone. I didn't feel even a fleck of disappointment in his body that I was crippled up in a chair. "You always seem to be indoors with everything you tell me about. Now I know why." We were silent a moment at the little pond, I felt a cool relief sweeping over me. "This doctor, what does he do for you?"

He's teaching me to walk again... well, maybe. I'm not certain that I can.

"I thought you said he was horrible?" Henri pressed, "That sounds very noble to me."

You haven't met him, I countered. Henri chuckled.

"Your illness," he began in a softer tone, "Does it give you pain?"

Yes. I felt his chest ache right in the centre.

"I'm sorry for that," he whispered.

Me too, I replied, *but it's been more than three years*

now, you get used to some of the pain over time.

Silence fell once more between us. Henri grew nervous, fumbling with the reed in his fingers until it slipped and swayed gently to the ground between his legs. He rubbed the dirty knees of his trousers thoughtfully and then let out a sigh.

"I have decided what to do, now that I've no work to keep me here," he said in a much more shaky tone.

What? I asked impatiently.

"I met some other young men last night," Henri explained, blinking down at the dewy foliage he was sat on, "They're going to escape from the city and travel north into the mountains."

I didn't like the sound of that; surely the icy mountains were far more dangerous than the Germans? *But why?* I asked. *Why would you go north?*

"Because boats have been arranged," Henri answered, his voice now a nervous low whisper, "There are boats to bring men to Scotland, men who want to join the British Army and fight."

You're coming here? I couldn't hide the excitement in my voice, but then I realised the risk in what he was doing. Crossing the North Sea would be a harrowing task, and that was if he made it out of Oslo at all without the Germans catching him. *Henri, isn't this all too dangerous?*

He waved his hand. "Everything is settled. I leave tonight."

117

I stayed as long as I could with Henri before the cold shiver in my spine told me it was time to come back to my own head. He wouldn't explain his escape plan since he was sitting in such a public place, but he told me the time that he was due to leave and I promised I would return to give him courage. It would be the middle of the night here, there was no reason I couldn't do it, even if I knew I'd feel awful the morning after. As I opened my eyes back at Ty Gwyn I was filled with excitement and dread in equal measure. I knew by Henri's watch that it was nearly nine here now, so I didn't bother with the clock.

Idrys was awake and watching me thoughtfully under his bushy brows. It made me jump when I realised he was still there and I winced with the sharp pain that shockwaved through me when I saw him. He scratched his bearded chin at me, smiling but with something serious in his eyes. I tried to rub my eyes, feigning sleep although I had actually been awake for hours.

"You do that a lot, you know," Idrys began, and to my horror he mimicked my motion where I placed my hands over my eyes when I let my mind travel. "I've seen you a few times in the sitting room, doing that, when you think no-one's come in the room." I swallowed dryly, but said nothing. "I asked Leighton about it the other day," the old farmer continued, "but he just told me you get funny headaches."

"I, um," I stammered. I didn't know what to say, the old man was looking at me in a whimsical sort of way, like he had yet more words ready to fall from his lips.

T.C. Finn

"The funny thing is," he added, leaning forward, "I used to know someone else who did that with his hands and his eyes. That fella I was telling you about in the army, the psychic spy."

I felt like Bickerstaff had when I told him what I knew, helpless and shocked and angry that my secret was out. But like the doctor I had no power to deny it; no words would come to find a good excuse. Idrys knew. He already believed that people like me were possible; there was no way I could talk him out of that.

"You moved your lips, you know," he said amusedly, "like you were talking to someone."

"I was," I replied, stunned.

"Who?" Idrys asked.

His old face was kind and curious. A weight that had been resting on me for a very long time suddenly disappeared. I took a very deep breath and told him everything.

CHAPTER TWELVE

The Escape

I stayed sat up in my bed all that day. The horrible Doctor Bickerstaff had not come to see me, but he had commanded three days' rest until the fever was definitely gone. I had slept through one and half of those days already, but Mam insisted on sticking to his word. I wondered if she would be so eager to please him if she knew about him and Blod, but any part of me that wanted to spill the beans on him was overshadowed by how much I cared for Mam. It would surely have broken her heart to know that Ness's father was the surly doctor living just over the hill.

Idrys left after breakfast to sort a few things out with the farm boys, but he promised he would return in the evening to advise me on Henri's escape. He said if I was going to be there, then maybe I could take some old military tips with me and be useful. Being useful to Henri was exactly the plan, so I was keen for him to get back. I tried to sleep a little but I was too worried to really relax even though I needed to build up my strength. I had just about drifted off when a great clattering and slamming of my bedroom door told me that Blod had arrived in her usual carefree style.

"Come on you, lunch," she ordered.

It took my weak limbs a little while to obey me and organise my body back into a sitting position. Blod huffed out her breaths as she stood with my lunch tray, tapping one of her heeled feet to a slow rhythm on the threadbare carpet. The very second that I looked like I was sitting right she dumped the tray over my lap so that soup dribbled out over one edge of the bowl. I righted it quickly, biting back my annoyance as my oh-so-gracious maid turned to go. A wicked thought hit me when she got to the door.

"Blod."

The blonde stopped in her tracks, throwing her head back in my direction with a roll of her eyes. "What now?" she demanded.

"If you had a secret," I began in a low, careful tone, "And someone else found out about it, would you want them to tell you that they knew?"

Blod's face didn't change at all. If I hadn't already known that she did have a secret, her perfect features would have given nothing away. She was much better at playing it cool than Bickerstaff. She looked thoughtfully at the wooden lintel of the door, running her fingers down the doorframe.

"Hmm," she mused, "I suppose if it was something shameful, I'd rather they didn't tell me they knew. It's easier to pretend then, isn't it?"

Blod's bright blue eyes became terribly pensive, focusing hard on the wood and wallpaper near her. I was dangerously close to feeling sorry for her, but I put that down to this being the first real conversation we had ever had.

"What if it wasn't shameful," I offered, "just sort of... unfortunate?"

Her rosy lip stiffened.

"I wouldn't want people feeling sorry for me," she bit the ends off her words as she spoke.

Before I could say anything else she swept her perfect frame from view and I heard her heels totter off down the stony hallway. She had left my door open and a little spring breeze filtered in, cooling my soup. As I ate I began to think that Blod and I weren't all that different sometimes. I knew exactly how awful it was to have people giving you their sympathy all the time, like it was going to be some comfort to me that these healthy, able-bodied people had taken time out of their active lives to take pity on poor sick Kit in her chair. It would be worse for her if people knew about Ness. Poor husbandless Blod and her child.

A shaky, bitter guilt hit my throat as I tried to eat. Perhaps I had made a mistake in threatening Doctor Bickerstaff, but there wasn't much I could do now to put it right except to keep my big mouth shut.

A whole day sat in bed was excruciatingly boring, save for the portion where Leighton came home from school and sat talking to me before dinner. Mam let him stay with me for the meal but I became more and more anxious as I wolfed down an overload of veggies and not much meat. Idrys had not yet returned. I had about five hours before Henri was due to make his escape from Oslo and no advice as yet from the only other person who knew of my gift. Leighton made a crumbly mess all over my covers with bread and I tried my best not to bark at him with my growing irritation.

"You're going potty in here alone, aren't you?" he observed brightly.

"It was bad enough when I was stuck in the chair," I moaned, tapping my knee rapidly, "but this is just awful."

"Mam says you're not allowed out of bed until two o'clock tomorrow exactly," Leighton said, shaking his little head with a smile, "And Doctor B said we shouldn't even talk to you very much until you were better, but Mam said that was going a bit far."

"Humph," was all I replied to that. I knew exactly why Bickerstaff didn't want me conversing with anyone, especially not until my bad temper had abated as much as my fever had. I wouldn't land him in any hot water now of course, for Blod's sake, but there was no reason that *he* had to know that just yet.

Leigh was telling me about his horrid teacher at school when Idrys finally poked his bearded head around the door. He picked my brother up off the bed in his massive arms and deposited him in the doorway with a pat on the head.

"Off you go bach, it's my turn now," he said. Leighton looked at me, shrugged, and went on his way. Idrys closed the door gently. "He's a bit easily led, your brother," he observed, "We'll have to work on that sometime."

The old Welshman settled himself in the chair beside my bed and I shuffled nearer to him, my eyes wide and waiting. Idrys steepled his old hands and leant on them thoughtfully.

"I been thinking Kit," he said slowly, "It's not doing all this psychic stuff that's making you so poorly, is it?"

My eager heart deflated. Wasn't he going to help me?

"No!" I insisted immediately, "No it's that awful Doctor Bickerstaff. He tried to make me walk for ages and it was so difficult."

Well, most of that was true, apart from my overwhelming, seething anger and the fact that we'd been arguing. Idrys considered that for a moment then released his hands with a flick. He broke into a little sigh.

"All right then," he said. Relief swept across my face. "I expect if this boy of yours is trying to get out of the city, he'll have to get past patrols and guards and things. It strikes me the most useful thing you could do is get into the heads of these guards and distract them long enough for him to get past."

I nodded, but with a frown. "That's easier said than done," I admitted, "I'm not exactly known for accuracy of getting into the right head at the right time." I didn't feel quite so confident any more. "But I have been getting better at it," I added quickly.

"Hmm," Idrys mumbled, rubbing his beard, "Maybe you need a little target practice. Why don't you try me?"

"What, right now?" I was a little startled.

The old man smiled. "Unless you've tried me before, of course?"

I laughed. "No, no I haven't. It's just strange for someone to ask me to... jump into their head."

"Well it won't be a new experience for me," Idrys replied, "That fella I knew in the war passed me a few mind messages back in the day. I remember how it works."

It was a strange and awkward experience, but Idrys had that comforting charm that only granddads have, which made it a little easier for me to relax and gather my thoughts. I felt self-conscious as I raised my hands up to cover my face but I tried to push embarrassment aside. I closed my eyes, taking my two deep breaths, and suddenly I was totally disturbed by the sight of myself sitting in my bed. I was right; I looked very peculiar with my hands up like that, but I could see how Leighton would have mistaken me for having a headache if he'd ever caught me that way.

This is so strange, I thought.

Idrys laughed. He felt warm, but a little tense. "Would you prefer it if I looked somewhere else?"

Yes please, I replied.

Idrys flicked his eyes over to the fireplace and I went with him. He folded his hands over his belly.

"Well, you did that well enough," he remarked, "So yur's the thing: can you now go from my head to someone else's? See if you can get to Ness without going back to your own head first."

I'd never thought of doing that before, but it didn't seem too difficult. Except that I couldn't close my eyes again, or raise my hands like I normally would. I was going to have to just concentrate and see if I could get there without any physical moves. I pushed myself away from Idrys and his warm heart, thinking instead of Ness's huge blue eyes, her joyous giggle and her precious Dolly. And I was in the kitchen. I could feel Dolly's hand in Ness's mouth. She looked up just in time to see Blod snatch the rag doll out of her grip. Ness dropped her mouth open in protest.

"Ych a fi!" Blod said, shaking her head. "This thing's dirty bach, you've got to let me wash her now."

I felt Ness's bottom lip quiver. Her little heart was turning hot and her brows were coming down hard into the tantrum of all tantrums, something I did not want to be sitting in her mind to witness. But instead of sinking back into the blackness that would pull me to my own head, I thought with all my strength of Idrys again. He was standing by the fire now, warming his coarse farmer's hands.

I did it! I exclaimed, making him prick up his ears. He looked around and I saw myself on the bed, still entranced. *I went to Ness's head and I came back to yours, without stopping off at my head at all!*

"Smashing," Idrys said, "Then you've got what you need. Now go back to normal so you can save your strength for later."

He was right of course, and when I got back into

my own mind I could feel the toll the new type of journey had taken on my already weak frame. Now I really wished I had been able to sleep better in the daytime. I cradled my tired head and wiped my eyes as Idrys came back to sit beside me.

"I don't know if I can do this," I said quietly, "It might be a lot harder in the dark when the minds belong to strangers. And in Norway too, it's a bit different to two rooms away, isn't it?"

Idrys reached out and patted my shoulder with a smile.

"I don't know a lot about this psychic lark," he said gently, "but I do know a thing or two about life. And life is about belief. If you've got belief in yourself, you've got a chance of doing great things."

I nodded, wanting desperately to believe him. But if life had taught *me* anything so far it was that my body had a habit of ruining all my chances at doing things, great or not. What was there to suggest that it wouldn't let me down now too, when I needed it most? Idrys didn't need psychic powers to sense my hesitance. He gave my shoulder another squeeze.

"This boy Henri, you care about him, don't you?"

"Of course," I said, a tiny smile creeping into my lips, "We're friends. He said he really needs a friend."

"Then you'll do your best for him, won't you?" Idrys pressed. I nodded fiercely. "Then I think you'll do fine. Now sit back and relax and I'll give you the rest of my advice." He let go of my shoulder but I felt all the heavier, laden with the new responsibilities of my gift.

The clock on my bedside table was lit by moonlight as the rest of Ty Gwyn slept. When it was nearing the time that Henri had set, I got to work unstrapping myself from the night splints that Mam had returned to me earlier that night. Nothing would get in the way of this mission; no torturous device from some evil doctor's mind would weaken me when I took my mind to Norway tonight. By the time I'd gotten the wicked things off I was ready to lie back and concentrate hard on finding Henri. I did my best to relax and be comfortable, freeing my body and mind from every distraction.

In moments I could see a damp grassy space in front of me in the dark. The wind howled as Henri shivered and there were many whispered voices around him talking in Norwegian. He was rubbing his hands together and taking furtive glances around at the murmuring group. They were all young men like him; some looked even younger than me, their faces contorted with worry in the dark.

Henri, it's me.

I knew by the jolt of surprise in his heart that he had heard me, but otherwise he didn't so much as flinch. I realised then that he wouldn't be able to just talk to me in English with a dozen other boys around him.

Listen, I have some advice from an old solider. Can you hear me ok?

He nodded very slowly, so slowly that the other boys would probably have thought he was stretching his neck.

Right, I began, trying to remember exactly what Idrys had said, *you should put your socks on outside your shoes so that you make less noise when you're running*.

I felt Henri break into a smile. He whispered in his own language to the other lads as he began to unlace his shoes. Everyone else quickly followed suit.

And rip anything off your clothes that's dangling or loose so it doesn't get caught on fences or wires, I continued.

Henri spoke again to his cohorts as they were taking their socks off. One of them gave him a huge smile and patted Henri on the shoulder. I felt that familiar swell of pride in Henri's chest as he checked his clothes for loose bits.

And this was the most important one, I said, *No lights, not even a cigarette, not even if you think there's no Germans around. There could be sentries anywhere with guns, if they see a light where it ought not to be, they might just shoot for it*.

Idrys had been very specific about that one; he had lost friends in the first war in that way. Henri gulped hard and did his slow nod again before addressing the boys one last time. When they had finished fumbling with their clothes, one of the elder boys took Henri off to the side, crouching with him in the wet grass. The older fellow spoke to him quickly and sharply, pointing with a flat hand off into the darkness. Then he gave him a hard clap on the shoulder and returned to the group, leaving Henri stooped alone in the black night.

What was that about? I pressed.

Henri gulped again. "They said I'm good with ideas, so they want me to distract the guards whilst they start the run."

That didn't sound good. My expert advice from Idrys had made Henri the least likely to get away safely now, but I wasn't prepared to accept that.

You take me to the guards and I'll do the rest, I promised.

There were four large German soldiers standing sentry at the border point the boys had chosen. Painted signs in both German and Norwegian glowed occasionally in the reflection of the soldiers' flashlights as they ambled back and forth aimlessly. They were young men, not much older than the boys trying to escape the city, and they were clearly bored beyond belief of being on guard duty. Henri was laid flat on the wet grass about ten feet from the nearest soldier where the wire fence ended to leave a space for cars to pass through. The most thickset of the four guards was training his flashlight on that gap, staring intently into nothingness whilst the other three smoked and talked.

Choose your moment carefully, I told Henri, my own nerves raging as wildly as his thumping heart, *That big silent guard is about to have a very funny turn.*

"Good luck." Henri mouthed it so quietly I couldn't be sure he'd even said it.

Keep looking at the guard for me.

I focused hard on the quiet man, glancing from his meaty hands gripping the light to his small, piggy eyes cast into shadow. I tried to imagine the mind numbing boredom he was feeling, the sheer pointlessness of standing in the damp, dark night with three other blokes that he probably didn't like very much, judging by the discontented curl on one side of his fat pink lip. I could feel his lip curling, and suddenly I felt terribly hungry. My vision was staring into the gap in the pass, following the beam of the flashlight. My flashlight. In my meaty hand.

Mission accomplished, but the real work was next. My distraction of choice was a tried and tested method; I had done it to Leighton plenty of times when I first got the hang of my gift, back before I realised how cruel it was to frighten my little brother like that. But my childish prank had not been in vain, for now it would give Henri the chance to escape.

Zzzzzzzzzzzzzzzzzzzzzzzzzzzzzzzzzzzzzzzzzz.

I buzzed like a bee, hard and loud and right into the centre of the guard's mind. He jumped immediately as I'd hoped he would, dropping the flashlight. It rolled away leaving the gap in total darkness. The guard fell about wildly grabbing at his ears, batting them with his huge hands as he tried desperately to flush the imaginary creature from his eardrum.

Zzzzzzzzzzzzzzzzzzzzzzzzzzzzzzzzzzzzzzzzzz.

I let my inner child take over, the buzzing grew wilder and louder still. The guard threw his gun off his shoulder and cried out which attracted the attention of the other three men. I grew dizzy as the meaty guard ran around in circles with his hands over his ears, staring at the dark ground. He ran up away from the pass in the opposite direction to Henri, along the fence a little until he turned, crying to his fellow soldiers to help him as he sank to the ground.

Zzzzzzzzzzzzzzzzzzzzzzzzzzzzzzzzzzzzzzz.

He looked up then, jumping up again frantically, and I saw all three of the others racing towards him. The sternest looking of them was shouting at the top of his voice. The other two were in fits of laughter; one of them had even retrieved a camera, but was laughing so much he couldn't focus it. Not one of them still had hold of a flashlight as they crowded around the now-cowering guard I was occupying. My view of the pass was completely obscured, but that meant theirs was too.

Zzzzzzzzzzzzzzzzzzzzzzzzzzzzzzzzzzzzzz.

I let the imaginary bee loose one last time in the meaty guard's mind; he was screaming so loudly that a hundred boys could have run through the pass unnoticed. The stern soldier leant over to grab the distressed guard by the shoulders. He shook us violently, making me feel sick as he dug his hands sharply into the guard's biceps, shouting over the screams to make his orders heard.

I stopped buzzing. The guard took a deep breath, his eyes clouded with water. He was shaking and breathing out ragged sobs. The laughing pair had finally gotten their act together to take an embarrassing photograph of him; the stern one shouted at them both when he saw the flashbulb go off behind his head. I receded gently back from the congealed humiliation building in the guard's stomach, thinking instead of Henri and hoping that he'd taken the right moment to dash by.

When I found him he was streaking across the pitch black fields, glancing behind him to the patrol and the soldiers. Another flash of the camera told me he was already a considerable distance away from them; the bulb was little more than a firefly sized burst. His feet fell heavily into the grass but the socks over his shoes dulled each leap into a tiny thud. I could feel every muscle in his strong body raging as he pressed on in the darkness and slowly I saw the shadowed forms of the rest of the boys running in a pack just ahead of him.

Well? I asked loudly over the sound of Henri's thudding heart. *Did I do all right?*

"You. Were. Amazing," he panted, half laughing and half gasping for air.

The cold shiver I knew only too well began to creep up the back of my spine and though I wanted desperately to stay with Henri until he reached the other lads, I knew my energy was spent.

I have to go, I said sadly, *but I'll come back as soon as I can.*

"Tomorrow," Henri gasped, "Promise me, tomorrow."

Tomorrow, I replied as the feel of his charging heart faded away.

CHAPTER THIRTEEN

Step By Step

Every time I visited Henri in the next few days he made me promise that I would come back tomorrow, which was actually not an easy promise to keep in a house full of unpredictable Welsh women. When Idrys was visiting he helped me to make excuses to get peace and quiet, but when he wasn't there I often had to retire to bed early to be undisturbed, pretending that I was tired or had a headache. Mam was starting to think that I was ill, which could only mean that a visit to beastly Bickerstaff was looming on the horizon and he was the last person I wanted to see. After about a week of visiting Henri for only five or ten minutes at a time I decided enough was enough. There was only one way to get peace from Ty Gwyn, and that was to get out of Ty Gwyn.

I needed to walk. I needed to get as far as the bank of the stream or to one of the trees where I could sit undisturbed and pretend to be taking in the fresh air. I told Henri of the plan early one night when I had feigned tired eyes and escaped to my room.

"I don't want you to hurt yourself," he murmured,

"Didn't you say the strain makes you ill for days?"

He was standing on the side of a large hill looking out at a stunning pink sunset. The lads were making camp every night in some secluded part of the mountains as they moved nearer to their target, but Ol, their self-appointed leader, had told Henri it would be almost the end of May before they could get where they were going. Every time I went to him I saw a new, stunning view from the higher altitudes of Norway and it often made me wonder how much he would miss that kind of beauty when he eventually made it to the rain-drenched shores of Northern Scotland.

We don't know that for sure, I argued, *Bickerstaff pushed me too hard. If I do it at my own pace I might be fine.*

"Or you might not," he added. It was hard to tell what was actual worry and what was just shivering in his chest from the cold evening air.

Have a little faith in me, I said sadly.

Henri put his hands up to his chapped lips and rubbed them gently.

"Since this war began, you are the only thing I've had faith in. Sometimes I still wake up afraid that you're not real."

Perhaps when you make it to Britain I can prove to you that I'm real.

It was a thought I'd been harbouring ever since Henri had told me his plan to get to Scotland. When I wasn't with Henri I often let doubts creep in, like doubts about whether he would ever want to meet me if he did make it across the sea. But, here with him, when he said such meaningful things, it didn't seem quite so impossible to believe that he would.

I felt him smiling even though it cracked his sore lip. "How far will it be from Scotland to North Wales?" he asked. There was no hiding the elation in my voice when I replied.

The huge wooden crutches that Bickerstaff had tried me on had been sitting in the corner of my bedroom ever since the fever. It was a bright warm Sunday after chapel when Idrys wheeled me outside whilst Leighton struggled along with the crutches, dragging their pointed ends across the cobbles of the farmyard. We found a soft patch of grass at the edge of one of the fields; it was a space I knew from my psychic travels, the place where the teenage farm boys threw their love notes up at Blod's window. When I glanced up at the window I saw Ness's little face peeping out at us with interest, thankfully Blod wasn't there to witness my struggling.

"Right, how do we go about this?" Idrys asked, perplexed by the triangular contraptions that Leighton was now trying to keep upright for me. I took them from him and stood them up either side of the chair, gripping the handles tightly.

"Just be ready to catch her if she falls on her bum," Leighton explained. I gave him a wide eyed glare but I couldn't hide my smile. His freckles were coming out in the spring sunshine and I thought the country air had done wonders for his growth. Mum was going to be impressed by both of us when she saw us next, that I'd make sure of.

With a massive heave I got from the chair onto my feet, wobbling for a few moments until I had the cushioned parts of the crutches under each arm to prop me up. I felt like a sagging scarecrow as I straightened up my frame, embarrassment forcing the red flush into my cheeks as I realised how silly I must have looked to my little audience. When I found Leighton's face again he was smiling, but thankfully not laughing. He rolled eagerly on the balls of his feet, clapping his hands together silently.

"Go on then, take a step." I could hear the anticipation hitching his breath.

Dragging the heavy crutches made my progress even slower than it had been when I used the wall of the bedroom to get about, but I walked seven snail-like paces to Idrys before I had to stop and heave out exhausted breaths. My arms were on fire and the jellyfish knees were back but Leigh and Idrys gave me a cheer all the same. The old farmer helped me back into my chair and said that we all deserved a drink and a biscuit, but as he wheeled me inside I waved a finger at him breathlessly.

"Only for half an hour," I heaved, "Then you've got to take me back outside to try again."

We went on like that for days, stepping in and out of the increasingly warm air as April turned to May. When Idrys was busy I managed to persuade Mam to tear herself away from her washing and cooking long enough to make sure I didn't collapse on the grass and when Leighton got home from school he watched me practice inside. At first he stood by the door of the sitting room whilst I walked in case he needed to shout to Mam for help, but I couldn't avoid feeling terribly pleased with myself when he finally plopped himself into a chair, deciding that I wasn't going to fall.

Though I hadn't quite gained independence with my steps, the rests I had to take in between practices were perfect opportunities to wheel off to my room and find Henri. We'd been exchanging stories every day of our progress and though he had trekked scores of miles over sheer hillsides and vast barren plains, my grand total of nineteen steps in a row was still the greatest achievement he had ever heard of. Every day he wanted to know the number of paces I could manage, so every day I pressed myself harder to take that one extra step so as not to disappoint him.

"This boy must be bloody good looking to get you working so hard," Idrys remarked one morning when the step total had reached twenty three.

I was inclined to agree, though I hadn't seen Henri's face at all since the day he'd been beaten up by Kluger and his mob. I found my motivation in the warmth in his chest when I told him of my success and in the wide smile he cracked when he heard me say hello. I needed his praise and his belief in me the same way I needed the crutches: to hold me up, to help me take on the challenge. Without them I could so easily be that tear-soaked little girl again collapsing on the floor of Bickerstaff's office and that was something I definitely never wanted to go back to.

The last day in May was a Friday which always signified Mam putting on a huge family dinner and inviting Bampi Idrys in for the evening. It also meant that Blod would be occupied with the dual tasks of helping Mam cook and supervising Ness whilst Leighton spent most the day at school. I disappeared under the pretence of practising a few careful steps alone in my room, but once I'd wheeled in there I took just four steps from my chair to the bed where I lay back and shut my eyes immediately.

I was surprised to find Henri indoors after so many visits to the beautiful mountainsides he had been traversing. He was in a little wooden room looking into a sink full of soapy water. He sloshed his hands into the sink and brought them up to his face with a tired sigh, obscuring my view as he washed his forehead before moving down to his cheeks. He looked up, but where I had been hoping for a mirror there was just a blank wooden wall that he stared at without focus. He slapped his wet face gently a few times then suddenly shook his whole head, droplets flying everywhere.

Henri you make me feel sick when you do that! I protested.

He jumped, then laughed in quick succession.

"Then you should tell me you're here instead of spying on me," he accused.

He had a point, actually, but I wouldn't let him win. *Oh yes,* I replied, *because feeling you wash your face is terribly exciting.*

"What do you mean 'feeling'?" Henri asked.

Um... In all our recent conversations I had managed not to let that slip yet, though I had often felt as though I ought to let Henri know I could feel everything that he felt. *Well,* I thought uncertainly, *I can feel what you do with your body, almost like it's my own body.*

He pinched his arm hard.

Ow! I cried immediately. He hissed at the pain he'd caused himself. *You didn't have to test it!*

"This isn't good news Kit," Henri mused sadly, "If you're with me and I get hurt, you'll feel it. I don't want you to suffer for me."

I wanted to gulp down my worries. *Are you likely to get hurt?* I asked.

Henri turned his back on the sink quietly as he reached for his shirt and swung it over his shoulders. For a brief moment he looked down to do up his buttons and I saw a flash of his bare chest, but he must have remembered quickly that I was behind his eyes because he looked up again at the wall while he finished getting dressed.

"Well, we've arrived at the place where the boats will come for us," he explained, "This is a small base made up by the Resistance."

When will your boat come? I pressed. He had ignored my last question, but I was too interested in how soon he could get across the sea to pursue it.

140

K.C. Finn

"When the water's right," he said, drawing in a sharp breath, "We just have to be ready to leave as soon as they tell us. It could be any night from now on."

That's brilliant, I exclaimed. He smiled a very small smile.

"Listen to me Kit," he said, his deep voice turning serious, "I don't want you to be there when I cross the water." I made to protest but he carried on talking. "It's going to be cold and dangerous and all kinds of hell to endure. I don't want to be the reason that you feel all that."

But it won't hurt me really, I argued, *I'll just–*

"No," Henri cut me off, shaking his head, "If you come to my mind and you find me on that boat, you leave again right away. And you keep leaving until I am back on land somewhere. If you don't, I won't forgive you."

I hadn't heard him speak this harshly since the night he cursed the Germans when his employer was taken away, and most of that had been in Norwegian. This was his warning to me and he meant it.

"If you care for me at all then you must do what I say," he urged.

He knew more than I did about the dangers on the water, someone had clearly warned him how bad it was going to be. I wanted to tell him to turn back, to not risk it, but now that he had vanished from a city riddled with German soldiers there was little choice left for him but to endure whatever the journey threw at him.

Of course I care for you, I said softly, *I promise I'll stay away until you're safely on this island.*

"Good," he answered quietly. I felt the heavy burden in his chest start to relax. "Well, do we still have time together now, or will you have to go soon?"

I smiled. *I think I'm all right for a while. Everyone's busy here today.*

Henri left the little wooden washroom and made his way down a pitch black corridor, turning instinctively to another tiny, dark room. Once inside he fumbled with a lantern until it came to life, illuminating a little bedroll on the floor. He lay down on it quietly and I felt the hardness of the floor behind his back. It was horribly uncomfortable, but it didn't seem to bother him.

"I've been wondering about your family in London," he said quietly, "Tell me, what does your mother do?"

Mum works in a factory that makes parts for bicycles, I admitted. I felt Henri smiling quietly to himself. *It used to be a tiny little job, but she started working millions of hours there once Dad went away, and now she says the factory's started making parts for aircraft instead.* I felt a sad sort of longing creeping into the back of my head. *That's why she can't get away long enough to come and see us up here, she's working very long hours for the war effort.*

"I think it's good that everyone does their part," Henri mused, "I want to do my part too when I come over."

He meant becoming a soldier, I was sure of it. The thought of Henri going to battle was both awfully brave and utterly terrifying to me.

They won't let you enlist until you're eighteen though, I answered, bringing myself some comfort.

"I know, but my birthday's in August, it's not that far away." He shuffled on the hard floor, resting his head on a rolled up jacket. "So your father is away at the war?"

Um... no. Not exactly.

"What do you mean?" Henri asked.

I hesitated, for a moment before I gave in and told him. *Dad went away about a year before the war started. Mum always says he's working, but we haven't heard a word from him in all this time.*

"I had a friend like that once," Henri began, "His mother told him the same thing."

And where was his dad really? I asked nervously.

Henri bit his lip. "I'm not sure I should say."

Go on, I pressed, *it can't be any worse than what I'm thinking.*

"In prison," Henri answered, "What were you thinking?"

Dead.

I could feel the shock in Henri's broad chest. "You don't really think your father's dead, do you?"

Sometimes, I said sadly, *then sometimes not. It's all so strange. We woke up one morning and he'd just vanished, he never even came to say goodbye to us. Mum just said he had to go, and that was that.*

"I think prison's more likely by the sound of that," Henri said. I felt his own grief matching mine as he gripped the pockets of his trousers tightly, his arms turning stiff. "I would have preferred to hope that my parents were still alive, if I could have."

I didn't want to press him to talk about them and he didn't volunteer any more information, so I tried to ignore the sadness rising within him.

If we were in the same place together, I said gently, *this would be a good moment to give you a hug.*

He broke into a grin as his gaze fixed on the black ceiling. "I have saved up a few hugs for you already," he revealed, "On the condition that you can walk up to me to get them."

A fluttery, wonderful feeling gripped my chest so strongly that I didn't know if it was me or Henri that was feeling it.

I did twenty seven steps last count, I replied, wondering if my voice would quiver in his head.

"Then I'm going to stand thirty paces away and hold my arms out like this," he laughed, pushing his long, strong arms up in front of him in a wide, welcoming gesture, "And you'll have to get to me."

Yours arms will be aching by the time I do, I giggled in reply, *I walk like a snail. A slow snail. A really elderly, slow snail.*

He fell about laughing with such abandon that all thoughts of the war vanished from our heads, so it wasn't until I returned to Ty Gwyn later that I thought again about the boat and the dangers ahead.

CHAPTER FOURTEEN

Sweet Sixteen

Henri and I had a few more precious days where we could chat and laugh together, but the night finally came where I closed my eyes and found him at sea. The thrash of icy waves shocked me so severely that I fell right out of his head and back into my own bed, but the few seconds I'd been with him were enough to tell me that every muscle in his body was straining against the North Sea. I wrestled with myself about going back to him, just to check that he was all right, but I had made a promise to him and it wouldn't be right not to keep it.

I told Idrys about the boat when we were practising my steps outside and he promised me that a good strong boy could make it across the water. Henri was a good strong boy if ever I'd seen one, but I took little comfort in the old Welshman's words. I didn't even need to step into his head; there was something behind his thoughtful eyes that told me he was worried for Henri too. I threw all my efforts into reaching thirty paces, which was about the distance from the edge of the field to the nearest tree, but I got stuck at twenty nine, my energy sapping away until I actually did collapse on the grass.

It had been three days since Henri went to sea when my aching body dropped into the long warm grass, spent from my futile efforts. Twenty nine steps weren't enough to reach him. Nothing was enough to reach him until the beastly sea let him go. Idrys rushed over to me and made to help me up, but I waved him off, looking up at the tree I had almost reached as my eyes began to water. He looked down on me, his bushy brow furrowed in concern.

"Just leave me," I sobbed, "I'm tired of this."

"Don't be daft," he said, crouching down to scoop me up in his hefty arms, "You're doing great, you are. Don't be giving up now eh? Not when you're so close."

I lay limp and upset in his grip as he took me slowly back to my chair, shaking my head.

"Everything'll come right soon," he promised, and I knew he didn't just mean for me.

That night I went to bed feeling sure that Henri's crossing would be over, readying myself to congratulate him on a mission well completed. He'd told me it would take about three days if conditions were good. I suspected that they weren't good from the brief glimpses of the crashing waves and hellish winds I had witnessed when I checked on him, but I was still hopeful that the boat might have kept to its timescale. I settled in my cosy bed trying to ignore the anxious pounding in my chest, focusing on Henri as hard as I could.

Everything was black, like it sometimes was if I had caught him sleeping.

K.C. Finn

Henri? Henri wake up, it's me.

Nothing happened. The world stayed black. I could feel someone breathing, but I couldn't tell if it was him or me. There was no movement of body, no light, no noise.

Henri, I pressed, pushing harder and louder into his head. *Henri please wake up. Please!*

I tried time and again but there was no reply. I came back to my own head to check nothing was wrong with me then tried Henri again, but found myself in the same blackness as before. I panicked then, sitting up in bed and throwing all my splints off with a mighty crash. He was hurt; I just knew it, knocked out or something. I swung myself to the edge of the bed, tears flowing down my face. Or worse still, he was gone. He had warned me about the dangers he would have to face; perhaps this was what he really meant when he said he didn't want me to suffer.

He didn't want me there in case I felt him die.

In spite of any weakness I leapt to my feet, racing on wild limbs to the nearby wash basin to throw up. I hadn't even realised that I had made the walk without aids until after I had spewed my guts out, crying and heaving into the bowl. The door burst open and a second later I felt Mam's warm hands on my shoulders as she guided me to sit and wiped my face. I could hardly communicate with her I was crying so much, which didn't really matter because I couldn't have possibly explained what had made me so upset. When my chest finally finished heaving I began to hear her soothing words.

"There, there, love," Mam said in her sing-song lilt,

"Bad dream was it?"

I just nodded, feeling hollow. I grimaced at the horrid taste in my mouth and Mam fetched me some water. When I tried to sip it my hands shook out of all control.

"Oh dear," Mam said quietly, "I hope you're not getting sick, not with your birthday the day after tomorrow."

I didn't care about my birthday any more, not if I couldn't hear Henri wish me many happy returns.

My sixteenth birthday began with the news that conflict had broken out in North Africa. The wicked war that had engulfed the whole of Europe was expanding to other continents now; I had a horrid feeling that no place on Earth would be left untouched before it was through. It had already gotten to me, that was for sure. I tried in vain the whole morning of the day before to reach Henri again, but every time I sank into the horrific blackness where his mind used to be it only cut away another part of my heart, so that in the end I became terrified to try again, since every visit only cemented my grief at losing him.

Mam still thought I was sick so she was being very tolerant about me crying all the time, tactfully ignoring it in that special way of hers. Idrys tried to take me out to practice my walking but I refused to go, even after he tried to persuade me that Henri was probably just unconscious. He didn't know that for sure, he couldn't possibly know that; I thought it was cruel to give me that kind of hope. In the end he gave up trying and just held my hand quietly for a while as Mam started to prattle on about the arrangements for my celebration.

"Now we'll set up the big tables in the field between yur and the barn, you'll do that Da," she said to Idrys, who just nodded, "And Blod can lay the table up for nine of us."

"Nine?" I said in a broken voice. If I was going to be made to suffer through a birthday garden party, I at least wanted to know the guest list.

"You, me, Bampi, Leighton, Blod, Ness, the two farm boys," Mam began, hesitating a moment, "and Doctor Bickerstaff."

"Doctor Bickerstaff?" I spat with rage. There could only have been one way to make my life worse right now and Mam had gone and done it. "Why on earth is he coming to my birthday party?"

"Nawr te," Mam warned with a patient finger, "I know you don't like him but he's done wonders for you, and I want to say thank you to him."

I couldn't think of anything worse than sitting at a table full of laughing, joking people when I felt like my whole world had fallen into a gaping pit. Idrys had a hopefulness that I just couldn't accept, so he was no help when all I wanted, no needed, to do was to be alone and think through the facts. I consoled myself at least that Doctor Bickerstaff would not be smiling and laughing at my party, in fact it would probably be just as much of a torture for him to attend as it was for me to have him there. He'd be sharing my misery, whether he knew it or not, and he'd probably spend the whole afternoon terrified that I'd let something slip about his secret to Mam. It was comforting to fix on his misery for a bit instead of my own, however selfish it made me feel, but then I tried my best to involve myself in setting up for the party in the hope that if I got really busy I might just be able to push my grief right out of my head for the rest of the day.

When the time came to sit at the head of the birthday table I had failed miserably in my attempt to not think about Henri. I plastered half a smile to my face as Idrys's two farm boys came to sit down, their mouths hanging open as they stared at the beautiful food Mam had prepared in my honour. I tried to appreciate it all but it was so hard to unearth any spark of joy within me, so instead I just took a sandwich and ate quietly as the table gradually filled up with the rest of our little family. The farm boys' mouths dropped once again at the arrival of Blod, apparently even more delicious than the party food.

I was surprised at how much she'd gone to town to dress up, especially considering it was for my party. She looked stunning in a little yellow dress that I knew she had made from an old pair of curtains a few weeks ago, all long legs and flowing blonde tresses as she came and sat on my left hand side at the table. She gave me a smile that felt as forced as the one on my own face, which I didn't really mind. I felt a lot less obligated to be happy and chatty with her sat beside me than anyone else; I could get on with my snacks in peace, willing the clock to run out so I could get back to my room and let my real feelings out again.

Bickerstaff was so late arriving that I'd actually convinced myself he wasn't coming. It was funny to see him out of his usual doctor-wear; he was dressed in a smart suit, too clean for a party in a field, with a crisp bottle green shirt and a stunning white tie. As he approached the table and shook hands with Idrys I heard Blod gulping down water beside me like a starved camel. Her eyes were fixed on him for quite some time before she realised I was watching her. The young doctor settled himself as far away from us as possible at the other end of the table and accepted a small beer as he enquired with one of the farm boys after his father's health.

"Well, now we're all yur," Mam began, rubbing her hands together excitedly, "How about some cake?"

Leighton and Ness cheered simultaneously; I envied their blissful ignorance to the horrible world around them. As Mam took some matches and started to light the candles of my cake, she smiled so warmly at me that for a moment I felt like things might get better again after all.

"Aw, sweet sixteen eh?" she said proudly.

"And never been kissed," Blod added. It didn't sound unkind, but I knew how she meant it by the glitter in her shiny eyes.

"Unlike you eh Blod?" said one of the farm boys, setting them both off into sniggers.

Bickerstaff choked on his beer, slapping his chest

hard to sort himself out. He caught my eye down the long table with a guilty look until Mam put the cake down in front of me, blocking his stare.

"Right, all together now," Mam said, holding up her fingers like a conductor, "And we're doing it the Welsh way remember. One, two, three:"

"Penblwydd hapus I chi, Penblwydd hapus I chi, Penblwydd hapus I Kit, Penblwydd hapus I chi."

Even Leighton had learnt it the Welsh way and it did make me break out into the first genuine smile of the afternoon, especially since Ness climbed up and stood on the table to belt out the last line at the top of her little lungs. Bickerstaff was mouthing the words, though I couldn't hear his voice, watching the little girl carefully in case he needed to leap up and catch her if she fell. I blew out my candles without making a wish. The partygoers broke into applause and hip-hip-hoorays afterwards, but when the clapping died out I caught myself thinking about Henri once again.

I looked away from the happy scene, feeling like my throat was going to close up, only to notice a figure I hadn't seen for a long time coming towards us through the old farm buildings. Officer Lewis, the local policeman, was ambling carefully over the cobbles and waving to get our attention. I tapped Blod's arm and made her turn to see Lewis in the hope that her usual loudmouth style wouldn't let me down. And it didn't.

"All right there officer?" she bellowed, rising from the table to return his gesture, "What's going on mun?"

"Idrys!" he shouted in his thick-as-gravy accent,

"Yoo hoo! Mr Pengelly!"

Idrys eventually heard him and rose from the party table, his wide strides taking him to the officer before he was in earshot. They had a very animated conversation which all of the people at the table were watching, until Mam decided we were all being terribly rude and told us to get on with eating our cake. I did as I was told but my eyes kept flicking over to where the two men stood. Idrys caught my gaze a few times; he kept turning his head back in my direction as Lewis was talking to him. Eventually he nodded and the two men started off towards the front of the house.

"Where you goin' Da?" Mam called.

"Be right back," Idrys answered with a wave.

The table fell into an awkward silence, an atmosphere so dead that I could hear every individual at the table chewing on their cake and swigging their drinks.

"So Doctor," said Mam, desperate to break the quiet, "Have you heard about Kit's walking? Da said he's phoned you a few times. She's coming on well, isn't she?"

Idrys had been phoning Bickerstaff about me? I felt a little betrayed and vowed to have that out with him when he was done with Lewis.

"Apparently so," the doctor replied like he didn't believe a word of it, "She's due for a formal review next week, so-"

"You shouldn't talk about her like she's not even here," Blod butted in bitterly, "It's just bloody rude, that is."

"Bloody!" Ness shouted gleefully, making Leighton

and the farm boys giggle.

"What's rude," Mam said irately, "Is you butting into other people's conversations, young lady."

I was put out at that, because Blod might have actually just done the only nice thing she'd ever done for me, and now she was being punished for it.

"I'm not a child, you know," she bit back at her mother. I wanted to stand up for her, but I didn't know what to say.

"All the more reason not to behave like one then," Mam answered sternly. There was a look in her eyes that told us all the conversation was over.

Bickerstaff drained his drink and cleared his throat to cut the tension. "As I was saying, I'll be able to make a proper assessment on *your* progress with the crutches on Monday, Kit, if that's agreeable for *you?*"

He was talking to me, not Mam. Blod had won the argument after all. I nodded politely to him.

"That's fine. Thank you doctor," I replied.

During the exchange, Idrys had returned but Lewis hadn't. Instead of going back to his seat at the table the old farmer came to my side and picked up my crutches, putting them across my lap. He took the handles of my wheelchair and began to pull me away from my place.

"Here what you doing?" Mam asked, half a smile on her lips.

"It's a secret birthday present," he said, his deep throaty voice filled with glee, "So keep your noses out, all of you."

"I never got a secret present!" Blod moaned.

"And you never will with that attitude," her Bampi replied, turning my chair so I couldn't see any of them anymore. "I'll bring her back in a minute, you lot stay put."

When we were far enough from the table to be out of earshot I demanded to know what was going on, but Idrys just chuckled and kept quiet. It wasn't until he had wheeled me back into the black and white hall of Ty Gwyn that he spoke again. He rounded my chair and crouched down, putting a hand on my knee with a wide, old smile.

"Did you make a wish on that cake?" he asked.

"No," I said, my brows tightening in confusion.

"Well you should've," Idrys beamed, "'Cause it's come true."

He left me outside the door to the small sitting room but pointed to it, like whatever he had planned was waiting right inside. I could hear Officer Lewis in there talking his head off about something ridiculous, like there was someone else with him to hear it all. I got up onto my crutches and approached the door slowly, knocking it with a kick of my foot. Lewis came to open it with his familiar grin.

"Wow Kit, you're looking well!" he exclaimed. "On your feet and everything!"

"Well I'm just-"

I forgot everything that I was about to say as the door swung fully open. Sitting by the fireplace in Idrys's usual chair was a boy with messy hair, both brown and black. He looked like he was wearing someone else's clothes; they

were a little too tight on his tall, long-limbed frame, the
trousers rising an inch too high above his shoes and socks.
He had high cheekbones and ears that stuck out a little, he
was rubbing one of them with a smooth hand as he turned
at the sound of my name.

"Henri!"

"Oh, so you *do* know each other!" Officer Lewis said,
oblivious to what was going on between us. "This young
man claims to be related to you, Miss Cavendish. Is he
right?"

I nodded fiercely, unable to say anything else. He
was all kinds of right. Henri rose out of the chair to his
full height; he had a good few inches on me even with the
crutches holding me up. He smiled with straight teeth and
chapped lips, rubbing his stubbly, chiselled jaw like he was
as dumbstruck as me. All I could fix on were his eyes the
colour of chocolate, those eyes I'd been looking through for
the last ten weeks. And now they were finally looking at me.

"They're very distant cousins," Idrys explained from
the door, "Best leave them to a reunion Lewis, they haven't
seen each other for... well for ages."

I just about managed to say goodbye to Lewis as he
doffed his helmet and left. Idrys gave me a knowing look
as he too exited, shutting the sitting room door behind him.
Then it was just us. Me and Henri and the fading teatime
sun outside the window. My arms began to shake under my
weight against the crutches and Henri took a step forward,
reaching out for me.

"Do you need to sit down?" he asked, his rich voice

K.C. Finn

shaking as much as my body was.

"That'd be a good start," I replied.

CHAPTER FIFTEEN

Home Truths

"I thought you were dead," I mumbled, "I tried to reach you and it was all just black, just nothing."

"We crashed on the rocks when we came ashore," Henri said, taking my shaking hand in both of his, "I was unconscious for a long time, up until last night. As soon as I woke up, I told them to put me on the train here."

"You must be so tired," I said, gazing at his strong, smooth hands clasping mine, hardly daring to believe I could really feel them there.

"Not any more," he said with a nervous laugh.

We were sitting together on the old sofa, which was very strange for me. The only chair I was used to sitting in always had wheels on, so leaning back into the cracked leather and feeling it under my legs was all very new. As was holding hands with a boy. And not just any boy at that.

"So you lied to them? Pretended we were related?"

I looked at Henri's face again, watching his warm smile and his sharp jaw as he sucked in his cheeks thoughtfully.

"Well how else was I going to find you?" he said

158

with a happy shrug. "The home guard in Scotland tracked down your evacuation home and gave me some train fare. I think it was cheaper than feeding me there, they had enough problems with the other boys that made it across."

"That made it?" I asked, feeling his grip on my hand tighten a little. "Did some of them... not?"

Henri nodded solemnly, his smile fading off. "I was very lucky," he whispered, "We lost half our own boat one night in a storm. It was a miracle the whole thing didn't capsize."

Without any warning I burst into tears, the culmination of two days of frantic worry and despair exploding in a fit of pure relief. I threw my arms around Henri so fiercely that he fell back against the sofa, cradling my head against his chest as I tried desperately to stop sobbing and looking like such an idiot in front of him. He stroked my hair gently with one hand, I felt the other hand hovering at my waist, like he didn't know if it was okay to hold me there or not, but eventually he put both arms around my shoulders instead.

"It's okay Kit, I'm safe now," he soothed, "I'm here now."

"It's hard to believe you're really here," I sniffed, drying my eyes as I listened to the familiar thump of his heart.

"Imagine how strange it is for me," he exclaimed, "knowing now that the voice in my head has a body and a face!" I looked up at him, laughing as he smiled down at me. "And a very pretty face, too," he added shyly, his brown eyes glittering. His heart rate quickened where I was leaning over it. I was about six inches from his lips.

There came a knock at the door and I sat up as sharply as my weak form would let me, drying my eyes just before Mam and Idrys came in. Henri stood up immediately and bowed his head politely to them both, but Mam was upon him in moments with one of her bone-crushing embraces. She kissed both his cheeks until he started to blush, holding his lovely face up for appraisal.

"Welcome young man, Da's told me everything about you!" she said.

Idrys, who was standing behind her, shook his head to us both as if to say 'Not everything, obviously'.

Idrys suggested that Henri could stay with him at the cottage across the pasture and help out on the farm, an idea that Henri and I were elated with. He came out to enjoy the rest of my birthday party, introduced to the assembled people as 'Cousin Henri', my extremely distant relation, who had just made the amazing journey across the North Sea, escaping the clutches of the Nazi swine like the hero that he was. Mam enjoyed embellishing the thrilling tale from the bare bones that Idrys had given her and Henri couldn't get a word in edgeways to correct any of the details, so the contents of my party were all terribly impressed with him despite the fact that he was rather shy of actually talking at length with any of them.

The only person who made it quite obvious that he disliked Henri was Leighton, which was terribly out of character for my little brother. Leigh was usually the first to want to make a new friend, but every time I looked at him he was giving Henri these nasty little sideways looks, most especially when Henri spoke to me or even just smiled in my direction. I tried not to waste much time worrying about Leighton when I could spend it returning Henri's smiles and conversation. He was very softly spoken compared to the loud Welsh contingent all around us, but his deep smooth voice was easy to pick out in the din.

"I'm not sure I'm going to be much good on a farm," he admitted, biting his lower lip. He had a little piece of cake stuck to it that I wanted to sort out, but the table was too wide to reach him. "I only know how to measure and cut."

"Idrys knows all that," I said quietly, "he's not going to expect miracles."

"So... he knows everything?" Henri's brown eyes were dark and round with interest.

I nodded gently. "More or less. I didn't mean to tell him, but it's turned out really well to have someone to help me."

"To help us," Henri corrected, "I don't think your policeman would have let me in if not for his influence."

We were leaning very close to each other over the table to talk in such low tones and a loud spluttering from Leigh's direction startled me backwards. I looked at him, panicked in case he was choking on cake, but all he did was

161

give Henri another of those rotten looks. I was about to tell Henri to take no notice when Doctor Bickerstaff rose from the far end of the table. He was looking straight over our heads, blue eyes flickering to Blod for just a moment as he set down his napkin.

"Excuse me a moment," he mumbled as he stalked off toward the house.

It was only a few seconds later that Blod started clattering about between Henri and me, collecting our plates despite the fact that we still had cake left on them. I gave her a knowing look and she scowled at me shamelessly.

"Well I'm going to get these washed up," Blod said all too loudly, "Since I'm everyone's bloody slave and it'll be me that's still doing them at midnight otherwise." Her complaints didn't have their usual confidence and her walk had less of its carefree sway as she too approached Ty Gwyn. Henri craned his neck to watch her go before turning back to me.

"It's not impossible to imagine them together," he whispered, shifting and sitting in Blod's space so that he was beside my wheelchair, "The little girl is the image of him."

I nodded quietly, but I wasn't really thinking about Bickerstaff and Blod. Henri was so close I could smell the freshness of his borrowed shirt. He leant casually on the armrest of my chair, the soft brown hairs on his forearm brushing against my much paler limb. I watched him rubbing his palm with his fingertips; a trait I knew was always accompanied by the prickle of nerves in his spine.

He smiled at me again when I had taken far too long to reply and I couldn't help the toothy grin that escaped. I wanted to giggle, even though he hadn't said anything remotely funny. There was something sparkling deep in his big brown eyes, like he too was in on the joke.

"Ouch!"

A bowl-cut hair style banged into my elbow as Leighton forced himself into the total lack of space between Henri and me. I rubbed my arm and curled my lip at him.

"What are you doing?" I snapped.

Leigh feigned complete innocence. "It's a bit chilly now," he suggested, "I thought you might want to go inside."

"No thank you," I said through gritted teeth.

"But you look cold," Leigh insisted, "I could wheel you."

"If I want to go inside I'll ask Henri to wheel me," I insisted.

But my brother wouldn't be put off. He put all his strength into pulling my chair back from the table and took me about ten feet away where we couldn't be heard. His little freckled face was livid.

"Look, I don't remember any Cousin Henri, Kit," he whispered viciously, "I'm not stupid you know; I want to know what's going on."

"He's come from a terrible place crawling with Nazis, Leigh," I pleaded, "Telling them he's family is the best way to protect him."

"But how do you know him?" Leighton pressed, his little hands balled into fists. "He's all... close to you. It's weird. Boys don't do that to you, Kit."

I didn't need reminding of that, but Leigh was all too happy to point out my total lack of a social life, especially where any admirers might have been concerned. When I'd started at grammar school there used to be a lot of boys who liked to talk to me at the gate at lunch, but that was before I started to walk funny and become known as 'the girl with the pink rash'. I was trying to appreciate Leighton's protectiveness, but frankly he was getting in the way of the precious time I had with Henri before Idrys decided to go home for the evening.

"We were pen friends," I lied irately, "We know a lot about each other, that's why he's so friendly. Now will you please take me back over there?" My brother's rosy lip fell into a frown as he grabbed the chair handles and started to obey me. "And whatever you do, don't tell anybody that we're not really related to him," I chided in a perfect imitation of Mum.

"Oops," Leigh said quietly.

"What?" I demanded, "What have you said?"

"Nothing much," he mumbled, leaning in near my ear, "But Doctor B asked me about Henri… and I think I said that I didn't remember him."

I said nothing else to Leigh as he brought me back to the table and he skulked off back to his place with his head down low. Henri watched him go with a sympathetic sort of look.

"Is everything all right?" he asked, turning back to me.

I nodded, but he must have already seen the worry on my face. Henri rested his smooth hand on top of mine and I couldn't help but smile as his warmth crept through my skin. Leighton was right, actually, I was getting cold, but if that meant Henri was going to warm my hand up then I wouldn't complain. But Henri snatched his hand away again as a loud cough caught us both by surprise.

"You're in my seat," Blod snarled.

Henri jumped away quickly with an apology as the blonde goddess threw herself down hard onto the chair. She too was shivering, though I was sure it wasn't just from the cold.

"Where's Bickerstaff?" I asked her gently.

A tear was gathering in one corner of her eye. She pushed it away violently.

"He's gone home," she whispered, her voice cracking.

I offered Blod the chance to talk to me that night but all I got in return was the usual abuse and a very clear message that her life was none of my business, thank you very much. I was therefore terribly surprised to find her waking me up the next morning. Blod didn't really wait for me to stir before she started to remove the night splints from my elbows; I came around fully when she was sorting out the ones on my knees.

"Why are you doing this?" I mumbled sleepily, "Mam usually-"

"Oh bugger Mam," she said quietly, "Come on, I said I'd take you out for a walk before breakfast. Hurry up and get a wash."

Blod gave me barely ten minutes to get sorted before she was back in the makeshift bedroom, rushing me into my shoes and grabbing my crutches and chair. I decided against questioning her any further until we were out in my usual practice space behind her bedroom window. It was a still, silent morning, so silent that I slowly realised we were awake and the rest of the house wasn't. Blod got me up onto my crutches at the edge of the grass.

"How far d'you usually go?" she pressed.

"Almost to that tree," I replied, and without another word we were off.

She let me do my first three, slow steps before she started to speak, all the while focused on my feet padding hard into the dewy grass.

"I don't want your opinion, right?" Blod began, half vicious and half afraid, "But I've been going mad about this all night, I've got to tell someone, and it's only you that knows what's going on."

I said nothing, finding it hard to focus on my balance at the same time as her words.

"Steven's told me that you know about us," Blod said, her low tone suggesting that she would even be afraid for the clouds to hear us talking, "I don't want to know how you worked it out; I 'spect you see a lot just sitting in that chair when no-one's looking at you."

I had never given Blod any credit for thinking about

me as a person rather than a hindrance and that annoying urge to feel sorry for her was slowly returning as I carried on my snail-pace trek.

"But he went mad at me in the kitchen last night," Blod continued, "He's worried that if you worked it out then I must be giving off hints or something. He's got a rotten temper."

"Well so have you," I muttered, instantly regretting that I'd let the comment slip.

Fortunately Blod gave off a tiny laugh. "Well yeah, he wound me up all right. I slapped him in the face actually. Just a bit, you know, but it left a mark and that's why he had to go home."

"That's one way to get rid of him," I supposed. Blod laughed again, this time brighter still. "Personally," I said gingerly, "I don't know why you ever got involved with him in the first place. Did he used to be nicer?"

"Oh God no," Blod answered with a half-smile, "He's always been moody. When he first came to the village all the girls fancied him, thought he was mysterious, you know?" I was surprised to feel her holding my shoulder steady as I struggled on towards the tree. "But most of them got fed up after a while; he was too temperamental for them. But not for me."

I could well believe it. Bickerstaff had the same hot-headedness as Blod, the same selective deafness, even the same wicked smirk when he knew he was in the right about things. They were peas in a pod, no mistaking it.

"The problem was I lied to him, see, about my age,"

Blod said, her golden hair falling down so I couldn't see her face, "Nine years is a big age gap, init? I thought if I added a couple of years on, he might be interested in me."

"And clearly he was," I added awkwardly, "What I don't understand is how it all went so wrong after... well, when you found out you were having Ness."

"Steven wanted to do it all proper like," Blod explained, "Especially when I told him my real age. He wanted to marry me, make it right."

"Why on Earth didn't you let him?" I asked in disbelief.

I stopped, realising we had reached the base of the tree. Blod turned on me, her angelic face hard and serious. Her blue eyes cut into me like diamonds.

"If he had, everyone would have known the reason why, especially with Ness coming along just four months later. They would have all said I'd trapped him." Blod's expression grew fiercer, her eyes both angry and sad. "I didn't want people to think I was that kind of girl." Blod took one of my crutches away as she helped me sit down on the grass. "Mam told everyone I'd gone to secretarial school until after the birth and we hushed it up, just kept it in the family."

"But no-one knows that Bickerstaff's the father?" I questioned.

Blod shook her head. "No, so don't breathe a word," she said harshly.

"I won't," I promised.

We sat together quietly for a moment under the

K.C. Finn

shade of the huge tree and I made a silent congratulations
to myself for making it the full thirty paces. Who would
have thought that Blod, of all people, would be the one
to get me there? As I looked across at the out buildings
a wheelbarrow came around the side of one of them. My
heart leapt into my throat when Henri appeared with it. He
was wearing borrowed clothes again, but these must have
belonged to Idrys since they were miles too big around the
middle. Henri had tied the huge shirt in a knot at his back,
leaving his chest and stomach exposed to the morning sun.

"It's a bit wrong to fancy your cousin, you know,"
Blod said, nudging me hard in the arm.

"We're not related by blood," I said immediately,
which was true, it just also happened to be true that we
weren't related by marriage either.

"He's a bit young for me," Blod mused. She too was
watching him push the barrow nearer to us, his slightly
tanned skin glowing in the sunlight.

"Good," I said sharply.

"Oh give over," Blod said with a wave of her hand,
"He didn't look at me once last night. All he did was smile
at you. You're well in there."

"D'you think so?" I asked all too keenly.

I half expected Blod to revert to form and tease me
about it, but she nodded with a wicked glint in her eye.
After a moment she got up and brushed herself down from
the dewy grass, cupping one hand around her mouth as she
started to wave with the other.

"Oi! You!" she called brazenly.

Henri caught sight of us, dropping the barrow instantly and starting to jog over. As he approached he undid the knot in his shirt and pulled the baggy fabric around him to fasten it properly. I tried my best to hide my disappointment, but it was no easy task.

"I've got to go in and get the breakfast started," Blod said as Henri arrived beside her, "You walk Kit in when she's done out yur, right?"

She leaned in against Henri's ear and whispered something to him, then turned and gave me a wink as she slunk away through the grass back towards Ty Gwyn. Henri's dark brows were knitted in confusion as he sat down beside me under the tree, hugging his knees up to his chest.

"Kit," he began with half a smile, "What does 'no funny business' mean?"

CHAPTER SIXTEEN

Walking On Air

I had hoped fervently that Doctor Bickerstaff wouldn't take Leighton's little slip up over Henri seriously, so I was suitably horrified when he turned up a few days later at Ty Gwyn asking to speak to 'the Norwegian boy'. Henri and Idrys were loading coal into the sitting room fire when Bickerstaff came in and Idrys wheeled me away quickly to leave the two chaps to converse. But Idrys must have known something was up, because he wheeled me right into my bedroom and told me to sneak back mentally and find out what was going on. It was much quicker to find Henri's mind with him in the same house, so the doctor had hardly begun speaking by the time I was listening in.

"You'll be pleased to know, Mr Haugen, that the local constabulary has accepted your identification papers as genuine," Bickerstaff said in his deadpan tone.

"I should hope so," Henri answered stiffly. I felt rather guilty that he'd inherited so much contempt for Bickerstaff from me before ever having a chance to actually meet the man in person, but there was a suspicious look in the doctor's eyes that told me it was probably best for Henri to be on his guard.

"Tell me, how exactly are you related to the Cavendish children?" he pressed.

"We're cousins by marriage, on Kit's mother's side," Henri explained, just as we'd rehearsed. "It's a very distant connection, but my parents are dead now, and I had no-one else to turn to." I felt that old sadness creep into Henri's chest as he spoke, knowing the sincerity would lend itself to Bickerstaff believing our story.

"On her mother's side," the doctor repeated, "Her mother being...?"

Gail, I whispered.

Henri did all he could to stop himself from jumping with the shock of my voice in his mind.

"Gail," he answered quickly.

"Her maiden name?" Bickerstaff pressed.

Arkwright.

The doctor asked question after question about my family to Henri, who repeated my answers to the letter. Bickerstaff didn't seem entirely satisfied, in fact he once or twice looked around him as though there were answers hidden somewhere on the walls, like he was trying to catch a schoolboy cheating on a test. After he had exhausted his supply of questions the doctor shoved his hands into his pockets irately. I could feel Henri's amusement at the sight of his defeat.

"Tell me then young man," the doctor said finally, "What are your intentions now that you're here?"

Henri was on his own now, for that was something

I had no idea about. I felt him stiffen his shoulders proudly.

"Well sir, I turn eighteen in August, about six weeks from now. My intention is to enlist for the British Army and fight the Hun like everyone else."

Something changed in the doctor's face, his steely resolve falling away slowly. He nodded ever so gently.

"I'm sure we're all keen to heed the call, when it comes," he replied solemnly.

Henri had mentioned fighting for us a few times before, but now that he was here in North Wales I couldn't bear the thought of having to let him go again. He was too proud to tolerate my attempts to persuade him not to enlist, so in the end I stopped talking about him going away and decided to enjoy whatever time I had with him, secretly praying every night that the war would end before he had the chance to go off to training. I thought perhaps my prayers were being answered as July rolled in, when the papers started reporting on a great on-going battle over the British airspace. It seemed like Luftwaffe planes were being shot down left, right and centre by the RAF, and every report that came in saw Mam and Blod punching the air with joy that Clive and the boys were part of that great success.

Despite the low rations and the lack of money, Idrys managed to get Henri kitted out with some proper clothes and put him to good use on the farm. He took over my afternoon walking practice, which generally ended with us sitting under the nearest tree and talking until Idrys called him back to work. Mam invited him over most evenings for dinner, but Leighton had got into the nasty habit of following us from room to room with his watchful little eyes. It was painfully ironic that the only real privacy we had was when I went to my bedroom and Henri went to his, where we were able to talk in his head across the pasture.

It was a too-warm night in the middle of July that I found Henri standing by his window trying to cool off. I waited for a moment quietly as he took in some deep breaths of the night air, but Henri gradually stopped what he was doing and started to smile.

"You're there, aren't you?" he asked.

How did you know?

"I think I'm learning to recognise the change in my head," he explained. Henri moved to lie down on his bed and look up at the cobwebbed ceiling of the Pengelly Cottage.

Listen, I began excitedly, *I didn't want to tell you when Leighton was there, but Blod told me there's a summer dance in the village hall at the end of next week. All the teenagers are going.*

"You mean somewhere your brother and Idrys can't get into to pester us?" Henri asked with a laugh. "We have to go, of course."

Excellent, I said, agreeing silently that between my little brother and the old farmer we couldn't get a moment to ourselves. *That's settled then, except for one little thing.*

"Oh?" Henri asked, waiting.

I'm not sure if I can actually dance, I admitted, *In fact I'm not sure that I really have walking mastered yet. But I'd still like to go, even if I have to sit it out and just watch.*

"Don't be silly," Henri said with a smile, "We'll figure something out."

Henri and I went to Mam with the suggestion of me learning a few dance steps, mostly because we knew that she would say yes without even thinking about it. Mam didn't disappoint us; in fact she took me off potato peeling duty for the rest of the week so that the time could be reserved for Henri and I to practice. Leighton was enlisted to move the furniture around in the small sitting room to make space, which left him with a wicked scowl across his mouth. When Henri offered to help move the chairs Leigh was so vicious in replying that I shouted him out of the room, which allowed me to watch Henri shove the sofa backwards with his long, strong arms. He turned and caught me looking with a smile.

"Idrys won't be happy, you know," he mused guiltlessly, "I'm supposed to be picking fruit or something right now."

"Mam's in control of him really," I replied, grinning from my chair and holding my crutches, impatient to get up and get started, "She'll talk him round."

"And who's going to talk your brother round?" Henri

asked, scratching his smoothly shaved chin.

I let loose a mighty frown. "He'll just have to grow up," I huffed, though I wasn't sure I was patient enough for that. It was like Leigh had taken all of Mum and Dad's protective instincts in over the years and now they'd all spilled out in one monstrous mood swing, one that was threatening to totally ruin my summer.

Henri broke my thoughts by taking away my crutches. I looked up at him with a frown as he threw them on the sofa.

"You're not going to use them to dance," he insisted, "You'll stab me in the toe."

"Then what will I lean on?" I asked, a smile creeping into the corner of my mouth.

Henri leant over my chair, his chin almost touching my shoulder, and wrapped his long arms around my waist, lifting me to my feet with ease. I gripped his shoulders hard as he let me take some of my own weight onto my legs. When we were settled I was looking up a little into his face, but he wasn't quite as tall as he always seemed when I was sitting down so low. If I had the strength to be on my tiptoes, we could have been nose to nose. I made a mental note to work on that sometime.

"Keep your strongest hand on my shoulder and give me the other to hold," he said, his rich voice so perfectly quiet. Even though there was always a ridiculous din from the kitchen and Blod's radio upstairs, I felt like every sound in Ty Gwyn melted off into silence when he spoke.

I did as I was told, wobbling slightly when he made

the transition to only having one arm around my waist. I had to lean on him an awful lot to stay standing, but the strain was well worth it when I found him smiling proudly at me. I caught myself staring into his deep chocolately eyes and tore my gaze away with a grin.

"Aren't we supposed to move?" I asked.

"Oh, um, yes," he mumbled, adjusting his warm hand at my waist and pulling me a little closer, "All right. How about you step forward with the left foot and I'll step back?"

He counted me in. I was about fifty times slower than his counting, but we managed it all the same.

"And now you bring your feet together again."

That was somewhat easier, but I could feel Henri half lifting me off the ground to help.

"Now we step to the right side, and feet together."

I dug my hand into his strong shoulder muscles to keep steady, feeling my face flush pink from more than just the physical strain. His nose bumped my temple as I stumbled; I could feel him grinning against the side of my face.

"Okay, this is the hard part. Now you step back with the left, but twist your body to face the left too."

There was a sweet scent on his breath like he'd pinched one of Mam's cakes that were meant for after dinner. I had hardly registered what he said before we started to move, and as I tried to twist my body my knee went to jelly and I started to fall backwards. I felt my eyes shoot wide open in shock, but it was only a moment before

Henri wrapped both his arms around me and pulled me upright. I let out a few sharp breaths, my face pressed down against his chest as my legs shook on their own. As we waited for them to calm down I felt one of Henri's smooth hands stroking the back of my shoulders, which made them feel weak all over again.

"Do you need to sit and rest?" Henri asked, his jaw moving against my hair.

I pulled back from his chest, shaking my head. I felt terribly weak and shaken in all sorts of ways, but there was no way I was ready for him to let me go. I couldn't think of anything worse in that moment than having to leave his warm arms, the way he scooped me up and held me, like I could almost be a normal girl that could stand on her own. I made to speak, but my breath caught in my throat when I realised Henri was leaning his head down, bringing me closer to his smooth lips and his cheeky grin. I felt like my heart had stopped, like everything on the planet had stopped. There was no war, no families torn apart, no lack of food or nice clothes, no planes shooting bullets into the sky. There was just us and this moment, everything I could ever have wanted.

"Ooooh!"

Henri's lips had barely grazed mine before he pulled his head away sharply. I craned my neck in fury to see Ness Fach in the doorway, waving Dolly excitedly. She pointed at us with a huge grin full of tiny teeth, then ran off at an inhuman pace.

"Mam! Maaaaaaaaaam!"

Henri scooped me up quickly and put me in my chair.

"I'll go catch her," he promised, kissing my forehead before he took off after the little tell-tale.

Which left me sitting alone with a thump in my chest so fierce I was sure my heart would just give up the ghost at any moment, but also smiling so much that I was sure it'd make my face ache for a week.

Henri had only just managed to stop Ness Fach from spilling the beans about our almost-kiss to Mam, but he hadn't got to her before she reached Leighton, which sent my little brother to an all new level of annoying. For the rest of the time between then and the summer dance, any time we practised a few steps Leighton was there watching Henri like a mangy guard dog, fangs out and ready to attack. Having him there did actually make me concentrate less on Henri and more on learning to dance, but I would much rather have sent Leighton away if I thought he wouldn't go straight to Mam and tell on us at once.

"The dance will be the place," Henri whispered to me once whilst we practised, "Whenever you get tired, we can find a nice place outside to sit alone."

"You know I get tired an awful lot, don't you?" I giggled into his ear.

"I thought you were supposed to be watching your feet?" Leighton demanded irately from his perch at the door.

When the morning of the dance came around I was surprised to find Henri and Idrys joining us for breakfast. Henri arrived with a suspicious looking parcel under his arm which he took and put in another room before he joined us at the table. Afterwards he asked me to come and talk to him alone, taking the handles of my chair with an audibly deep breath. Leighton protested heavily, but Idrys insisted on taking him outside to calm down and get some air. To my surprise Henri wheeled me into my bedroom where the parcel, wrapped in brown paper, was waiting on my mattress. He passed it to me eagerly, sitting down on the corner of my bed with a glint in his eye.

I must have had the stupidest grin all over my face whilst I was opening the paper, but it was nothing compared to the Blod-like squeal of delight I gave when I finally found what was inside it. A dress. A beautiful new dress, navy with white polka dots. I spread it out over my knees to see the wide, flowy skirt part, perfect for dancing. It had a bright white ribbon around it to bring in the waist.

"I hope it's all right," Henri said quietly, "I didn't have your measurements."

Realisation set in slowly. My mouth fell open at him for a few seconds.

"You made this?" I asked. "For me?"

"Idrys thinks it very strange that I can tailor for men and women, but Mr Hoffman always liked us to do things that way." There was a sad drop in his tone for just a moment when he mentioned his old employer. "If the waist is too big you can pull it in there." He pointed at the ribbon as I nodded.

"What was it, before it was a dress?" I queried, inspecting the polka dots again.

"A tablecloth belonging to Mam's mother," he explained, now grinning as widely as me, "I did ask her permission, of course."

"I love it," I said brightly, "Oh I love it so much. It's wonderful."

I wanted so desperately to leap out of my chair and hug him, but all I could do was reach for his hand and give it a big squeeze. He took the dress from my lap and laid it out on the bed for me to admire. I'd be wearing it soon, in just a few hours' time, dancing with Henri and sneaking off somewhere to finally claim that very first kiss that we'd been waiting for. The most perfect of all days had just begun.

As I started to speak again a terrifying cry shocked us both. A high pitched, screaming sob, like someone had just been stabbed, followed by a low, animal sort of wailing. It was how I used to cry when I first had the pain all over my body, but somehow this cry was much deeper, much worse. It sounded like someone was dying. My heart started to race as Henri grabbed my chair and we careered out of the bedroom, racing through the black and white hall to reach the source of the cry in the kitchen.

Mam was on the floor with her head in her hands. Her usually rosy face was bright crimson, flushed all too bright. Her calloused hands shook as she covered her eyes, sobbing and wailing. Blod stood beside her with a letter in her hands, her pale Celtic face now white and lifeless as though her soul had just upped and left her body. She raised a hand to her mouth in slow motion, looking at me with a terrifying emptiness in her crystal blue eyes. Her lips moved but no words came out, the only sound was her mother sobbing uncontrollably beside her in a heap.

The kitchen door burst open as Idrys came marching in; he too had been alerted by Mam's wild cries. Leighton was behind him looking younger than I'd ever seen him, his face white and full of terror as his eyes took in the sight of Mam and Blod in their tableau of shock. Idrys was demanding an answer from the pair of them as to the distress, but all Blod could do was give him the letter from her trembling hand. She turned away slowly in her ghostly fashion, facing the wall, shaking her head of blonde curls. Mam slowly retreated into silence; it shook me to my core to see such a strong, proud woman curled on the floor like a frightened animal, shuddering with a river of silent tears streaking down her face.

"What is it?" I said fearfully, looking up at Idrys as he studied the letter.

Every semblance of joy in the old famer's face was gone. He looked grey and bleak; his usually sparkling eyes were empty when they found my gaze. He let the letter flutter slowly to the floor, clearing his throat.

"Clive's dead."

Mam let out another huge shriek at hearing the words out loud. Suddenly I didn't feel like dancing ever again.

CHAPTER SEVENTEEN

Days in Black

The letter had come from Thomas, who was a ground mechanic now stationed in Portsmouth. Clive and Ieuan were on a plane together that went out to battle the Luftwaffe, but it had been shot down over the English Channel in the early hours of yesterday morning. Boats supporting the battle in the air had pulled Clive's body from the wreckage, only to find that he had taken almost the full blast of the attack. He'd died on impact, before the plane even started to go down. Most of the other men had been pulled from the sea, just barely alive, and taken to hospital, but worse news still awaited the Price family. Two crewmen had not been recovered at all, and Ieuan was one of them.

For once Leighton didn't complain when Henri wrapped his arms around me, in fact when I sat down later on the sofa with my head on Henri's chest, my brother curled up in front of our feet like a kitten. I stroked his sun-bleached hair as he shuddered out tiny tears. For my own part the tears wouldn't come, it was like my eyes were too shocked by it all to realise they were supposed to be crying. Henri sat in a thoughtful silence for the whole afternoon, only speaking when I asked him things; I rather thought he'd seen enough death on his way to me, perhaps he hadn't imagined that the reaper's cold shadow could reach us in the sunny mountains of Bryn Eira Bach.

Idrys made the decision that he and Henri would abandon the cottage over the pasture for now and come and stay at Ty Gwyn to care for Mam. I couldn't even bring myself to be happy that Henri and I would be under one roof when I thought about Mam and Blod and the hell they were going through. For the first day in all the months I'd lived in the farm house, Blod's radio was silent. Fourteen hours passed between the arrival of the post and me settling into bed for the night, yet I was sure that I could still hear Mam crying through the ceiling above my head. I wondered how there was any water left in her body at all.

Leighton's eleventh birthday was August 4ᵗʰ, just four days before Henri was due to turn eighteen, but neither boy was keen for a party, especially when it was announced that Clive's funeral had been arranged for a date smack bang between the two. Idrys was making all of the arrangements to spare his daughter the horror, so when Henri was occupied with picking up the slack out on the farm, I started spending a lot of time with Ness Fach in the summer sun where I could see him going by as he worked.

"What's he doin' now?" Ness asked, bouncing on my knee and waving her Dolly in Henri's direction.

"He's picking up the yucky weeds," I explained, "So they don't make all the nice flowers…" I stopped myself before the word 'die' fell out of my mouth. "… get poorly."

"That's boring," Ness said.

I found the strength for a sad smile as the little girl threw her head back onto my shoulder, looking up into the sky with her huge blue eyes. I watched her small face as she followed the clouds, one finger outstretched to point at them. She wasn't smiling.

"Daddy's up there," she said suddenly. I froze, my heart held in an invisible clamp. "He's always up there flying in the sky. But Blod says he won't come home no more. He's going to live up there now."

"That's right," I whispered, my throat feeling tight and dry.

It was now that my body had decided it finally wanted to cry, but there couldn't be anything worse for Ness Fach than having the whole house blubbering, especially since she didn't have much clue as to why everybody in her life had suddenly fallen silent and tearful. I sucked up every drop of water and shook the hotness from my face, cuddling her up in my arms.

"Blod says Ieu might go live there too," Ness added.

"We'll see," I choked, "He might want to come back here, with us." I felt awful as a flash of Ieuan's cheeky smile and ginger hair crept in behind my eyes.

"Can I go and live there if I want?" she asked thoughtfully.

"No," I said all too quickly, burying my head against her long tawny hair to hide my tears, "It's only for people who can fly, sweetheart."

"All right then," she replied. I felt Dolly being flung

to and fro in front of me.

Ness had lost two fathers already in her short little life, two men who made it clear that they adored her, that neither one had ever wanted to be separated from her. It made my thoughts turn inwards to London, to Mum and most especially to Dad. If my father was out there alive somewhere, then he had made the choice to stay away from us all. Bickerstaff clearly hated his life in the village, but he was here all the same, perhaps only here for stolen glimpses of the little girl playing with Dolly in my arms. His little girl.

There were a lot of things that couldn't be put right any more at Ty Gwyn, but I thought there was at least one thing I could do.

On the day of the funeral it seemed as though the whole of Bryn Eira Bach had turned out to cry and sing and hang their heads in unison for the great man that was RAF Flight Sergeant Clive Price. I could hardly bear the kind words and hopeful wishes in the preacher's service; I spent most of it with my head buried in Henri's shoulder trying not to make it too obvious that I was covering my other ear to block it all out. It was so wrong for us even to be sat there, so wrong that such a good man had died defending his country from the murderous horde that were still trying to claim the skies over England.

I caught sight of Doctor Bickerstaff walking through

the graveyard after the burial, his black suit shining in the glare of the August sun, and knew that my opportunity had arrived. I got onto my crutches as fast as my newfound strength allowed and called Ness over to me. Blod gave me a watchful, tearstained look over the assembled family, but she couldn't intervene. Thomas was home temporarily for the service and he was clutching her hand so tightly that the tips of her pale, perfect fingers were tinged with blue. Ness took hold of my left crutch as though it was as simple as holding my hand and we set off at a snail's pace towards the lonely doctor.

Bickerstaff was alerted by my ragged breaths and thumping footfalls long before I got to him, but he waited patiently with his usual expressionless face until we made it closer to him. Ness hid behind my leg at first when we reached him, peeping out through the gap in the triangular wooden frame to watch him with interest. He gave her a quick glance, his stiff lip softening. He scratched under his chin thoughtfully, taking in a deep breath like he was preparing himself for a great undertaking.

"How's Blod?" he asked quietly.

"Frantic," I answered, "Mam just keeps shutting herself in her room. Blod's been trying to run the house, but she can't cope with it all. We've all tried to help, but she won't let us."

"Perhaps she wants to be rushed off her feet," Bickerstaff supposed, "Some people prefer to bury their grief in keeping busy. I know I do."

Ness was slowly coming out from behind me. She

ambled forward, Dolly in the one hand as always, but she took the hem of her dress in her other hand and swished it about. It was a black dress recycled from one that Blod had worn some years ago to her grandmother's funeral.

"Bampi says I look pretty in this," she mumbled, mimicking the little twirl she had done for us that same morning in the kitchen.

Bickerstaff's resolve broke entirely. He wore a massive smile, but his eyes were growing damper by the second. He crouched down to the floor to be at eye level with the little girl, steadying her as she started to get dizzy from the twirling.

"You do," he said gently, "you look pretty as a picture."

Ness crinkled her nose. "Which picture?"

The doctor faltered for a moment, but Ness was patiently awaiting an answer.

"All the pictures," Bickerstaff answered, I could hear the break in his throat where tears were threatening, "Every picture you can think of, well you're the prettiest of them all."

"Ooh," said Ness, smiling all over with her tiny teeth, "I'm going to tell Blod I'm the prettiest!"

Before either of us could stop her she was jogging away on her small, unsteady feet back towards the family. Bickerstaff rose again and looked down at me, sucking in a breath. His watery eyes were threatening to set me off again, but I did my best to hold it in. I had done enough crying to last me a lifetime and a fair chunk of it had been in front of him already.

"Blod's not really up to looking after her at the moment," I began, looking away from his unbearably sad face to focus on the chapel, "So I've offered for Henri and me to bring her along when I come to see you next, to get her out of the way for a bit."

"Thank you," he said quietly. A short silence passed between us. "Henri knows, doesn't he?" The doctor asked.

"He does." I didn't see much point in lying.

"I hope you can trust him, whoever he is."

I looked back to Bickerstaff, whose emotions had receded to leave his usual stern face. He wasn't used to believing in people, not like Mam; he still wouldn't entertain a word of Henri's story.

"I know I can trust him," I said. It was meant to come out fierce, but I was too weak for the full emotion to find its voice.

"He's a stranger," Bickerstaff challenged.

"Not to me," I replied.

"But how? How can you be sure of that?"

"I have my reasons," I replied, my face suddenly as stone-like as his.

Bickerstaff narrowed his eyes at me. "You know something we don't." It wasn't a question.

I nodded, but gave no reply.

We spent Henri's birthday under a tree drinking orange pop and trying to talk about subjects that didn't lead back to the war. The news of Clive and Ieuan had shaken Leigh out of his selfish reverie, so if one good thing had come from the darkness it was the fact that my brother had finally actually gotten to know Henri. He even sang Happy Birthday in what he called 'The Proper English Way', laughing so hard he could barely get the words out for lack of breath:

"Happy Birthday to you, Happy Birthday to you; you look like a monkey and you smell like one too!"

Henri laughed for the first time in what seemed like forever and a warmth settled in my chest, like things were finally going to get back to normal. I sat in the dehydrated grass supporting my back against the tree trunk, looking out across the pasture at the now-empty Pengelly Cottage. Henri was sleeping in what was usually Ieuan's room at Ty Gwyn, but he didn't seem to like spending much time in the room at all when he was conscious. I could relate, knowing now that I was sleeping in the sitting room of a man who would never come home to it again was a hard thing to bear if I dwelt on it too much, but I was getting better at not letting those thoughts ruin every day. We all were, except for Mam.

When Leighton went to get more pop, Henri came to the tree and sat down beside me, putting a long arm around my shoulders and pulling me in. He kissed the side of my head gently, his warm breath sinking into my hair. He hadn't tried to kiss me properly again even when there had been opportunity for it, and I was sort of grateful for that. As much as I wanted to feel that tingling, only-us-in-the-world sensation again, right now the atmosphere just wasn't right. But we were always close to one another when we had the chance, I had gotten so used to his arms around me that it felt like some part of me was missing when he wasn't there.

"I'll have to go into the village tomorrow," he whispered, "to pass my enlistment papers to the right people."

An invisible blade sank slowly into my fragile heart, but I had always known this day was coming.

"It'll take them a while to process it," I said hopefully, "I bet they've already got loads of boys waiting to go to basic training."

"Perhaps," he said softly, his lips still resting against my head.

I turned sharply to face him, searching his deep brown eyes. "I don't want you to go," I said, racing to find his hand to hold it tightly.

"I won't really be gone," he replied, "You'll always be able to find me."

"That's not the point," I said, my curls shaking as I trembled, "This is dangerous Henri, this is war."

"You forget where I've been already," he said, turning his face away to focus hard on the distance. He kept a firm hold of my hand and gave it a good squeeze. "You came to my head in the quiet times, the safe times. But I've already seen the destruction, the danger and the death, Kit. I think there are two types of people during war: those who see the horror happening and run away, never looking back, and those who want to do something about it." I felt his other arm pull me in closer against his strong body. "You know which type I am, so you know I have to go."

I couldn't say anything, because it was all true.

The days flew by in a similar way until my next appointment with Bickerstaff came around. Now that almost any short distance was doable on my crutches and my arm strength had finally improved I was fairly certain there was nothing the once-wicked doctor could do that would overstrain me, especially since this time Henri's watchful eyes would be there to see the check-up. At any rate I was fairly certain it wasn't me he really wanted to see. Ness was terribly excited to sit in the doctor's lovely white car when it came for us, the whole journey over the hill she crawled around at an uncatchable pace to look out of every window and sit on every seat. By the time we got to the cosy little waiting room Henri was exhausted from trying to keep her still.

"How does Blod cope with this?" Henri said as he brought the struggling infant to sit on my lap, one of the few places she would willingly stay still, "I'm going to have bruises all over my arms, she's a kicker."

I gave him a little smile and he put his hand on my shoulder, until we both saw the old receptionist watching us, her eyes bright and her mouth hanging open ready to gossip about us to whoever came in next. Henri went to sit opposite us on a comfy looking chair, but no sooner had he sunk his back into it then Bickerstaff poked his head out of his office door.

"Miss Cavendish, please."

He wasn't smiling, not even at Ness. Not a good sign at all.

I let Ness wriggle off me and amble towards the office whilst I wheeled behind. When we were settled in our usual places Bickerstaff's expression softened for just a moment as he crouched down in front of his little girl, silently presenting her with something yellow.

"Lolly!" she cried happily, grabbing the confection and stuffing it into her mouth. Bickerstaff picked her up awkwardly and set her down on the edge of his desk, patting her head just the once.

"Sit still here," he chided, "While I talk to these two."

Ness nodded and obeyed, which was most unusual given her wriggle-fest in the car. Henri looked a little annoyed that she didn't listen to him that way, but I put it down to the fact that she was too concentrated on slurping her lolly to want to do anything else. When I looked back to the doctor he hadn't sat back down. I followed his grave expression to two brown letters on the desk in front of him. He slowly picked one up and passed it across the desk, right over my head, offering it to Henri.

"I've been to billeting office today, I took the liberty of picking this up for you," he explained, his tone worryingly dark.

The other letter had already been opened, but

I heard Henri ripping the seal from his. He came to sit beside me as he started to read it.

"It's my call up," he said, and for all his bravery there was something hollow in his words.

"Already?" I exclaimed, my mouth suddenly dry, "But..."

"The training doesn't start until October 1ˢᵗ, you've got some time yet," Bickerstaff said in what passed for a soothing voice.

I looked down at the other letter again, then back at his empty face.

"You're going too, aren't you?" I asked.

The doctor nodded, his eyes flickering away.

"We'd better get on with your assessment," he said flatly.

Henri rose, still studying his letter. "I'm going to read this properly outside, if you don't need me?"

I shook my head, trying desperately to hide my sadness. October was almost six weeks away, there was still time for the war to end, for Henri to no longer be needed to fight. I watched him go, my breathing growing heavier, until I realised that Bickerstaff had rounded his desk ready to examine my walking. Ness Fach watched him as she sucked on her lolly, her huge eyes travelling over his face with the same keen interest she reserved for clouds and farm animals.

"She likes you," I said, smiling at Ness.

"Don't," Bickerstaff snapped, his stern exterior returning in full force.

I wrenched myself up on my crutches without a lick of help from him, my lip curling irately.

"You could at least be grateful," I bit back, "I didn't have to bring her, she's been a right handful today."

"It's not that," he whispered, turning his face away from both of us, "I just don't want her to get too attached; not now I've had the call."

I didn't understand. It was a bad do to be sent out to battle, I knew that, and dangerous too, but nothing was a certainty any more.

"It's not like you're going to prison," I supposed as I started to walk towards him, "You'll come back."

When I reached him, Bickerstaff looked deep into my eyes with that soulless sadness I remembered from my first accidental trip to his head.

"Henri's a strong boy," he began, again in a whisper, "he'll do all right. But there's a very good reason they're calling on more medics." He gulped with a painfully dry throat, the sound was strained, it made me want to cry again. "It's because they're the first to go."

I shook my head ferociously. I wanted to grab him to make him see sense, but the crutches were always in the way.

"You don't know that," I protested.

"Yes I do," he answered through gritted teeth.

Bickerstaff let out the deepest breath I'd ever heard, his propriety falling away to leave just the face of a young man. He gave me a hopeless look.

"I have every certainty that I will die out there, Kit.

You'll see me proved right before Christmas. Your walking is rather excellent, by the way. It's just as well that you don't need me anymore."

It was the first praise he'd ever given me, and now it seemed that it would also be the last.

CHAPTER EIGHTEEN

London Rain

I didn't dare tell anyone what Bickerstaff had said in case it got back to Henri. He was building his muscles up every day under our tree, pulling his full weight up to his chest where he hung from a very thick branch. He was so confident that he would do well at training and that he'd be able to go anywhere and do anything the British Army asked of him. I couldn't bear the idea that Bickerstaff felt so opposite about his chances. Whilst I prayed every night for Henri's safety, now I also spared a thought for the doctor I'd hated for so long, hoping that perhaps somehow he would be stationed on our side of the water and not thrown right into the field.

Now that October 1st would see Henri taken away from me the days seemed to rush by all the quicker. The summer leaves started to turn their auburn and golden hues and when the first cool breeze of autumn crept into my bedroom one morning there was little I could do but force the worries as far out of my mind as I could manage. Luckily I wasn't left to think about them for long as a familiar sound travelled down through my ceiling whilst I took off my splints. Mam.

She was crying this morning. She wasn't always crying now, but she had only been out of her bedroom twice since the funeral, so I had hardly seen her face in the last four weeks. Blod said she couldn't bear to face a world that didn't have Clive in it. I understood that fairly well, but it was hell to think that Mam would never step out of her home again and I was sure that wasn't something Clive would have wanted for his wife. If he'd been here to have his say he'd have marched her downstairs at a pace and wrapped his mighty arms around her. Idrys had already tried to do the same, but even he had given up and decided that his only daughter needed 'her own time' to work things out.

That morning saw me in one of my determined moods. I was feeling strong, so I managed to wash and dress by myself before Blod or Leigh came to find me, then I took off on my crutches to the foot of the steep black stairs that led to the other floor of Ty Gwyn. I had seen what it all looked like by being in the minds of other people, but now I decided it was time to see it for myself. Each movement of the crutch left a clunk on the stone and the old burning agony returned to my arms and legs as I made it up each step, but I made it halfway up before I would even concede to stopping to catch my breath. My ascent was neither smooth nor silent, however, so by the time I was two steps off the top both Henri and Blod had woken up and come to see what the noise was.

"What're you doing, you mad thing?" Blod accused

K.C. Finn

in a whisper.

"I want to see Mam," I urged breathlessly.

Henri was grinning at me as he straightened out his stripy pyjamas. He held out his arms like he'd promised he would all those weeks ago.

"Come on Kit, you can do it," he beamed.

Blod let off a sigh. "If you fall down them stairs I'm not patching you up." She glided past me, already dressed in Mam's apron to start on breakfast, but I caught her smiling a little as she went.

When I reached the top Henri scooped me up into his arms and my crutches dropped with a clatter on the landing. I felt his just-out-of-bed warmth spreading through my aching limbs and he held me tight to keep me standing as I leant on his chest for support. He was grinning at me like a Cheshire cat and he suddenly buried his face against my neck and let out a little laugh.

"You're so brilliant," he murmured, "You surprise me all the time."

"Oi!" whispered a voice nearby. Idrys's sleepy, bearded face was poking out of Thomas's room. "Just because you can get up the stairs, it doesn't mean you can sneak around to see your boyfriend, young lady."

I felt my face flush crimson. My boyfriend. I bet that's what they were all calling him when we weren't around. Henri held onto me with one strong arm whilst he retrieved my crutches.

"I came to see Mam actually," I explained with a little smile, getting back on my own two feet as Henri slid

199

the rests under my arms.

"Make sure she gets back down safe," Idrys warned Henri, giving us both a roll of his tired eyes.

With that I was left at Mam's door, listening to her quiet sobs. Henri retired to get dressed as I pushed open the door gently. It felt invasive, like I shouldn't be there, but I had come too far to turn back. The bedroom she and Clive had shared was a tribute to their lives. Photographs of all their children littered every surface, with Clive and his boys in their RAF uniforms taking pride of place on the wall above the fireplace. Right beside the bed was an ornate frame with a wedding photo inside it. Mam had never been quite as beautiful as Blod, but her young round face was a picture of perfect happiness where she stood in her white dress beside her man.

Now she was curled under her covers with her back to me. I knew she'd heard me come in because her sobs had stopped. She reached for a hanky and took it under the covers to find her face, then waved a hand at me without turning over.

"I don't want no breakfast Blod, you just see to the others, don't worry about me."

"It's not Blod," I said gently, "It's me Mam."

"Kit?"

She turned then and sat up in her bed, looking me over with sore red eyes. Her hands rose up to her mouth wordlessly as I stumbled to her and sat down on the edge of her bed, my chest heaving with exhaustion. She reached out and touched my shoulder, like she wasn't sure that

I was really there. Then she shook the whole bed as she shuffled towards me and threw a strong arm around my head, pulling me in against her chest. I had always been protected by my chair from Mam's full-on assault hugs, but secretly I'd always wanted one, no matter how much it hurt. It took ages before she released me and I felt a cold shiver all over me as I was set free from her warmth.

"You came all the way up yur for me," she sobbed.

"I miss you," I said, trying my best to smile.

That set her off crying again for a few minutes, so I rubbed her shoulder gently until she was ready to speak again. Mam pushed herself out of her covers and hung her legs over the edge of the bed to sit beside me, catching sight of the lovely wedding picture for a moment. There were all kinds of things I could have said to her, but I thought that everybody had probably said them already, so instead I just held her hand in the dark little room.

"I've missed you too, love," she whispered. The sing-song lilt in her voice was not gone, just replaced by a more sombre melody.

"Do you feel like helping me back down to breakfast?" I asked with an eager smile.

Mam's kind face looked older than I remembered, but when she returned my smile I could see traces of the rosy youth she'd had when we were first introduced.

"Ie, all right then," she replied, unleashing a mighty sigh, "I suppose it's time I took a look at the damage Blod's done to my kitchen eh?"

I knew full well that Blod had been keeping her

mother's kitchen pristine since the day of the funeral, but I said nothing, enjoying the idea that Mam would find that out for herself soon enough.

Life was slowly returning to normal at Ty Gwyn as September rolled in, but even though Mam was up and about Idrys was reluctant to return to his own cottage. She was leaning on him and Blod a lot more now to cope with the duties of running the home and her emotions were fragile at best. When Henri broke the news to her that he and Steven Bickerstaff were both due to leave for basic training in three weeks' time she went back to her room and cried an afternoon away, leaving Blod to scrub the lunch dishes, her own tears falling into the soapy sink. I hadn't seen the doctor in ages, since our conversation over the call-up he had even stopped coming to chapel. I pleaded with Blod to telephone him at least, but her will was as rottenly stubborn as his on the matter.

My fears for him and Henri were overtaken one day when Idrys burst through the back door of Ty Gwyn and hurriedly wheeled me off to the sitting room without so much as a word of explanation. Henri followed us in carrying a newspaper and when we were alone and the door was closed he thrust the paper into my lap. I stared down at the front page, my eyes first catching a picture of a whole row of houses on fire. I struggled to refocus on the headline: LONDON BLITZED BY JERRY BOMBS.

Idrys crouched in front of me and grabbed my shoulders. "It's happening day and night love," he pressed, "Use your mind and find your mother, make sure she's all right."

My heart threatened to batter its way out of my chest as I nodded too many times. Idrys and Henri sat themselves down on the sofa whilst I took a few deep breaths, trying desperately to gather my thoughts. In her letters Mum had told us that there were special shelters all over the city now in case of these attacks and that she'd be able to hide in the London Underground stations if the threat of bombs ever became a reality. I wondered sadly what Clive had really died for, why we had beaten them back once just for them to regroup and start destroying us again. I tried to push the anger aside as I raised my hands up over my eyes, shutting them tightly against the afternoon sun.

I heard the echo of what I thought was thunder as I looked into a totally black scene. My mother had her hands over her ears and her eyes tight shut. She was trembling all over, but right in the centre of her chest was a flush of anger I couldn't understand. When she opened her eyes I looked out into a dimly lit underground station that I didn't recognise. It was packed with hundreds of people in wet raincoats split directly in half: into those who were looking up to the sound of the thunder and those who were burying their faces down towards the ground. Mum joined the ones looking up, until another clap of the horrific noise came echoing down the stairwell nearby.

It wasn't thunder of course. The bombs were bigger

than I could ever have imagined, louder than if you'd
flown a biplane straight through a thunderstorm. Most of
the women in the makeshift shelter were on the ground,
huddled with their children, trying to soothe them. I could
hear their little cries reverberating around the station. It
was strange to see this many people gathered without the
faintest sight of a train. On the other side of the tracks
they sat in rows along the wall, some people were even laid
out trying to sleep on their wet coats. Another bomb went
off overhead and the collected people shook like they were
of the same mind, my mother rubbed her arms, holding
herself steady.

Dad should be there to hold you, I thought.

I realised I'd become far too casual with my
thoughts, it had come from spending all my nights talking
to Henri. Mum stiffened, raising a hand to her face to cover
her mouth.

"Kit?" she whispered. "Was that you?"

I was surprised by the total lack of shock in her
voice, or in her body for that matter.

Yes, I said unsurely, *I suppose I should explain?*

Mum took off at a pace to an abandoned block of
telephones nearby. As she reached one she put it to her ear
and I heard the tone that meant the phones were out of
service. My mother deftly slipped a pair of sewing scissors
from her handbag and snipped the phone line so the noise
died out. She held the two ends of the cut cord in her hand
where no-one could see the break. I watched in fascination.
Mum had always been a confident, no-nonsense sort of

woman, but I had never witnessed such a cool and collected display from anyone I knew, least of all her.

"You don't need to explain to me sweetheart," she spoke as though she was using the phone, "I know what you can do."

My first reaction was not relief, but betrayal. *Why didn't you tell me you knew?* I demanded. *All these years that I've been wondering who I am, what I can do? And you've just been keeping it a secret!*

"I had to darling, or they would have enlisted you!" Mum toyed with a long curl the same auburn colour as mine, I could feel her agitation.

Who would have enlisted me? I pressed. *Enlisted me for what?*

"People like us are exploited in times like these," she replied.

People like us, I repeated, stunned. *Then… you can do it too?*

"I suppose it's time to tell you love," my mother began sadly; "I don't work in a factory. I have never worked in a factory. I do what I can for the War Office."

Did Dad know what we are? I asked fearfully. *Is that why he left us?*

Mum's whole body changed, every muscle growing tense. "That's not a conversation we can have in public, Kit. You never know who's listening." I tried to speak again but she cut over me fiercely. "Look Kit we're not supposed to talk like this. People with our abilities shouldn't link up, it causes problems."

I know, I answered, *It always gives me headaches, finding you.*

"And when I find you it makes you very ill," Mum said, a bitter taste of guilt catching in her throat, "I'm so sorry about that by the way, I stopped peeking into your life as soon as I realised what it was doing to you."

The fevers! I exclaimed as explanation dawned. I was excited by the deduction for a moment, until I realised that meant that Mum had been a witness to me threatening Doctor Bickerstaff that time. I didn't even have time to feel ashamed before she was talking again.

"I've been using Leigh to keep an eye on you both since then; he's not getting ill is he?"

No, he's the same as usual, I answered.

"Good," she said with a nod, "Look you really must go darling before it hurts you too much. Your granddad used to spy on me years ago and it set me off with migraines for days sometimes. I'm fine here; they'll keep us all night if they need to, until the city's safe again. Just keep yourself and everyone else there safe and well." She paused a moment, a grin slowly forming on her lips. "And give my regards to Henri."

When I returned I was weak and aching like someone had hit me in the back of the skull with a brick. Idrys and Henri took me to my room and heaved me onto my bed, shutting the curtains to let me recover in the dark.

After some of the ache had subsided I told them what I'd seen and most importantly heard. Idrys reclined in thought in the chair, rubbing his beard, but Henri came to sit beside me on my bed and held my hand. He grinned with a flushed face, shaking his head.

"I'll bet she watched us dancing," he mused awkwardly.

"How embarrassing," I said, throwing my free hand up over my face with a sigh.

We descended into bashful giggles until Idrys cleared his throat.

"What was your mum's maiden name Kit?" he asked.

"Arkwright," Henri answered for me. I gave his hand a squeeze, impressed that he'd remembered.

"I wish I'd known that before," the Welshman mused. We both gave him a curious look. "That fella from the Great War that I told you about…"

"The psychic spy," I filled in, turning my head on my pillow to see his face properly, "What about him?"

"His name was Reggie Arkwright."

"My grandfather," I replied. It wasn't even worth being shocked anymore; I just had to accept the fact that my whole family had been keeping secrets around me all my life. It wouldn't do to be bitter about it, I was just grateful that it was all finally coming out for me to put the pieces together. "I guess that means this psychic thing is an inherited gift."

"If you have children, they might have it too," Henri said excitedly. I couldn't help but return his grin.

"Fate's a funny thing, init?" Idrys asked, "Makes you think there's a plan for us all."

I didn't care what the plan was, so long as it involved us all surviving this war so I could finally interrogate my mother about everything I needed to know. And the first thing on that list would be what had really happened to Dad.

CHAPTER NINETEEN

Two Desert Rats

The blitz of bombs in London raged on all through the month of September. Mum sent me and Leighton a huge letter telling us that she was all right and how good the air raid wardens and the shelters were in the city, but made no mention at all of any of the questions I wanted her to answer. Henri suggested that she must be doing it to protect me, but I waved that off angrily every time he said it. I was sick of everyone trying to protect me, I wanted answers about my gift, my family, my father, and the war was getting in the way of it all. Worse than that, time was running out even faster than before for me and Henri.

I cried buckets when he came home with his train ticket to get to Essex for basic training. He'd leave at lunchtime on September 30th to get there for the start of the next day and Bickerstaff had booked the same journey. Mam was the one to find me sobbing over Henri's imminent departure, which made me feel all the more awful since she was still doing plenty of sobbing of her own when she thought no-one could hear her. She put her arms around me until I quietened down, whispering that everything was

209

bound to be all right. I wasn't sure which one of us believed her words less.

In our remaining days together Henri and I did the usual things that teenagers did, which was a whole new experience for me since I'd been confined to my chair, shying away at home for so long. We walked in the hills, the flatter ones at least, looking at the orange blanket of autumn that had settled over the village. We went to the cinema and sat holding hands as some dashing romantic heroes pranced about on the screen. We even did the shopping for Blod a few times, just to be out and about together. Nobody seemed to want to intercept us anymore and we were alone together often, but I was growing impatient now that Henri hadn't kissed me. Or wouldn't kiss me, to be more accurate.

We were about a week from his departure when I decided I'd tackle the subject. He watched me walk to a spot beneath our usual tree and I managed to get down into the crunchy leaves all by myself. Instead of leaning on the trunk I lay flat amongst the foliage and grass, looking up into the colours of the branches overhead. Henri lay down next to me and took hold of my hand, stroking along my knuckles with one of his fingers.

"Are you trying to stop me from getting too attached?" I asked suddenly.

"What do you mean?" he replied.

I gulped, steeling myself for the important question. "Do you think that if you kiss me, it'll be too much for me to cope with when you go?"

He let go of my hand. My heart sank for a moment

when I thought he was moving away from me, but he shuffled his long body onto its side and slipped his arm over my stomach. He held my side and pulled gently until I grabbed his shoulder to turn and face him. His black hair and lightly tanned face shone against the leaves as he let his fingertips stroke my cheek.

"If I kiss you," he began slowly, "It's me that won't be able to cope." He let his hand fall back to my waist and pulled our bodies close together until I couldn't see his face. I nuzzled my nose into his collarbone and kissed him there lightly through his shirt. "The promise of your kiss is what I'll live for out there. It's what will help me come back home to you."

It made me feel special, but I was happy and sad in the same moment. He sounded like he used to when I was in his head, the Henri surviving hard times who had relied on me to be there for him. But that was also the Henri who'd been beaten and harassed by Nazis, the Henri who had streaked past armed guards and almost been tossed out of a boat to his watery grave in the choppy North Sea.

"Don't you need to know what kind of kiss it is you'll be coming back to?" I pressed, playing with the button on the pocket over his heart. I tingled all over when he held me even tighter.

"The curiosity is killing me, I promise you," he chuckled. He let out a deep sigh against the top of my head. "Do you think I'm going to die out there?" He asked the question quietly, but he didn't sound worried.

"No, of course not!" I exclaimed, pulling back so I

could see his face.

"Then there's no urgency, is there?" Henri said with a soft, level tone. He started to stroke my face again, calming my frayed nerves. "I'll go and I'll do my part for the war. And when I come back, you and I will always be together."

There were so many things I wanted to argue against, so many worries I had that he just couldn't soothe. But the moment between us in the autumn air was quiet and precious. I didn't want to remember any part of my time with him ending in a fight.

"Okay," I said weakly, trying to smile, "In that case, shall we steal Blod's radio and try to have a dance?"

No-one could have made better use of their time than we did during that last month; I had bucket-loads of laughing, smiling memories of Henri to see me through the times when he wouldn't be there beside me. But it was still a shock when there came a knock at the door on the morning of September 30th. I was in the little sitting room alone when I heard Idrys answer the door and caught wind of Doctor Bickerstaff replying to him. The two men went upstairs and Blod came to find me from the kitchen, taking off her apron as she entered the room.

"Was that Steven?" she urged.

I nodded. "Henri said he was bringing him his uniform so he could get changed here, instead of on the train."

Blod nodded, her beautiful brow creased in worry. She had hardly mentioned anything about Bickerstaff to me since that one morning under the tree, but any time Henri or I mentioned his name we always got the sense that she was suddenly eavesdropping on us very carefully. She rung her hands together and took a few sharp breaths before she was off out of the room again like a shot. I was left listening for Henri and though I was tempted to step into his head I resisted the urge. Today was not the day for that kind of prying, I would wait for him to come and say a proper goodbye.

Eventually the feet on the steep stone steps caught my ears. I turned my wheels to face the door and smoothed my hair and dress down tidy, admiring the polka dots draped over my knees. It was the dress he had made me, the one we had saved for an opportunity that never came, and though Henri might have been willing to wait until after the war to see it on me, I was not so patient. I heaved up out of my chair and onto my crutches, swishing the dress with a swing of my knees so it fell nicely around me. I found I was surprisingly weak for the time of the morning, like the core of every limb was made of jelly.

The trembling weakness only increased when a slow creak indicated that the door was opening. A pair of long legs in brown boots stepped through it, shortly followed by the rest of Henri's strong body and his wide, shining smile. I smiled back proudly at the sight of him in uniform, but my face dropped into a frown when I realised he wasn't wearing the green shade I'd been expecting. His fatigues were a dusty, sandy sort of brown. Henri slipped an arm around my waist to help me stay standing, following my gaze to his khaki lapels as I reached out and touched the thin, coarse fabric.

"You like the colour?" he asked playfully.

"What's it for?" I answered, looking back up to his deep brown eyes.

"North Africa," was his reply.

"The desert!" I exclaimed.

I didn't know as much as I should have about all the places on the globe where this beastly war was being fought, but I knew that the sandy belt of countries flanking the north coast of Africa weren't the safest place to be even in peace-time. I couldn't find any more words to say, so I just buried my head in Henri's shoulder and tried not to cry. He wrapped his arms around me tightly until a second set of footfalls entered the room.

I pulled away from him to see Bickerstaff wearing the same coloured clothes, save for a few big red crosses sewn on that indicated his position as a medical officer. He had a smart little hat sticking out of his pocket which he toyed with as he tried not to process the sight of us wrapped up together in affection. Henri put me back down into my chair, his hands running up the torso of my dress as he let me go. He pointed at the fabric wordlessly, his eyes roaming over his creation, and I smiled.

"Did you tell Kit where we're going?" Bickerstaff asked, perching himself on the corner of the sofa opposite us. We both nodded. The doctor's big blue eyes found mine.

K.C. Finn

"We're going to be with the 7th Armoured Division, that's tanks and things."

"Exciting eh?" Henri asked, taking hold of my hand. Dangerous more like. I could tell Bickerstaff was sharing my opinion. Henri turned his head to the doctor eagerly. "Will we be on the ground or might they teach us how to drive the tanks?"

"You'll go wherever they think you're best suited," Bickerstaff replied without a chance of a smile, "I'll be on the ground, though. I have to be."

I could hear that same defeated tone hiding in the shadow of his words. When he said on the ground, he didn't just mean on foot. I wanted to comfort him, to tell him some great lie that would give him the same eager spirit that Henri had, as though spirit might just be enough to get them through the hell they were headed for, but anything I might have said was lost when the door to the room opened again.

"I'll bring the old truck round to get you lads to the station," said Idrys, stopping to give me a cheer-up kind of smile, "You just come out when you're ready, right?"

As the men nodded and the old farmer disappeared from the door, he was replaced by Blod with Ness held against her hip. The little girl looked strangely nervous as Blod brought her in and shut the door. Blod lifted her up a bit and gave her a squeeze.

"Right now," she said gently, her eyes travelling instantly to Bickerstaff, "You've got to say goodbye to the boys, see? They're going to bash the Germans."

215

Ness made a fist with her tiny hand and punched the air in front of her slowly. Blod took her first to Henri and passed her over, but as soon as she was in his arms she became the rowdy, wriggling mess that she always was for him. She punched him in the cheek gently and he said 'Ow' in a high pitch squeak that made her laugh.

"Give him a kiss and cuddle and wish him good luck," Blod pressed.

Ness planted a tiny, shy kiss on Henri's face and mumbled something against his ear as he squeezed her up tight. He wore a grateful smile as he handed the wriggling infant back to Blod, returning to sit beside me and hold my hand. I wondered if we ought to have excused ourselves before the next part of the farewell, but Blod and Bickerstaff were far too preoccupied with their daughter to notice either of us watching. When the doctor took his little girl into his arms she fell into that familiar calm state, watching his face with interest. Bickerstaff watched her for so long that Ness got a little bored and took hold of his face with her hands, poking him in the nose.

"Pob lwc," she said happily.

Bickerstaff grinned confusedly. "Welsh?" he asked Blod. She just nodded, her eyes shining a little. "Give us a cuddle then," he said.

Ness wrapped her tiny arms around his head as Bickerstaff swung her to and fro tightly. He closed his eyes against her little mop of tawny hair, not too far from his own blonde shade, and then gently kissed the side of her head. Henri and I wore the same warm smile at the sight of them together, but I wondered if underneath it Henri was as worried as I was that this man might not ever see his daughter again. When Bickerstaff finally released Ness he gave her straight back to Blod, trying to keep his eyes off her smiling face.

"Good girl," Blod said quietly.

She gave the doctor one long, sad look that he returned, then swiftly took herself out of the room. Bickerstaff started to speak, but then coughed loudly and violently for a few moments against the wall. When he spoke again his voice was lower and gruff.

"We ought to be going soon Henri; that train won't wait for us."

Henri checked his beautiful brass coloured watch and from this close I could read the name 'A.P. Haugen' on its side. His father's watch, most likely. Something dark came over his young features as he looked into the clockface.

"We have ages yet," he protested. His other hand clamped tight around mine.

Bickerstaff sat down again and rubbed his face. He was pink in the cheeks and I was pretty sure he didn't want to get to the station any faster than Henri; he just needed to get away from what he was leaving behind at Ty Gwyn.

"Did you say goodbye to Mam and Leigh?" I asked Henri.

He nodded, smiling again, but something deeper had settled behind his happy eyes. "She's getting him ready for school," he explained, "but I think my uniform upset her."

"I'll bet she crushed your bones all the same," I answered, trying to chuckle.

"Oh yeah," Henri replied, "I'll go to training with bruised ribs now."

I wanted to give him some bruised ribs of my own, but it was awkward with Bickerstaff still in the room. I rather thought he was sensing that himself when he rose from his perch and made a start towards the door, but he'd hardly reached the handle when it swung open at him again. The doctor leapt back in shock as a flurry of tears and flowing blonde hair rushed back into the room and accosted him. Blod wrapped her arms around Bickerstaff tightly and started kissing him before we'd even had the chance to look away. It all happened so quickly that I saw his hands rushing up into her hair before I even registered that I shouldn't be watching.

I looked at Henri who was also watching-but-not-watching the sudden outburst of affection. He gave me an awkward smile, his gaze fixing on mine thoughtfully as the half-grin fell away. Bickerstaff's lungs heaved when Blod finally released him from her marathon kiss, but before he could get breath to speak she was stepping away out of his arms. Her mouth was open a little, her bright eyes streaming with tears as she turned and suddenly ran away. Bickerstaff gave us both a fleeting, red-faced look, and then went after her with haste.

As soon as he was gone Henri picked me up out of my chair and took me over to the sofa, setting me down before he knelt on the floor in front of me. He put his smooth hands on my knees, feeling the fabric of the navy dress, staring at it thoughtfully. When he finally looked up at me again his face was serious, the kind of looks he'd worn when I first met him.

"You'll wear this again the day I come home," he said, "Promise me."

"Promise," I answered, "Even if I'm ninety six."

He half smiled, leaning up towards me, pulling my arms close to wrap them around his neck. I tucked my legs under the sofa to bring him closer still until our noses were touching.

"I thought you were saving this kiss for... after?"

"I've changed my mind."

His kiss was deep and sweet, warm lips and steady breaths as he squeezed me close to him. It felt like someone had released a flock of birds into my chest; every part of me trembled and fluttered as I firmly decided that this was the best feeling of my life. Until I remembered Henri's claim the week before, that he didn't need to kiss me yet because he had faith that he'd be coming home. If he'd changed his mind about kissing me, had he changed his mind about his chances of returning too? I thought he must have felt my hesitation when he broke our kisses, searching my face desperately like he wanted to recall every freckle.

"I'll be with you," I promised, "I'll be right there to talk to you, to help you through everything."

"I know," he nodded breathlessly.

He was scared suddenly; I could see it in the widening of his eyes, the way his hands were quivering where they held my waist. I stroked his dark hair down from its usual sticky-out mess.

"You're going to be fine," I soothed, sucking in a deep breath, "You'll get through it, just like everything else so far."

"With your help," he added quickly, his lips trembling.

"With my help."

I pulled him to me and kissed him again; trying to kiss away every frightening thought that was rushing through his head. We stayed wrapped in each other's arms until Idrys came back to drag him away. I followed him out to the car in the fastest crutch-walk I'd ever done. Bickerstaff was sitting in the back of the truck with his head in his hands and Blod was nowhere to be seen. Henri got in beside the doctor and waved to me as the farm truck set off down the cobbles. I waved long after he'd gone out of focus, so hard that my arm burned with the effort for days after he'd gone.

CHAPTER TWENTY

S.W.A.L.K.

Blod hardly spoke to anyone for three full days after Henri and Bickerstaff had left for training. The only person permitted to enter her radio-filled room was Ness Fach and even she was unceremoniously kicked out after about half an hour at a time. I made the strenuous walk up the steep stairs to try and show Blod that I wanted her to talk things out with me about Bickerstaff, but all I got for my gargantuan effort was a door slammed in my face. The only upside was that her tantrum had forced Mam back into her proper role running Ty Gwyn, which resulted in a lot less crying as she redirected her emotions into producing a new series of 'rationing recipe' cakes and biscuits recommended by some of the other ladies at the chapel. They tasted foul, but Leigh and I praised her efforts all the same.

As much as I still disliked Blod intensely most of the time, I felt rotten that I could see into the places and know the things that she must have been wondering alone in her room. I had visited Henri several times already at the training camp but now that he was regimented we couldn't seem to get a single moment where there wasn't someone else in the room with him or, more usually, where he wasn't running, leaping or aiming to shoot at something with a beastly drill sergeant screaming down his ear. I had come to know this master of torture as Sergeant Cross and so far there hadn't been a single moment where his face didn't suit his name. I was actually starting to enjoy Doctor Bickerstaff's company too, now that he was a couple of hundred miles away, especially when he railed about Cross and the abuse he was throwing at Henri on a daily basis.

"He doesn't like it because you're foreign," Bickerstaff said one night as he lay on his simple bed looking up at the ceiling.

"The French are foreign and they're dying for our cause," Henri murmured.

He was lying on his side on the next bed, fumbling in a drawer for something irately. I'd noticed the drop in his mood since he'd stopped being able to speak to me. When he looked down into the drawer I looked with him to see a brand new pad of paper and a pencil just as he pulled them out of the darkness. Henri sat up to put the pad on his lap.

What are you up to? I asked.

I felt him smile for just a second, then he picked up the pencil and started to scribble, focusing hard on the page.

I found a way to talk to you.

The words lifted my heart. *You're brilliant,* I thought, *you're just brilliant.*

I know. So are you.

"What are you doing?" Bickerstaff asked.

Henri looked up from the page for a moment to

focus on him, but the doctor was unbuttoning his shirt to get ready for bed so Henri looked away again sharply, probably thinking more of what I'd be able to see than of the other man's privacy.

"I'm writing a letter to Kit," he lied expertly.

"You've got it bad for that girl, haven't you?" Bickerstaff asked in a less than kind tone.

I felt Henri grin. "I really do," he answered. His cheeks were burning just a little in the seconds after he'd said it out loud.

"She's trouble," the doctor warned, but then I heard him let out a sigh, "They're all bloody trouble."

"You'd know better than me," Henri retorted, chancing another look at Bickerstaff. He had gotten into bed, but he continued to gaze upwards and broke into a sad little smile at Henri's words. Henri gulped dryly before he spoke again. "You should write to her, tell her how you feel."

Bickerstaff laughed a little. "The only thing that's important is how Blod feels, and she doesn't feel the same way I do. That ship has very much sailed, Henri. You'll understand when you're older that some things just can't be fixed, no matter how hard you try."

She's crying over him, I told Henri, *in her room, with the radio blasting where she thinks we can't hear her.*

"She kissed you goodbye," Henri pressed, "Don't tell me that means nothing."

Bickerstaff turned his head, his eyes narrowing at Henri. "I think it's time you kept your advice to yourself," he spat, his nasty side rearing its ugly head. He turned over in the little bed and slammed his head down on the thin pillow like a petulant schoolboy. Henri sighed and went back to his pad of paper.

So much for brothers in arms.

He's as messed up as she is, I thought, *they deserve each other, no mistake.*

I'll work on him another time to write that letter. I think he's tempted.

Do, or I'm going to get hell here for months the way Blod's going on. I want to smash that radio to bits as it is.

Please don't. You are not famed for keeping your cool.

You're a cheeky devil on paper, you know.

Henri grinned widely for just a moment before he went back to his usual expression. He looked up into the bunk house full of beds that were slowly filling with countless other young men. I knew that the lights would go out soon, removing any chance of reading his page. I waited, watching Henri stare at the paper, those familiar nerves creeping into his spine. He tapped his pencil on the page a few times like he was going to start writing, but then, very slowly, he brought the nib around and drew a very faint heart instead.

Henri had just a fortnight of training before he'd be shipped off to join the 7th Armoured Division trudging through the sand in the African heat. I spent some time out by our tree trying to convince myself that there was no need to worry about him, but the season's shift sent a cold breeze to numb my skin as if to tell me that my warmest wishes were not enough to keep him safe. I pulled my knitted cardigan tight around my shoulders, hugging my arms around my body and wishing that Henri was there to hold me instead. It was painful to think of his strong arms and warm kiss when I could no longer reach them.

Whispers in his head and scribbled words on paper were all I had now to keep me sane. I knew full well what I'd be like if I didn't have those at least; the prime example of separation and grief was still stomping around Ty Gwyn in her beautiful high heeled shoes. I shuddered in the cold under the leafy canopy that rustled with the wind, but I held fast to my promise. I had asked Blod to meet me out here and I was certain that she'd give in to curiosity eventually. I heard her disgruntled huffing for a long time before she came into proper focus as she clomped across the field.

"Mam says if we die of pneumonia she won't be held responsible," Blod griped as she sat herself down beside me and leant against the tree.

"I can't risk showing you this in the house," I said, biting my lip a little.

The Celtic beauty's interest was piqued, I could tell, though she continued to scowl and narrow her eyes at the cold wind whipping up around us. I steeled myself, taking a deep breath before I flung my hands out and steeped my fingers to the bridge of my nose.

"Okay," I began, "This is going to sound complicated

and impossible, but what I'm going to tell you is true, and I can prove it to you."

Blod was already judging me, her eyes shone with interest and a mocking sort of amusement, like she was ready to pounce with every wicked jibe she knew. I could feel my cheeks reddening before I'd even really said anything, not a good sign, but I pressed on against my will and my pride.

"Henri and I aren't related, not at all."

"Then how do you know him?" Blod demanded, slapping my arm a little.

"I found him… with my mind." I tore myself away from Blod's face so I wouldn't have to see the look she was bound to be giving me. "I have, well, your Bampi calls them psychic powers."

The snort that escaped Blod was both unladylike and extremely loud.

"What a load of rubbish!" she exclaimed gleefully.

"I can prove it," I said quietly. Blod calmed a little and I looked back in her laughing eyes. "I can step into your head; speak to you in your mind."

"Oh yeah?" She folded her arms and set her mouth in a smirk that reminded me of a certain doctor. "Go on then."

So I did. Without another word I put myself quickly into the right frame of mind, slipping out of my consciousness and directly into hers. For a moment she was still watching me, my skinny form hunched over and wrapped in a cardigan with my hands over my eyes. She felt like she was going to burst out laughing, prideful and fairly cruel.

Do you believe me now?

All mirth and mockery went flying out of Blod in the huge shriek that she gave. She scrabbled away from me on the grass, gasping and watching me carefully.

Check my lips, I thought, *they aren't moving. I'm in your head.*

A fluttering of panic gathered on Blod's chest.

"You can't hear my thoughts, can you?" she asked fearfully.

Fortunately for both of us, no. But I can see through your eyes and feel your emotions. Don't panic so much. I can't hurt you.

Blod took a moment to gather a fair amount of oxygen back into her throbbing lungs before she could think straight again. She did all the things to test me that Henri had first tried, how many fingers behind her back, what was she looking at, did she have her eyes open or shut. It was all easy, and when she was as convinced as I could make her I left her mind again and shook out my body against the numbing cold of keeping still for so long.

"So you can see Henri any time you want?" she asked. I didn't miss the bitter note in her tone. I nodded, trying not to smile quite so happily. "How is he? What's the place like?"

"It's all very hard and physical," I explained, "He's always aching and tired. Bickerstaff says Africa will be much worse, but frankly I don't see how."

Blod's lip dropped, her expression one of utter hurt. "Steven spoke to you?"

"No of course not," I added apologetically, "He doesn't have a clue I'm there. But he speaks to Henri, when he's not in a mood." I hesitated a moment, looking down at the dying autumn leaves under my hands. "I think he misses you terribly."

"Did he actually say that?"

"Well, no," I mumbled. I felt Blod's posture drop beside me. "But it's so obvious. He snaps at Henri like a bulldog when he even mentions your name. He's tormented."

I saw a flash of satisfaction come over Blod's perfect features, but it soon faded to leave her deep in thought again.

"I can't stand seeing you upset like this, thinking he doesn't care about you," I rushed on, trying to get all the explanation out before she could stop me, "But please don't tell anyone about what I can do. Mum says it could be very bad for me if people found out."

"It's not that I think he doesn't care," Blod said quietly, "I know he cares." She pulled her knees up to her jaw and rested on them, hugging her flowing dress to her legs. "When he left the other day, he gave me these papers. Bank papers, they were. He's sold his house and put all this money away, see? And if he dies out there, Ness and I get the lot."

"I suppose that's quite sensible," I said, though I didn't believe that was the only reason Bickerstaff had turned in all his worldly possessions. According to our last conversation, the young doctor was completely certain that he wouldn't survive his post in the war.

"But he actually sold the house!" Blod said in less than a squeak, tears forming slowly at the corner of her eyes. "He's made it feel like he won't be coming back." I put out a hand to pat her knee and to my surprise she grabbed it and held onto me tightly. "You'll keep an eye on him for me, won't you?"

"Of course," I promised, "I'll tell you everything I can."

We sat in a silence for a few moments until Blod seemed to realise that she was still latched onto me. She let go and dusted herself down proudly, pushing the water from under her eyes as she stared at the ground thoughtfully.

"Can you find anyone you want to with this psychic lark?"

The sudden question made me stammer. "Well, um, more or less. I've been getting better and better at sort of... targeting people."

Blod paused fearfully, taking a little breath.

"Can you find Ieuan?" she asked.

It wasn't as though the thought hadn't occurred to me. In fact it had come to me no sooner than I'd heard he was missing, but I had pushed the idea of looking for him deep down into my head and tried not to feel the guilt pressing in on my thoughts every day. In truth I was scared to do it, scared to search in case the worse had come true. I had no way of knowing what it would be like to put my mind into the head of a dead man and absolutely no desire to find out. Idrys hadn't asked me to look for him either, some silent understanding between us, perhaps, that it was better to hope than have one's worst fears confirmed. Blod clearly didn't have those kind of concerns.

"I can try," I said, voice trembling. I wasn't sure that I wanted to, but there was no way that I could say no to Blod, she'd lost so much already this summer.

She sat patient and silent as a child whilst I wrapped myself up warm again and settled, heaving out my shaking breaths. I closed my eyes along with the usual moves, concentrating hard on Ieuan's ginger head of hair, his low lilting voice, his eyes the same bright blue as the rest of the Price siblings. I thought about the jokes he'd made at the dinner table, the wink he'd tipped me about the rationed chocolate what seemed like forever ago. All around me was blackness for a terrifyingly long time, but I focused harder still on the youngest brother, the long nose and square jaw that smacked of his poor father.

The blackness evolved into something, though it was still a terribly dark place to be. I could see a crumbling, impossibly dark wall before me, I felt cramped, afraid, like I couldn't breathe. I panicked horrifically as I realised I was underground. Was he dead? Buried? Was this his body, deathly still, laying in the earth forever more?

"It's all right lads, they've moved off."

Ieuan started to move suddenly, digging something sharp and cold into the wall of earth in front of him. Now that he was moving again I could feel him crouching, his long legs tangled up underneath him, his head craned to the side against the confines of the space he was in. He looked down as a torchlight flashed somewhere behind him. There was a small, metal pan like you might use for cooking which he was filling with earth with a tablespoon. When he'd piled the last bit of soil on top of it he passed it back behind him.

"Pass us another empty, mun," he said gruffly.

He felt exhausted, but there was something steely and angry coating his heart. When Ieuan looked behind him to find another pan I was shocked to see a huge line of men all crouched in the badly lit passage. They were all kinds of ages and all in vests and underwear, their white garments smeared with the earth that surrounded them. Every man was digging out beside him, making their tunnel wider whilst Ieuan pressed on at its head.

"We're going to have to stop soon chaps, inspection in twenty minutes." A posh kind of voice came echoing down the long underground dugout to give the warning. "Five more minutes, then everyone up and back into uniform."

I wasn't all that sure about what was going on, but wherever Ieuan was he and the other British men around him were trying to tunnel their way out. He was captured, but alive, and the relief I was feeling would be nothing compared to how Blod would react to the news I could now give her. The old cold shiver hit me as thoughts of Blod sitting in the autumn leaves captured my attention; I left Ieuan in the tunnel and when my eyes reopened at Ty Gwyn, a huge smile erupted before I could even speak.

CHAPTER TWENTY-ONE

Reunion

We consulted Idrys about my visit to Ieuan as soon
as we could and he gave us the good news and the bad: Ieuan
would be well-looked after, he was in no immediate harm,
but he was also in a prisoner of war camp. There would be
no way for him to get out until the war was over and the
fact that he was tunnelling was a very dangerous sign. If the
Germans caught him trying to escape, the consequences
would be as severe as we could possibly imagine. It was a
wrench not to be able to tell Mam that her youngest son
was alive and well, but Idrys warned me that she wouldn't
be likely to understand my gift.

"You young people are more accepting of these
things," he said to Blod and me in a whisper, "It's best
not to burden Mam with talk like this. It might upset her
something awful."

Blod went back to her duties in the household so
that I'd have more free time to check on Henri, Bickerstaff
and Ieuan during the day. Mam was too grateful for the
help to question Blod's change of heart, putting it down to
her ever-altering moods, but she was disturbed by the way

Blod kept suddenly running off into my bedroom to ask me whispered little questions. I gave her what snippets I could from my visits to the POW camp and to the Essex barracks, but we had learned very little except for the fact that Ieuan's camp was located somewhere near Toulouse, which Idrys later informed us was quite far south in France. The fact that he wasn't in Germany boded quite well, I thought.

Henri's training days were coming to an end and the evening talks between the boys in the barracks were becoming more sombre by the day. Most of the soldiers and medics in training in Henri's living space were dressed in the same sandy brown uniforms as him and Bickerstaff, marking them all as 'Desert Rats', the new wave of aggression that was supposedly going to get North Africa under control at last. Most of the young men in the barracks were, like Henri, enthused about the prospect of battling alongside heavy artillery and tanks; it seemed like such weapons would offer them a great deal of protection. But there were a few agitators, Bickerstaff included, who were all too keen to remind the others that the Germans had cannons, shells and tanks of their own.

I didn't know whether it was better to be optimistic like Henri or keenly aware of the dangers like Bickerstaff, so all I could do was urge Henri to stay friendly with the belligerent doctor in case he needed him one day soon. For all the faults in his mood, Bickerstaff was an intelligent man, perhaps too smart for his own good; he would spot problems and risks where Henri might not. Henri wasn't keen on the idea of palling up with the most cynical and unpopular chap in the barracks, but for my sake he promised he would stick as close to the doctor as he could.

In return, however, I had to promise something of my own. It was going to take the boys two days to cross to their new post in Libya and Henri made me swear I wouldn't go poking into his head until they got there. Now that he had developed a keen sense for when I was actually there in his mind, I couldn't even pretend I hadn't visited him. I swore I'd keep my word and said a strained goodbye and good luck to Henri the night before the departure. He drew another little heart on his page for me, then scribbled underneath:

Tell Blod to look out for the post.

The news sent Blod into a frenzy, she practically attacked the postman the next morning asking repeatedly if there was anything for Ty Gwyn, even when he'd already gone past the cobble path that led up to the little white farm house. Idrys was even more anxious for news of Ieuan; every time he arrived at the house for a meal or a cup of tea he always came to me before anyone else to ask for an update. Mam quite often remarked on how popular I had become with everyone, though I knew she hadn't the faintest clue as to why.

I wanted to give Idrys more interesting news, but the life of a prisoner of war was not half as exciting as I'd expected it to be. The tunnel Ieuan had been digging had collapsed after a few days, forcing the prisoners to rethink their plans and start over again in another direction. Other than that his life was a series of inspections by official looking Nazis and surly guards interspersed with idle chit chat amongst fellow airmen and soldiers as they smoked and played cards, waiting for their next shift to dig a few more inches out of the ground beneath their feet. I had considered trying to talk to Ieuan to get a message to him from his family, but Idrys forbade it, fearful that the Germans might shoot him as a spy if they heard him talking to an invisible person.

It was a rainy afternoon, the day before I could visit Henri again, when the post arrived. Blod squealed at first, but she stomped into the kitchen and dropped a soggy brown thing into my lap with a huff moments later.

"Typical," she spat, "It's for you." She hurricaned out of the room again instantly.

I looked down at the marred envelope, reading my name and address in Henri's scribbly handwriting. This wasn't right; he had told Blod to wait for the letter. I looked up at Mam, her back to me as she did the washing up, and suddenly two and two made four. I wheeled out of the kitchen as silently as I could to catch up to Blod.

"Wait, wait!" I said in a hoarse tone, not wanting Mam to hear me.

I heaved and panted to get to Blod before she could march up the stairs, grabbing the sleeve of her cardigan as I wheeled straight into her leg. She kicked me away with a loud 'ouch' but I shushed her, beckoning her to come close whilst I spoke in a low whisper.

"Henri and I speak all the time. We don't need letters. I think this is really for you."

Bickerstaff clearly didn't want to raise Mam's suspicions, but it would look perfectly normal for Henri to be sending me a note before he was shipped off. Blod's eyes widened excitedly and she took the letter back, holding it tightly with both hands. Without a word she scampered up the stairs and I heard the door to her bedroom slam behind her. I smiled, proud of Henri and pleased for Blod.

As I made an awkward turn in the black and white hall the wide front door burst open with a bang. I was horrified to find the violent noise was made by Leighton, who was huffing and puffing with a round red face. Before I could even speak he found me and grabbed my arms, shaking his head in amazement.

"Kit! Kit!" he heaved, hardly breathing.

"Close the door Leigh it's freezing!" I ordered immediately, wrenching myself out of his frantic grip.

Leighton shook his head repeatedly, clutching at his chest and gasping. "Kit it's… it's…. I've run all the way from… She's coming! She's coming now!"

"Who is?" I demanded, rolling my eyes.

My little brother grinned as he got back his breath. "Mum!"

Mam and Mum were a funny sight in a room

together. My mother sat upright with her finely curled hair, gripping her tea mug and sipping the liquid gratefully as it steamed against the cold air around her. Mam relaxed, her face rosy from her day's housework, hair flapping out of her practical bun in wild directions. And yet they smiled together and talked incessantly, like they might have known each other for years. I supposed quietly to myself that if Mum had been visiting us in Leighton's head, she probably knew a lot about Mam already, perhaps more than she ought to. I watched them together for a moment more before I properly entered the room, my crutches resting on my knees as I wheeled in.

"Go on then," Mum said, taking in a big breath, "Let me see you."

Proudly and expertly I rose from my chair and onto my walking aids with relative ease. Shoving the cushioned parts under my arms I was able to walk right up to Mum and look down at her where she sat, beaming my best golden smile. She took my face in her hands and admired me with a grin that matched my own. I knew she had probably seen me on my feet before in her mental visits, but there was something different about the experience of actually being here and feeling her pat me on the back for my success.

"My goodness," she mouthed, looking to Mam to find her beaming too, "I must thank that doctor of yours, dear."

My smile flickered away. "You can't Mum," I said sadly, "he's in Africa now."

"Poor soul," Mam whispered, "I do hope he'll be all

right. And Henri too, of course."

Though the mood was a little more sombre, Mum still quirked an eyebrow at me.

"Yes," she said slowly, cracking a tiny smile, "We mustn't forget Henri."

"Brave boys, both of them," Mam said, suddenly rising to clear away the tea cups. She was holding something back in her voice; it quivered like a dam waiting to burst. It would be a long time before those tense moments were a thing of the past, I knew.

"Shall we go sit in the other room Mum?" I suggested, eyeing Mam carefully where she was scrubbing the life out of a cup.

"That's a great idea love," Mum replied, "Come and join us when you're ready, Gladys?"

Mam nodded, forcing a smile back to her face. "Yeah of course, Gail love," she choked, "You'll stay for your dinner tonight, won't you?"

"If you'll have me," Mum answered with a humble smile.

It was a well-known fact that Mam would feed anybody who came to Ty Gwyn, so she only bobbed in and out of the sitting room whilst Mum sat with Leighton and me, joining our conversation in between the mashing of potatoes and the roasting of meat. Leigh had run into our mother walking up the big hill to reach the farm house and

then run all the way on to be the first one to tell us all of
her arrival, so after he had heard the tales of the on-going
bombing in London he abruptly fell asleep on the old sofa
next to Mum. She put her coat over him and shuffled away
a little to be nearer to me.

"I have to go back right away tonight, sweetheart,"
she warned quietly, "but I came as soon as I could manage.
I know I've left you for so long without any answers." She
rubbed her pale hands together slowly. "But it would have
been far too risky to put anything in a letter."

I frowned, trying to organise my thoughts to work
out what questions I really needed answering. There was
the big one, of course, the D word, the one that I still didn't
think she would tell me about. I decided on building up to
that slowly.

"So have you ever worked in a bicycle factory, or was
that all a big lie?"

Mum gave me an apologetic grin. "I don't even
know how to ride a bicycle darling, much less manufacture
its parts."

"Who is it you work for then?" I pressed eagerly,
"The government?"

She nodded. "Whoever needs me. At the moment
that's the War Office."

"Why didn't you ever explain to me? You must have
realised I was getting these powers, surely?"

"I was hoping you might stay in denial about them
a bit longer, actually," Mum admitted, reaching out to take
my hand, "I assume you've been poking around in Norway,

what with Henri and all. You're much more advanced that I would have expected."

"Am I?" I found myself smiling at that. "Well I've been working on it very hard, and Idrys had helped."

Mum's face fell. "How many people know about this all together?"

"Three," I replied.

"Darling you must keep it that way." She squeezed my hand again before taking it back to tap her own knees impatiently. "This war, this situation… It isn't a good time to do what you can do."

"But Idrys knew Granddad Arkwright!" I protested. "He helped in the first war, you're helping in this one, and-"

"And nothing," Mum interrupted, her young face suddenly stricter than usual, "Your time to help will come when you're older, I'm sure, but not now."

I folded my arms at her. "You can't stop me," I said plainly, "It's my power."

My mother's slim shoulders drooped and she shook her head just the once. "No, I can't stop you," she conceded, "All I can do is ask that you be sensible."

She let out a long, low sigh, reclining on the sofa, pulling away from me. Leighton stirred a little, huffing out a short breath. She started to stroke his hair.

"I'm afraid of the things you might see, Kit." She spoke quietly, like every word might explode if its volume was too high. "This Henri of yours has been trained, but he doesn't know what's really out there, the horrors he's going to have to face. You shouldn't be facing them with him; you

K.C. Finn

should be here where I put you, where it's safe."

I was sure that Henri and Bickerstaff had both told me about the prospect of what was out there too. I hadn't listened to either of them and this third warning felt like a record on repeat.

"But I can help Henri," I protested, "I helped him before, when he was still in Norway!"

"This is going to be very different," Mum said with a grave, pale face, "If you do it, there won't be any going back. You can't un-see the places that your mind might take you to. You won't ever forget. I know I haven't."

She looked older than the last time I had seen her when she waved us off at the station more than a year ago. She was still my prim and proper mother with her careful balance of compassion and caution, but as she looked down at Leighton curled up beside her there was something so exposed in her face. Raw emotion had bubbled up into her eyes, striking every nerve, setting her up like a rubber band stretched to its limit.

"I understand what you're saying," I began cautiously, though in truth I really didn't. How did she know that I couldn't handle the sight of the war? How did any of them know what I could manage unless they let me try it? "But I can't turn my back on this now. There are people here depending on me."

"Don't say I didn't warn you."

Mum didn't say it in a nasty way; it was more like she just had to get the words out. Leighton uncurled himself from his cat-like position near us, rubbing his eyes.

241

"Oh no," he mumbled, "sorry Mum, I just-"

"It's all right darling," she soothed, stroking his hair again as he sat up and shuffled closer, "I've missed watching you sleep."

The conversation was over and I hadn't even reached the part about Dad. Every time I looked at Mum that evening I felt something different, sometimes anger, sometimes fear. Pity, loss, duty, guilt, I could hardly process the gambit of emotions running amok inside my head. I tried my best to push them all away, to just appreciate my mother for the few hours we had before she was due to set off on the midnight train back to London, but I was still riled that she had kept so much from me. She was still keeping things from me and worse she was telling me not to go looking for the answers myself either.

By the time she had gone that night I knew what I wanted to do. It was the ultimate betrayal, I was sure, but it was time to stop letting other people dictate my actions. I was going to do it. I was going to find my father.

CHAPTER TWENTY-TWO

Blood and Sand

My first attempt to find Dad resulted in blackness, but if experience had taught me anything it was that black didn't ever seem to mean dead. Everything was still; I was in that conundrum where I couldn't work out if my heart was beating or his, if those were my limbs twitching, my lungs expanding slowly. He might have been asleep. I didn't dare call out to wake him up, deciding instead that I would just keep coming back until he was awake. The next morning I thought about trying him straight away but my energy felt low. Saving my strength was the best move, especially since I needed to be in Libya after breakfast.

Blod came to sit with me in the little sitting room whilst I made the journey, desperate to ensure that we would not be disturbed. She was visibly uncomfortable with having to watch me travel, but she did her best to sit still and not fidget. It took me longer than usual to calm myself down, every time I closed my eyes all I could think of was how constantly I was disobeying my mother. My own guilt made me angrier than her so-called advice; I wished desperately that I was confident enough to believe that I was doing the right thing by stepping back into the war.

Africa was a beautiful place. I got to Henri at the same time for three days running when he was on patrol, looking out to the empty, sandy horizon. Though I couldn't feel the heat that rose in waves from the golden desert dunes, I felt the sweat pooling at the back of Henri's neck, his dusky fatigues sticking to his aching body. Training had been hard on him, but the journey had apparently been even worse.

How are your bruises? I asked when Henri had walked to the farthest part of his patrol route. He had to time his replies for the moments when no-one else was in earshot; turning his face away from the base so no-one saw his lips move.

"I'm learning to load this huge gun," he murmured, "Every time I load a shell it falls back on me. Damn heavy things, my arm is black."

Any sign of the Germans?

Henri shook his head. "We're not looking for Germans. It's the Italians that are fighting out here, but of course they're all still the enemy."

I bit my lip. *Is that better or worse than facing the Nazis?*

I felt his chest deflate. "I suppose when they're pointing a tank at you it's all the same."

You sound like-

"Bickerstaff, I know," he intercepted sadly, "Unfortunately the man makes a lot of sense to me now."

Henri gripped his rifle tightly, scanning the bare sands around him once more. "When you hear the gunfire at night, it's hard not to think about the fact that you'll be out there in it soon enough."

Where is Bickerstaff? I pressed, trying to steer away from the growing fear in Henri's ribcage. *Blod wants to know how he's doing.*

"He's out today with a special group," Henri said, licking his chapped lips in the unbearable heat, "They're scouting to find out how close the Iti's are. I'm supposed to watch for them returning. I'll have to go back to the other side now."

I knew that meant he couldn't talk for a while, but he was so sad, so lonely, that I couldn't bear to break the link.

I'll stay and keep you company, I offered. He nodded and set off back towards the other soldiers.

Henri was patrolling a section of wire fence that led down to a pair of huge iron gates where trucks and cars pulled into the base day in, day out. There were other guards who were permanently stationed at the gates, ready to open them at the sign of an allied group, but also sporting rifles to tackle any hint of a threat. The base itself was all done out in stone, like the British Army had overtaken some great Libyan mansion and filled it with their troops. Henri and his brothers in arms blended seamlessly with the sandy stones and dusky ground, their brown uniforms were already caked with squashed fly stains and tiny drops of blood that seeped out of their mosquito bites. I felt the serious set jaw on Henri's face as he reached the gate and nodded to the other guards, I ached to be able to take that jaw in my hands and kiss out his tension.

I love you, you know.

The thought had escaped before I had a chance to rein it in. Henri caught his breath in his throat; the sombre weight in his chest lifting away like a pressure valve had been removed. He couldn't reply, certainly not with the two gate guards standing right next to him, but I felt his face relax into a smile. His nerves danced in his arms and shoulder, racing back and forth to his heart as he let out a few breaths. Then, very slowly, he put his hand up to his mouth and kissed his own palm silently.

I knew what it meant.

I was all the more eager to stay until he'd be able to talk again; I'd been waiting about ten minutes for him to shift position when a speck in the dunes caught my eye.

Henri there, I directed, *coming over that big hill in the middle. What is it?*

He had found the sight a few seconds after me, his eyes focusing hard on the dark dot as it charged toward the base. He spoke to the other guards as they all raised their guns, eyeing the approaching threat. The sight of a uniform the same colour as their own meant nothing, they kept their rifles trained and the gates firmly locked until the blurry brown shape was in better view.

One man was carrying another across his shoulders, trudging through deep sand with staggered strides, his head down as he raced on towards where we were watching. The man being carried was in better view; his sandy uniform was coated in blood. I wanted to be sick, but there was no way I could look away. Pain and nausea ripped through my chest as the men came closer and closer, but I stared on, transfixed by the sight. His face was cut, his trousers ripped, his jacket sliced open right across the chest where a mighty gash oozed with red liquid. I had never known that blood could be so thick.

Once the guards had realised that the soldiers approaching were indeed their allies, the gates flew open and more men were alerted to rush out and help the injured fellow. They rushed him past where Henri stood watching then they burst out of the gates and raced towards the man who had been carrying him, who collapsed into the sand the moment his charge had been lifted. Henri found him and flipped him onto his back as the fellow heaved. He knelt back, aghast as I too reeled in shock at the sight of him.

"Bickerstaff!"

"Good morning," he choked, spitting out a mouthful of blood and sand beside him.

The handsome doctor had a huge laceration running down the left side of his face, now caked with bits of sand and dirt that were soaking up the deep red ooze all around the wound. His chest hammered visibly until he had caught his breath, I noticed the fearful tears streaming from his eyes. Eventually he sat up, thumping his torso to cough any sign of weakness from his voice.

"We were set upon," he breathed, "They killed Carter, took Briggs away. Cooper was the only one I could help."

Henri clapped him on the shoulder, his head flooded with pride, relief and an overwhelming sense of terror.

"Let's get your face stitched up."

He threw an arm around Bickerstaff's middle and hauled the other man up as fast as he could. I felt the sticky, sickly touch of the doctor's bleeding face as it grazed Henri's ear. I didn't know which one of us felt sicker at the sensation. Either way it was becoming too much, despite my desperation to stay, that old cold shiver in my spine told me it was time to go. In truth a big part of me was glad it had come, though I felt so selfish, just melting away to safety whilst Henri had to go on alone.

Blod was hysterical over Bickerstaff's injury; she kept making me describe it until I felt unbearably queasy again, so much so that I actually hobbled off to the kitchen for fear I'd have to throw up in the sink. These were the things Mum had warned me of, the things that I couldn't un-see. I was scared, trembling all over, but it wouldn't stop me going back there at the same time tomorrow, nothing would stop me from letting Henri know I was always there for him. He was growing more fearful every day of what fate had in store for him. But fate had brought us together once, so I was willing to trust it to do the right thing and I needed him to feel that way too.

When my nerves had recovered I spent some

time checking on Ieuan, only to find that his tunnel had collapsed yet again and he was in a secret meeting with some angry looking fellows who were trying to decide on a new location to begin another dig. They were interrupted briefly by some vicious looking guards who snooped around their room, perhaps looking for signs of the dig. They built their tunnels under the floorboards of course, and they never used their uniforms whilst they were digging. All the dirt was hidden away on their vests and other underclothes, to the untrained eye they were just bored players that had been removed from the great game in the outside world. To me, through Ieuan's eyes, they were cunning heroes waiting for their moment to strike.

Happy that I could report Ieuan as safe and well to Blod and Idrys, my thoughts wandered back to the other task at hand. I closed my eyes again, searching desperately for Dad. It had been more than two years since I had seen him, I wished I had taken better notice of how he looked the night I saw him last. He had hair a darker shade of brown than Leighton, cut in an elegant but very old fashioned sort of wave. I remembered his dark moustache shaped like the whiskers on a fox, how his brown eyes used to crinkle when Leigh and I tried to make it stick up the wrong way towards his nose.

Black again, but this time the body I was in was moving. I had no way to tell if this was my father, but I hadn't been wrong about my targets in a long time. I waited excitedly, focusing on every feeling this man was having. His arms were stretched out in front of him, moving with strain against something ahead in the pitch darkness. He was on his knees; they dug into hard, stony ground, aching like he'd knelt on pins and needles for hours. His toes were numb inside heavy boots, his head bowed down towards the ground beneath him.

He blinked something out of his eye, a vague shadow telling me he was wiping his face. So his eyes were open, but wherever he was there wasn't a flicker of light to be found. I heard scraping sounds where his hands were, sounds that I had learned to recognise lately. His chest was starting to ache from his task, but he made no other noise at all. There was just him, his silent breaths and the scraping. He was alone. And he was digging.

No matter how I tried the timing I could only find Dad asleep or in the tunnel. I was beginning to wonder idly if he was sleeping in the tunnel itself, but the thought of all those other passages that had collapsed for Ieuan told me that he probably wasn't. I was just unlucky with my visits. It was possible that Dad was in a POW camp too, but if that were true then I didn't understand why Mum would want to keep it such a big secret, or why Dad had left us so long before the war actually broke out. There was something more to it than what I knew so far, I supposed I'd just have to keep trying.

Bickerstaff's face was slowly healing with each day that I saw him, but it looked as though the blade that had cut into his cheek was going to leave a permanent scar on his pale skin. He and Henri carried on their duties as normal despite the shockwave running through the base about the attack, until one day I found Henri patrolling in a particularly nervy mood. He had his rifle on his back and he was rubbing his palms down the sides of his trousers over and over again, the skin of his hands turning raw. A bad sign, a very bad sign indeed.

Tell me what's the matter, I demanded.

"I love you too," Henri blurted a sharp whisper, "I've been meaning to say it. I was waiting for a nice time, but I have to say it now or I'll burst." His spine prickled with electricity.

For God's sake Henri, what's going on?

"They're sending us out there, to that same place where Carter got killed the other day." I froze, waiting desperately for an explanation. "About a dozen of us, we're going to ambush them at night."

Do the others have to go too? Bickerstaff and Cooper? I thought of the sheer horror of the injured men, those who had just managed to escape, having to go straight back to the scene where their ally had lost his life.

"Cooper's dead," Henri said softly, "His injuries got infected, they were too… Bickerstaff tried to help him, he really tried." He attempted to clear his throat, but I could feel how difficult it was, the invisible blockage of grief and fear had made it impossible to swallow. "But yes, Bickerstaff has to come with us. He's our medic, he has no choice."

An ambush, I mused, *Do you think I can help?*

"I don't think you should," Henri began, but then the tremble in his heart grew larger, "but I need you there, Kit. I-"

His voice cracked and heat rose in his already sweating face. He kept his back to the base, looking out through the fence at the seemingly harmless sands. I wondered how many vicious killers were hiding just over those distant dunes.

I'll be there, I promised, *I'll help you no matter what. You know that.* I couldn't stand the feel of his terrified body any longer, the way even his strong legs were quaking in his hardy boots. *I can feel your emotions, Henri,* I confessed.

His eyes widened. "Can you always do that?" he breathed.

Yes.

"Then you know, without me saying it," he whispered, "You know how bad this is going to be."

I'll help you to get away if you need to, I swore, *I'll help you to hide, to survive this.*

Henri sucked up his strength and forced himself to stop shaking, trying to be stronger than he seemed. His heart betrayed him though as it went on pounding away at his ribs. He shoved his hands deep into his pockets to remove the temptation to rub his palms. I wanted to hold him, to pull him in and never let go, but despite our mental closeness I was just too far away. All I had were the words I could whisper in his mind.

I love you so much.

"I love you too."

CHAPTER TWENTY-THREE

The Wee Small Hours

The ambush was scheduled for two in the morning. I was there early, watching Henri get kitted out with guns, grenades and all sorts of nasty looking things that I didn't want to investigate. I could tell by his occasional smiles that he knew I was with him, though I didn't speak very often. He and Bickerstaff were the last ones left in the barracks as they prepared themselves for the operation. I caught a few glimpses of the doctor with his pink scar; his face was grave and hollow. He looked like he hadn't been eating or sleeping at all.

"Just get out if things turn sour," Bickerstaff said in a low murmur, "Don't worry about helping anyone else. Run like hell, due south brings you back here after about an hour."

"I wouldn't leave any man behind," Henri protested, "You didn't last time."

"And a fat lot of good it did," Bickerstaff spat, "Cooper would have been better dying where he fell. At least the Iti's would have made it quick."

I felt my stomach give a lurch. His wicked temper

was a hundred times worse in the face of war.

"It's not about cowardice, Henri," the doctor added, strapping a case full of bullets into place, "It's about what's practical. If you stop to help someone else, then two men die instead of one. You can't win a war like that."

"Don't you mean 'we'?" Henri pressed.

Bickerstaff kept his blonde head down, refusing to answer.

He doesn't think that he'll live through this twice, I thought. Henri nodded imperceptibly.

He approached the doctor where he was lacing his boots and put a hand on his shoulder. I could feel Bickerstaff shaking at the touch. Henri leant down against his scarred face, trying to make him see that he was smiling.

"Remember your girls at home," he whispered. Bickerstaff shut his eyes tightly. "If there's any way to get home to them, you have to strive for it. I know that's what I'm doing."

Bickerstaff froze in place stubbornly until Henri broke away, defeated. The call came for the dozen selected men to form ranks and soon the pack of Desert Rats were off, streaking silently out of the gates and into the dark sands. They walked slowly and determinedly for almost an hour, their guns held tightly and their eyes darting everywhere at once for the signs of a threat. I could hear Henri's heartbeat, quick but steady as he went. He was trying to be brave, trying not quake or tremble because he knew I would feel it if he did, and I was content that his pride was also helping him not give in to fear.

K.C. Finn

The marching slowed suddenly as the boys got nearer to their target. I watched with fascination as the leader of the pack had them all lie low in the sand, shuffling on their hands and knees until they were lined up on the crest of a large dune. Over the dune they peered down into a deeper sand valley where two tents sat about three feet apart. A single man was sitting between them, his head nodding up and down as he dozed. Signals were given that I didn't understand but I felt Henri and the other slowly creeping onto their knees and clutching their guns again. The objective was capture, not kill, but Henri kept his finger on the trigger all the same as he snaked down the side of the dune.

One dark figure apprehended the sleeping guard first, knocking him out with the back of his rifle with a swift thud. He fell to the ground unconscious and the soldier began to restrain his hands behind his back. The others made a circle each around the two small tents, their guns trained on them from every angle. The captain of the squad was right opposite Henri as he cleared his throat loudly and kicked the tent before him.

"Come out with your hands up," he ordered into the night, "We have you surrounded."

But nothing happened. The captain poked his rifle deeper into the wall of the tent, but I could see there was nothing inside it to hit. It seemed strange that the Italians would leave a guard to watch over two empty tents.

"It is we that have you surrounded, Englishman."

Henri whirled on the spot to a voice behind

him. From the top of the dune a row of black figures had appeared as if they had emerged from the night sky itself. Their faces were smeared with black paint, their uniforms abandoned for all black fatigues to make them look like mere shadows on the sand. They were armed with much large guns than Henri and the others, some of them had great tubular barrels resting on their shoulders.

"Drop your weapons."

The same man who had spoken before ordered with his shadowy mouth. His accent was as thick as the dark beard all over his chin.

"No," said the captain from behind Henri.

A shot rang out from one of the black figures. Henri didn't look around, but I heard a body crumple to the floor. He was frozen with fear, his gun falling limply from his arms as his breath caught repeatedly in his mouth like he couldn't seize control of his lungs any more. The other men dropped their weapons too. The black crowd descended from the top of the dune to retrieve the guns, only to be replaced by another wave of heavily armed men who looked down on them from above. They were outnumbered at least two to one.

When Henri was forced to turn by one of the Italians I saw the other villains dragging the poor captain's body away. Even in the dark night I saw his glassy eyes, wide open and reflecting the tiny sliver of moonlight behind the clouds. His corpse was hauled past my vision slowly. I wanted to scream. Henri's heart beat so fast it was humming as a soldier grabbed him and twisted his arms behind his back. I felt the sharp agony of the violent move as though it was my own body being wrenched into a helpless submission.

I'm still here Henri, I said in my best calming tone, *They clearly don't want to kill you, so just don't make them angry. It's going to be all right.*

I couldn't know that, of course, but Henri's breathing came back to normal all the same at my words. He watched tensely as the other men were being jostled about, the Italians forcing them into a huddle in the darkness where they could keep control of them all. I hoped that this enemy was a civil one, that if Henri was to be taken by them he might just end up locked away like Ieuan. It wasn't a great prospect, but it was a good deal better than death.

Everything went wrong so quickly that I didn't have time to register it all at once. A scuffle started with one of our boys at the edge of the huddle, he managed to break out and kick the nearest Iti in the gut, sending him flying into the tent where he became tangled in the crumpled mess of canvas. Shooting broke out and the cluster of men began to scatter. Henri struggled against his captor until they both fell over the body of the unconscious guard that the poor dead captain had knocked out, but Henri got out of it first and scrambled to grab hold of the Italian's gun before he could get it back.

"Run man, run!"

Bickerstaff's voice carried over the din of the guns. He grabbed Henri by the elbow and pulled him down against a steep dune where the Italians couldn't aim, then they streaked out in the valley until it rose back onto the steady plane that would take them back to base.

Keep running, I pressed deep into Henri's mind, *don't think, just keep running.*

There was no time even for fear; the two men were at the forefront of the other Desert Rats as they all bolted back towards the distant promise of safety on the dark horizon. Half the Italians were giving chase when Henri glanced back; the others with the larger guns were taking up positions to fire from farther away. Every thump Henri's boots made into the sand sent a jarring pain into each rattling bone of his body; I ached as he carried us on through the random deadly bullets that were being fired wildly by the pursuers.

A huge boom broke the sound of heavy breaths and tiny bullets and someone cried out not far behind Henri. He stopped running and turned, other men flying past him as one of the Desert Rats lay bleeding on the ground. The clouds had cleared to shed more moonlight on the scene: his foot was bloodied and he lay in shock where something much larger than a bullet had hit him. Henri looked up to see the pack of Iti's catching him up, then raced forward to help yanking the shocked fellow to his feet.

"You're an idiot Haugen!" Bickerstaff shouted as he came to take the man's other side. He too had turned back at the injured chap's cry.

"What does that make you?" Henri replied, his usually rich voice wild and terrified.

They pulled the injured man on until he came to

his senses and though his foot was leaving a trail of blood, eventually they were all running again. Except now they were at the back of the pack. Another boom hit out, firing a shell that thankfully didn't find them, but when its echo died out I could hear the grunts and foreign shouts of the Italians closing in behind them. Then it happened, the horror, the thing I was wishing against with every bit of strength I had.

A hand grabbed the back of Henri's uniform. He struggled to break free but he was pulled to the ground, a mighty hand gripped hard over his mouth so he couldn't even cry out for help. The man with the crippled foot went charging on ahead of him, the rest of the escapees were already lost to the dark night. But Bickerstaff was looking back. He hauled himself around and started running back towards danger, towards Henri. He had no gun, no way to tackle the man now pulling Henri back up to his feet, just a grimace like a bulldog and a will like steel in his eyes.

Another boom deafened us all; a wind flew past where Henri and his new captor stood. The moonlight caught Bickerstaff's outline as the shell whizzed straight towards him. Everything was strangely slow as Henri's wide; disbelieving stare let me take in the whole gory scene. Bickerstaff tried to leap away from the shell, but the blur of speeding metal was faster than he was. Thanks to his leap it found its mark not in his chest, but in his shin. His leg came away from his body like some great invisible child had snapped the limb off at the knee. I watched in silent horror as what had been his calf and foot flew out into the darkness. He screamed out in agony, dropping to the ground, reaching out towards Henri desperately.

Henri was trying to shout, biting into the hand that blocked his mouth, but the man who held him now wore thick leather gloves. He pulled Henri's body securely against his, but both of them looked up sharply as a set of shining lights suddenly flashed into life in the dark night. A truck. And then another. British Army vehicles, driving towards the Iti's at full pelt. The one who had Henri threw him up over his shoulder in a fireman's lift, finally releasing Henri's mouth for him to cry out for aid. The Italians took off running as the trucks got closer to where Bickerstaff lay, but he was out of focus with the way Henri was banging back and forth against his captor's back.

"Henri!"

The doctor shouted, but he could do little more. One of the trucks had stopped beside him but the other was still pursuing the pack of Italians. Henri bashed hard against the back of the one carrying him, trying to reach anywhere he could to batter him, weaken him somehow so that he would be let go. The Italian shouted something in his own language and after a few seconds Henri's eyes showed me someone else coming into view. The wicked leader with the dark beard had jogged back to the rear of his men, and with a hard thump on the back of Henri's head; I lost sight of everything going on.

When I returned to my bed, sweating and panting, I knew there was no point going back yet. They had knocked him unconscious, but perhaps the army truck would catch up with them yet. All the images of the carnage in the night flooded my mind, I held my head tightly to try and push them away. The cold dead eyes of the captain and his crumpled body. The trail of blood from the soldier's foot as he ran on through the sand. Bickerstaff. The way his leg had come away like a loose part. His deafening scream. Henri's fear. The aggressor's iron grip, the leather gloved hands he had bitten into in desperation. The cruel, smiling face of the Iti leader as he brought down his fist to make everything black.

I was crying, screaming, tearing off my splints and throwing myself out of the bed to be sick. The sight of it all burned into the back of my eyes, my body shivered with the strain of racing unaided to the basin, everything was too much. I collapsed onto the ground with a hard crack to my back, crying out and sobbing loudly as my limbs bent under me. My fears for Henri's safety made me shake all over, and now I wished I didn't know what I knew. Until he came to I would be haunted, not knowing if he'd been recovered or thrown into the hands of the enemy for good.

The whole household was alerted to my terrified sobs, but nobody could help me to calm down. I shook uncontrollably as Idrys and Mam got me back into my bed, Leighton and Ness watched with terrified faces at the door. Most fearful of all was Blod, who sat beside me clinging to my hand. I had news, terrible news, and she knew it all too well. But Mam was fussing far too much to get rid of her; I couldn't explain anything until she was gone. I wasn't sure I could even make my mouth form the words yet.

"It's a night terror," Idrys insisted, though his blue eyes gleaming with concern told me he was lying.

Mam held me down as I shook and cried. Idrys and Blod left and returned almost instantly with a large bottle of something. Idrys poured a measure of yellow liquid into Blod's shaking hands as she held the glass. She brought it to my lips, forcing the drink into my mouth. It was beastly, sour like glue and it burned my mouth all over. I tried to resist it but Blod pushed my head up and tipped the whole thing into my mouth. I had no choice but to gulp it down before it burned a hole through my head. As it settled in my stomach I gave a great lurch and after a moment my head flushed with dizziness.

The ceiling melted like water above me and my eyes flickered shut, trying to contend with whatever that dose of liquid was doing to me. Every limb felt heavy, like they didn't belong to me anymore. I tried to speak but my mouth was a limp, slurring mess. I needed to stay awake; I needed to get calm, to tell Blod and Idrys what had happened. I needed to be there when Henri woke up.

But now, like him, my world was fading into inescapable blackness. Pain surged though me like a knife had cleaved my heart open and slowly, but gratefully, I gave in to the urge to fade away.

CHAPTER TWENTY-FOUR

Hospital Corners

When I awoke I had a pounding headache. Someone had put a cold cloth on my brow that flopped down into my lap when I managed to haul myself up. Though my head was raging like a brass band conducted by the Devil himself, I started to push off the tight covers where I'd been tucked in, looking around for my crutches and clothes. It was time to find Blod; she had to know what had happened to Bickerstaff. At first I was relieved that the Army truck had picked him up, thinking that meant that he'd be fine, but slowly the thought of Cooper dying a painful death from infection had crept into my thoughts. The doctor himself had said it would've been better to leave him for the Iti's to shoot. I coughed with a horrible bitterness in my throat, clutching it as I shuffled gradually towards the edge of the bed.

Where do you think you're going, young lady?

Instinctively I looked around, but I already knew the voice was not in the room.

"Mum?"

Get back in your bed this instant.

The Mind's Eye

Being on the receiving end of psychic words was not something I'd ever thought about experiencing. I knew of course that most teenagers had their mothers' voices in the back of their minds telling them what to do, but this was taking the concept a bit far. I sat back against the headboard of the bed, letting my head fall against the wall above it with a dull thump. Pain surged from the point of impact.

"Aren't you worried you'll give me a fever?" I asked, checking my hands quickly for any signs of the salmon pink rash. I loosened the collar of my nightie, feeling slightly warm.

I'd do a damn sight more than that if I was there with you right now! Mum was fuming; every frantic intonation in her voice came through loud and clear. *I told you to stay away and what did you do?*

I knew exactly what I'd done, so I bit my lip and ignored her question.

"How do you even know I've been using my powers?" I demanded.

Because I was fast asleep last night, minding my own business, when suddenly I was in the head of a crying, screaming sixteen year old who wouldn't stop raving about the war. Can you guess who that might have been Kit?

Mum's voice started out in the same angry boom, but gradually I could hear it breaking down into sobs. I had done exactly what she didn't want me to do, seen things that would burn themselves permanently into the back of my mind for the rest of my life. But though those horrid sights were making my insides squirm even as I sat listening to her words, I knew already that I wouldn't regret them. Now that the shock had passed, I was all the more intent on doing what I could to end the senseless carnage I had seen.

"Henri told me once that there are two kinds of people in war," I said, looking down at my hands as they balled into weak fists, "People who run away from the truth of what's happening and people who want to make a stand and make things stop." I steeled myself against the heat rising up the back of my neck. "I know which one I am now."

I don't care what you think you know, my mother replied, *I care about keeping you safe.*

"What I *think* I know?" I answered, enraged. Tiny beads of sweat collected at my hairline. "What I thought I knew was that my mother and father were normal people who didn't lie to their children!"

There was silence for quite a while, but I knew by the growing heat across my forehead that Mum was still with me. I put the cold cloth back on my brow to try and fend her off.

"Look Mum, people I care about are in real trouble right now," I snapped, "There's no way I'm not going help them."

I'm afraid you're wrong there, sweetheart, Mum answered sadly.

I raised a weak hand to adjust the cloth, only to find that my old pink rash had formed in the crook of my elbow. I watched as it spread, starting to pant as my mouth ran dry.

"No please!" I cried, "Please don't! It's not fair. You're making me ill, Mum!"

I'm sorry darling, she whispered, and it actually sounded like she was, which made what she was doing all the worse. *I'll try to help Henri for you if I can, but I have to keep you out of the way for now.*

My vision grew cloudy as I threw off my covers to see my legs. A salmon coloured blotch the size of a dustbin lid had wrapped itself around one of my knees. I couldn't move; I sat there staring at my leg as my damp neck grew weary of holding up my head. I was going again, back to the blackness, for how long only God knew. And possibly my mother.

"I won't forgive you," I murmured, my teeth sticking to my top lip as I fought to speak, "If someone bad happens to Henri, I won't-"

I'm sorry, Mum said again, *but I have my orders.*

I tried desperately to say 'Who from?', but there was a surge of heat in my face. My body slumped over against my will and soon-after I was gone.

Though I didn't hear Mum's voice again, the fever plagued me for over a week, which told me she had found a way to stop me from using my powers, however unfair it was. When Mam was in the room I felt clear headed and almost well, but any time that Blod or Idrys came to check on me I almost always went under the fever's heated grip before I could answer anything more than their first question. I started trying to pass quick bits of the story to them before the fever could take me down, but I wasn't sure if they were getting through.

"Bickers..." I slurred, my eyes half closed, "S'okay."

Blod pressed me for more, but I couldn't reply.

My days in the sickbed were degrading at best after all the progress I had made. I shuddered to think how weak I would be when Mum finally allowed me to come to again, if indeed she didn't keep me raging like this until the end of the war. The rash gave me sore skin, Mam said she even thought it had got inside my throat and my fluctuating temperature meant that my head spun every time I even adjusted it on my pillow.

But most disturbing of all were my dreams. I knew, sometimes, that when I was half asleep I stepped into other people's heads by accident, but in the delirium of the fever I couldn't be sure that anything I saw between my waking moments was real. I thought that Blod was crying in her room at night, which might have been real, but I also had visions of a grim grey place where someone in horrific pain was biting so hard on their lip that they cracked it open. I could taste the blood when I woke. I saw the dark black tunnels under the POW camp, felt the cramped little walls closing in until I screamed myself awake, terrified that they were going to bury me there before I could get out. I dreamt of lying flat and being told not to move whilst the floor beneath me bobbed to and fro like I was riding a huge wave. I dreamt of people in a dimly lit café talking in a foreign tongue.

And I dreamt of running. There was so much running, day and night, a speed so fast that the buildings, fields and forests around me were nothing but colourful blurs. Aching lungs sagged like they were filling slowly with sand, but I kept on running, wild eyes searching in the blur for the next direction to take. A strong, hammering heart raged in my chest, thumping loud in my ears every time I stopped to hide. The hiding was never for long before I took off again, seeking the next target. When I woke from the running I could never remember enough; I lay frustrated and crying day after day.

Until the fever just stopped. It was night time when I opened my eyes and felt that the pounding in my head had finally abated. I sat up immediately, my limbs floppy and raw as they were finally able to obey my wishes. I didn't have the strength for anything more, so I cupped my freezing cold hands to my face to call out for help. For the first time I noticed that the nipping frost of winter had set in on the dark windows, when I shouted out my breath followed in a stream of condensation.

It was Blod who heard me first; she burst into the room clutching a long letter on bright white paper. I smiled at her weakly and her sparkling eyes lit up. She rushed to sit down beside me on the bed and flapped the letter at me with a fearful, nervy smile.

"He's home," she said in barely more than a whisper, "This just got yur. Mam said he don't have any family, see, so they wrote to us after they asked him."

I didn't quite follow her, but I nodded all the same, reaching limply for the letter. She held it up for me to read, her hand quivering so much it took me ages to make out the words. Steven Bickerstaff was in a military hospital in Llandudno, which was about as far north as you could go in wales without falling into the sea. He was recovering from undisclosed injuries and the doctors needed someone to bring him home to the village.

"I didn't know he didn't have any family," I said sadly.

"Neither did I," Blod answered, taking the letter back to read it again. Her eyes drank in the words and a wicked jealous moment hit me where I wished it was Henri coming home instead.

But then the scenes from the night in Africa replaced my selfish wish, I saw Bickerstaff's silhouette illuminated by the light of the oncoming trucks, the gut wrenching sight of the remains of his leg flying yards away from his body. I could still hear him screaming. I looked at Blod again. Undisclosed injuries, the letter had said. She didn't know what had happened to him.

"Mam says we have to pull together and help him," Blod said with almost a giggle, "No complaints here of course." She hugged the letter to her chest and gave me a secretive little look. "I've missed his surly, rotten face so much, you know."

I couldn't help but smile. "Don't phrase it like that when you see him," I advised.

The Mind's Eye

I made a few difficult decisions between my first moment of feeling well again and the time that we got on the train to Llandudno. The first decision was not to go looking for Henri. Mum had perhaps decided that I had learned my lesson about staying out of the war and I hadn't felt hot or headachy at all since the fever had left me, so I had a feeling it wasn't a good idea to go looking for him right away, no matter how desperately I wanted to. The other thing that helped me resist temptation was the prospect of being allowed to go to the hospital with Mam and Blod to bring Bickerstaff home. Having seen what the poor man had been through, it seemed selfish to risk putting myself back in a sickbed when I should've been there to help him.

The other decision was to tell Blod what had happened to Bickerstaff. At first I hadn't said a word, but she was so excited to see him that I knew she'd think I'd betrayed her if I didn't tell her he was missing half a leg. Our friendship had never felt particularly secure and we'd only really come together once I'd offered to use my powers to help her. Besides which it was only right that she knew what she'd be getting herself into if she went to Llandudno ready to shower the bad tempered solider with affection. He had surely been through hell in the last ten days and even being back in Blighty couldn't solve the problems he now had.

The hospital was what I had expected, a proper sterile space with that cold, clammy feel to it like rainclouds were forming overhead. It was absurdly busy; every

K.C. Finn

corridor was full of people chattering away in English and Welsh, sometimes at the same time. I saw flashes of men in uniform, some visitors and some patients and several outside courtyards where men in pyjamas were gathered in clouds of cigarette smoke, their faces grim as they nodded to one another in hushed tones. When we reached the section we had been guided to there was a pretty nurse at a desk who gave Mam a pile of forms to look over before Bickerstaff could be released.

"While you do that, shall we go in and let him know we're here Mam?" I asked as Mam sat down with the paperwork, a puzzled look on her rosy face.

"I s'pose so," she muttered, leafing through the pages, "This might take a bit of time."

Blod beamed at me, helping me out of my chair and onto my crutches. She grabbed the green grapes that Mam had paid a fortune for and led me off into the ward. I was smiling too until we crossed through the double doors, when a tidal wave of sadness seemed to hit us without warning. Faint cries came from behind screened sections as we passed the first few beds. A young woman passed us in silent tears. The men that were in full view were an atrocious sight, their once youthful faces marred by scars and burns. They had casts and splints and great metal contraptions that seemed to be holding their injured bodies together; one even had bandages all over his face. I feared what might have been underneath.

I spotted Bickerstaff at the very end of the ward by virtue of the fact that he once again had his nose in a file.

271

I noted the empty tray at the end of his bed and supposed it was probably his own file that he was analysing. Typical. The ward was far too noisy for him to hear us coming, even with Blod clicking along in her best heels and me clunking my huge heavy crutches all the way down the perfectly clean path. He was in plain white pyjamas with the covers pulled up to his chest and as we got closer I saw once again the huge scar that marred one side of his face where the Iti blade had slashed him. All the same he looked rather well compared to the other men suffering around him, it was no wonder that they wanted to pack him off home.

"Oi," Blod said once we were at the foot of his bed.

Bickerstaff's blonde head shot up at the sound of her voice. His mouth dropped open a little and let his file fall into his lap. His eyes flashed to me briefly before they settled completely on Blod.

"I," he stuttered, "I thought Idrys might come."

"You're stuck with us and Mam to get you home on the train," I informed him.

He was still staring wide-eyed at Blod. "That'll do, I suppose." His scarred face expanded into a sheepish grin before he gulped nervously.

Blod pushed the grapes at me, which I barely caught without dropping my crutches, then rushed to sit beside him on his bed and threw her arms almost violently around his neck. Bickerstaff reached out and hugged her to him, looking at me awkwardly and then out into the ward.

"Steady on," he said quietly, "What if your mother comes in?"

Blod mumbled something about Mam against Bickerstaff's neck that I thought sounded extremely offensive. I ambled over and dumped the doctor's grapes on his bedside table, waiting until Blod released him from her grip. When she came away there were tears collecting in her eyes. Bickerstaff wiped them away with his thumb, looking to me with a frown.

"You won't know about Henri," he said in a breathy tone.

"Did they recover him from the Italians?"

Bickerstaff's mouth dropped open again, his blonde eyebrows dropping to frame the confusion in his eyes.

"No, they got away," he said in disbelief, "How do you-?"

"But they haven't found a body? There's been no news of him since the ambush?"

I didn't care what he thought of me or how suspicious he would be. Mum might have been able to stop my mind going to Henri's, but she couldn't prevent me asking these kinds of questions in person. Bickerstaff looked at me like I had three heads, but he replied all the same.

"Nothing," he said, shaking his head, "I think if they'd killed him we might have had a body back to bury. That particular team had a penchant for that sort of thing."

I thought carefully. "They sent Carter back to you?" I asked.

At the mention of his fallen ally Bickerstaff dropped his head. "What was left of him," he muttered. As he spoke Blod's hand snaked across the bed to hold his. He clutched it tightly, giving her a small smile before he looked back to me. "How do you know all this?"

"I'll let Blod explain it to you when we get home," I replied, content at least that there was a fair chance Henri was alive. *Where* he was alive was now the problem. I found my eyes travelling down the bed to where one solitary foot was poking out of the covers. "You don't have to explain what happened to you, either," I added gently.

Blod's hand moved out of Bickerstaff's grip and touched his knee under the hospital blankets. "Mam doesn't know anything, as usual," Blod explained, "So we'll keep it that way, and you'll have to explain to her about your leg when she comes in."

"But you know?" he asked, his face young and helpless. Blod leaned in and planted the tiniest kiss on his lips. Bickerstaff straightened up and took a deep breath, looking down at his hands. "In that case, it's a good job I taught you to walk, Kit. I'll be needing that chair of yours now."

CHAPTER TWENTY-FIVE

Burning Questions

I was both put out and extremely pleased to be told I'd be sleeping in Ieuan's room from now on. Knowing that the young RAF officer was alive and well in Toulouse had taken away the creepy atmosphere of his little room; it now felt as though I was keeping it tidy for him until he came home. It was also the room that Henri had used for the few weeks he'd stayed here, which was usually comforting, but sometimes very sad when I thought about the threat hanging over my head if I tried to contact him again. I was also daunted by the prospect of tackling the stairs every day, but Idrys promised he'd carry me if things ever got really bad again.

Leighton loved the idea that I was upstairs again, in London we had always had rooms next door to one another and now we were back to that arrangement. I, in truth, had been avoiding my little brother for fear that Mum was sitting in his head keeping watch on me, but now that I wasn't using my gift I thought it couldn't hurt to be around him again. I let him help me move my clothes and things upstairs to make Clive's old sitting room look as little as possible like a teenage girl had been living in it before Bickerstaff wheeled himself in to inspect his new quarters.

"I can't understand why he sold his house," Mam said one morning before the doctor was up and about.

She was sitting at the table with Idrys and me as we cradled cups of steaming tea against the cold November wind that was cascading through every crack in the doors and windows of the little farm house.

"I don't think he thought he'd be coming home," Idrys supposed. I knew he was right but I said nothing.

"Poor soul," Mam said, looking down at the table, "He'll have to start all over again now. New house and everything."

"Does that mean he's out of the war for good?" I asked.

"I spect the home guard will give him a clerical job if he wants it," Idrys mused, "I can't see him going back into medicine after what he's been through."

Blod entered the kitchen quietly, apparently surprised to find us all sitting there so early in the morning. She went to the sink to fill a glass of water.

"What you up to, love?" Idrys questioned, giving her a careful eye.

"Steven wants some water," she muttered, her cheeks flushed pink. She disappeared again swiftly, the glass dripping as she went.

"She's been ever so good with him," Mam said proudly.

"'Course she has," Idrys added with a wry smirk,

"He's still a handsome devil even with that godawful scar down his face."

"Don't be daft," Mam said quickly, but in the silence that followed I could see her mind turning things over behind her glassy blue eyes.

It was true that Blod had suddenly engaged in a life-changing transformation to take on the role of dutiful nursemaid but it didn't seem to be achieving the effect she desired. Bickerstaff was more miserable than ever. Most days he wheeled himself outside despite the icy fingers of winter that were slowly getting a grip on Ty Gwyn and sat contemplating the pasture until someone came to bother him. The young doctor continued to dress in his old smart suits, one trouser leg hanging down limply from the front of the wheelchair, a great gaping hollow where his foot ought to be.

The kitchen was beastly hot where Mam was making dinner and I was too tired to brave the stairs to retreat to my room, so I hauled outside on my crutches intending to limp off in the opposite direction to the moody physician. But something caught my eye, specifically the arms and legs of a certain rag doll being waved in his face. Bickerstaff had his back to me in his chair, but as I approached I could see Ness standing in front of him talking his head off, Dolly flying in all directions as she used her to punctuate her speech.

"But Mam says I can't have a house for Dolly 'til I'm five," she was explaining, "Bampi's going to build it, but he wants to build me a farm."

She crinkled her nose up at the notion.

"You don't want a farm," Bickerstaff said thoughtfully, "Dolly needs a proper house with carpet and curtains and windows."

"Ie!" Ness said, bouncing on her heels. "Could you build it instead of Bampi?"

"We'll see," the doctor replied.

My crutch hit a heavy stone and alerted them both that I was nearby. Bickerstaff struggled to wheel around on the small cobbles with Ness attempting to push the side of his chair to help. What she was actually doing was pushing the side of the chair into Bickerstaff's side, but he didn't tell her off.

"Afternoon," he said, inclining his head a little. I did the same. He looked me over with a thoughtful frown. "Quite the reversal, this," he added, sweeping a hand over what used to be my chair, "Are you having any problems just being on the aids all the time?"

"I have to sit down a lot," I replied, wary that he seemed to have reverted to his surly doctor mood for the moment, "But actually it's quite good. I didn't know I had the strength until I was forced to do it."

Half a sad smile pushed one side of his lip up. "It's like that with a lot of things," he mused.

"Are you going to try that fake leg the hospital sent you?"

Bickerstaff looked away. "I'm not sure." A chilly wind whipped up around us and Bickerstaff turned to Ness, patting her gently on her crown. "Go inside for a bit and warm up."

She took his gentle words with a nod and scampered off down the cobbles, falling over once on the way. We both made to go after her but Ness was a tough little thing, she picked herself up, giggled and ran off back into the house.

"I've been thinking about this gift of yours, Kit."

Bickerstaff had been with us for almost a week and he'd said nothing thus far about what I could do. I'd almost started to think that Blod hadn't told him.

"You could see into the ambush in Africa?" he asked. I nodded, swallowing back the images that threatened to flood my head. "Were you in my head or Henri's?"

"Henri's," I answered quickly.

Bickerstaff looked down at the hollow trouser leg now flapping in the wintery breeze. He caught it and tucked it up under his leg.

"Then you saw…" he began, but then fell into silence. I could imagine how hard it was to find the words, to actually say "You saw me get my leg blown off", when it was you that had to sit there looking at the empty space where your own foot should be.

I just nodded again. Bickerstaff sighed.

"Well there's one good thing that's come out of it," I said shakily. He raised a quizzical blonde brow at me. "You and Blod," I explained.

He sighed again, his features soft but still ultimately moody, then shook his head.

"I don't think that's going to work out very well," he muttered.

"Why not?" I exclaimed, thinking of all the trouble Blod had put me to, keeping watch on him across continents. "Don't you love her?"

Bickerstaff gave me a brief angry look like the one he frequently gave Henri when he was about to tell him to mind his own business, but then it fell away.

"I do, but it's not as simple as that."

"It should be," I insisted.

"You see, you're exactly like her," he complained, waving a hand at me, "All women most likely. She has this great romantic idea that she can take care of me, but she hasn't thought about the reality of it." He hung his head down, rubbing at his temple. "At the end of the day, if she marries me, she'd be married to half a man."

I couldn't stand his defeatist attitude any longer. He had been wrong about me, wrong about Henri and about the war, and he was most certainly wrong about this too.

"Better to have half the right man than the whole of the wrong man," I supposed.

He caught the judgemental sort of look I was giving him and started to wheel away. I was terribly pleased when I caught up to him despite the crutches and the cobbles.

"God I wish I hadn't agreed to help you sometimes," he muttered, trying to get to the door. I blocked his path with a well-timed crutch that hit his shin.

"Well you did," I answered, "And now I'm going to help you. And unlike you, I'm going to try and be fairly human about it."

Blod didn't like the thought of being shut out of what the doctor and I were doing, but she eventually agreed to give Bickerstaff some time un-nursed and we retreated to the dark little sitting room at the front of the house. The fake leg, which he insisted on calling a prosthesis, was mostly made of wood but it had some clever joints in the ankles and where the arches of the foot should be that shone silver. The proud doctor made me look away when he attached the thing to the stump at his knee and when I looked back he'd let his long trouser leg come down so that only the dark brown wood of the foot was showing. Once I'd put a sock and shoe on it for him, you would hardly have known the leg was false at all.

That was, until he started trying to use it. We had to be careful when he tried to walk because there was no way I'd be able to pick him up if he fell and that last thing he wanted to do was have anyone in the Price family see him flat on his face on the floor. I secretly thought it might serve him right after all the times it had happened to me under his guidance, but since I was trying to be the bigger person I kept my mouth shut. I sat on the old sofa whilst he borrowed my crutches for balance, finding that with just one aid under his left arm he could manage quite well.

"I'll call the place in Cardiff where they made yours," he said, the first true smile on his face in weeks, "He's a friend from medical school, I'm sure he'd do me one outside of the practice."

"Blod would hardly have to do anything for you," I observed, returning the grin, "All I've done is passed you the crutch."

"You've done quite a bit more than that," he said, turning away again to try another lap of the room.

Pride settled in my chest. It was perhaps the first good thing I'd ever done without using my powers; it gave me a funny sort of satisfaction to think that I had value beyond them. Bickerstaff was almost laughing as he rounded the room quite quickly. He had a clunky sort of walk, but he was spritely and bright compared to the forlorn figure sitting out in the winter wind a few days ago.

"So what do you think then?" I pressed, taking advantage of his rare good mood, "About you and Blod?"

He spun on his good leg and leant on the crutch, looking down at his feet. Then slowly he nodded and gave me a tiny smile.

"Well," he mused, "it's certainly going to put a new spin on 'going down on one knee'."

I knew the proposal had happened by the high pitched squeal that echoed through Ty Gwyn after breakfast one morning. I was upstairs when I felt the vibrations of Blod's heels trampling all over the house to make sure that everyone had heard the good news. By that point of course no-one was really surprised, especially considering she'd been giving every spare second of her day to him for almost three weeks. For his part Bickerstaff managed to keep a smile on his face for nearly the whole day before I caught him returning to his pensive and moody self just after dinner. He had a long chat with Idrys that night; they were still in the small sitting room when I struggled up the steep stairs to bed.

I hadn't thought about eavesdropping with my powers in quite a long time, it was as though being restricted from them now made things like that seem frivolous, selfish even. When I settled into my borrowed bed I thought sadly of Henri. Mum had promised to try and look after him, but what if she hadn't succeeded? Was I supposed to go on living this normal life, ignoring the abilities I had to help and comfort him, and if so until when? The end of the war? It had been a month since I'd used my powers last, when Henri and Bickerstaff were still in the desert heat of Africa. What on earth would Henri think of me for abandoning him for so long? Would he even forgive me?

I reasoned sadly that he probably wouldn't. But either way, it was time to try and find out.

CHAPTER TWENTY-SIX

Big Plans

I decided to try Ieuan first since he probably wasn't quite as punishable an offence as looking for Henri or my father, if indeed I were to get caught. The advantage of now being upstairs was that all the bedrooms had bolts on the inside of the doors, so I feigned tiredness the day after the marriage proposal and shut myself away for the morning. Leighton was at school, so I hoped there was little chance of Mum stopping by to see what I was up to. I had been very good this month, after all, and done exactly as I was told. Until now.

I found Ieuan sitting at a table in one of the bunk houses of the POW camp; they were having one of their strategy meetings, which usually ended in arguments about who was to blame for the latest tunnel collapse. But this time there was a different atmosphere between the men in their old uniforms that they had been wearing for months on end. There was no belligerence between them. They seemed hopeful. Ieuan sat across from a man who was usually only referred to as Wing Commander, today he was giving his men a satisfied smile.

F.C. Finn

"This could be it boys," he said in a proud Scottish boom, "our salvation has come."

The WC pulled a crumpled square of paper from a hidden fold inside the lapel of his tattered uniform. It was a tiny sheet with miniscule writing upon it. He showed it around, I felt Ieuan leaning forward eagerly at the mere sight of it.

"The Gaullists are working to free us," he explained, producing a pair of spectacles to inspect the tiny print on the paper, "of course their tunnels will be much sturdier than ours, they've got the materials."

"Another tunnel?" someone questioned behind Ieuan. Everyone shushed him.

"Yes," the WC answered with gritted teeth, "but as I say, a much better one. It leads out into a village quite a way from here. All we have to do is dig due north to try and meet it. It comes out here two days from now if they keep up their speed."

Ieuan filled with excited nerves, but I could feel myself frowning. This was no doomed attempt; this was a proper, full-blown escape. If he made it out of the camp and into the rest of France, the consequences of breaking out would be severe. Idrys had maintained that it was sensible for him to stay put, but here these gents were, risking their safety to get home and start fighting all over again. The men in the camp reached an agreement that they would all help to find the entrance to the new tunnel, but their smiling faces filled me with dread.

I decided not to tell Idrys anything that I had

discovered yet; there was still every chance that the plans of the prisoners of war would change and therefore no need to worry him. He'd have enough trouble trying to reign in Mam and Blod now that they had a wedding to organise, after all. With the door to my room still locked I sucked up my strength for another trip, my heavy heart settling on Henri as I focused hard.

"You shouldn't be here," he whispered immediately.

How do you know that? I asked, a desperate relief spreading through my whole body.

"It's for your own protection," Henri answered angrily, "Gail says so."

So Mum had found him after all. Henri was sitting in a dusty cupboard, his knees almost up to his chest. A book was open across them and he had a tiny torch which he settled between the pages, illuminating his ragged trousers and sore, calloused hands.

Where on earth are you? I asked.

"I can't tell you anything yet," he said sadly, "I'm trying to get home."

And Mum's helping you?

"Mum?" Henri asked. I felt his eyes flicker to the side as he thought. "Gail is… your mother?"

She didn't tell you, I mused, *of course she didn't tell you.*

"Why did she keep it from me?" Henri whispered.

Because that's what my family does, apparently. I felt the old resentment creeping into my head. *What did she tell you about me?*

"That the psychic trips were making you ill," he said,

"please don't make yourself sick for me Kit, with any luck I'll be home soon and–"

She's lied to you, I interjected. Henri froze, I felt him rubbing his palms on his knees like he always did when his nerves were up. *She was the one causing my fevers. She's afraid of people finding out what I am, in case the government pick me up to work for the War Office like her.*

"I suppose she's trying to protect you," he murmured.

Don't defend her, I insisted, seething inside. This wasn't the time for his forgiving nature. *And if she comes to talk to you, don't tell her I'm back in your head.*

Henri nodded. "So you're really not in any pain?"

No more than usual, I replied, *I'm not even using my chair any more. Bickerstaff's got it at the moment.*

"He's there?" I felt a rush of relief in Henri's chest. He felt thinner than he had been, more frail somehow. "Thank God."

Yes he's fine. He and Blod are getting married.

"I don't know which to feel more sorry for," Henri whispered, half a laugh in his words. I laughed too, a warm smile overtaking my bitterness for my secret keeping family.

I've missed you.

"I should hope so," Henri replied with a smile, "It would have been much easier to get back to Norway from here, the Resistance are struggling to arrange my passage to England."

Where are you exactly?

"Somewhere in France, I shouldn't say more," he answered, "Look, don't be too hard on your mother, Kit. She has all kinds of contacts with the Free French; they rescued me when the Italians were transporting me to Egypt. Gail directed me to all these different safe houses until I could get to this restaurant. I ran miles every day from one to the next, avoiding the German patrols. I've been well looked after."

The constant running in my feverish dreams suddenly made far more sense to me. I wasn't sure I could forgive all of the secrets and lies my mother had told Henri and me, but she had kept her word to help him to safety and that was something I would always have to be grateful for.

"I've missed your voice so much," Henri said gently, "I... I love you still, you know."

I love you too Henri.

I felt him tingle all over, a warm happiness rising in his cheeks. Then he gulped and something awkward twisted his expression.

"I think I might have told your mother some things I shouldn't have," he mumbled, "she asked about us. It's quite embarrassing now that I think about it."

I don't care, I answered, *if there's one thing she can't get in the way of, it's me loving you.*

"Even if I've been living in a cupboard for two weeks?" Henri asked with a chuckle. "I think I smell like the restaurant downstairs."

Even so, I replied.

All my doubts about Henri's feelings for me had melted. As much as I had missed him desperately, I hadn't realised quite how much it meant to talk to him until now. My hands felt wet at home like tears were dripping onto them, but I forced my thoughts to stay with Henri and his warm, smiling lips.

How soon can you be home?

"A meeting is happening here tomorrow," he explained, "They don't usually tell me anything until it's time to actually do something. But I've been invited to the meeting, so that's a good sign I think."

Perhaps I'll drop by.

"Be careful," Henri warned, "Gail might do the same thing."

I will be careful, I promised, *but it won't stop me now.* Nothing was going to stop me from seeing that Henri got home safe.

I composed myself and washed my face after I finally let Henri go. We talked at length about nothing at all until I slowly realised it would be time for lunch at Ty Gwyn and tore myself away from the feel of his smile and sound of his laugh. The Free French were in the business of sending Allied forced home so that they could get back to fighting against the ever-encroaching Nazi threat, so by the time I left Henri I was almost certain that he'd be coming home sooner rather than later. All the same, one tiny doubt remained in my head, alerting me to the risks he'd have to take in order to cross the channel safely.

Downstairs there was a huge commotion at the table as we all sat down to lunch. I had been clunking down the stairs and missed the beginning of it, but the middle was clear enough to catch what was going on.

"Next Friday?" Mam bellowed, "And how do you propose we get everything ready in seven days' time?"

"I've done most of it already on the phone this morning," Blod explained, "My old friends from school are coming tomorrow to fix up the dresses, Steven's still got his best suit and he's had a word with our preacher up at the chapel."

"He took pity on me," Bickerstaff said with a smile, but I couldn't miss the bitter note in his words.

"Don't knock it boy," Idrys replied with a warning finger, "you've had a hard time of it, take what you can while people are feeling generous."

Mam and Blod were buzzing around the table laden with lunch foods as Idrys, Ness and I sat beside the doctor and started to tuck in. Bickerstaff didn't seem to like Idrys's advice much but he was respectfully quiet and gave the old farmer a nod.

"But people won't be able to travel up in time," Mam protested, "Your Auntie Gert and-"

"Oh bugger them, I don't want them yur anyway," Blod said, waving her off. She brought Bickerstaff a cup of tea and kissed his scarred cheek gently. "Them aunties always cause trouble, nosey things. Besides which Thomas is already coming up on leave next weekend, and he's the only one I really care about being there."

"At least you don't have to worry about my side," Bickerstaff added with a laugh that nobody returned, trying to hide their pity for the man with no family ties.

"No friends from medical school or nothing?" Mam asked, giving him a kind smile.

He shook his blonde head. "I'm sure they're all frightfully busy with the war, I don't expect they'd be free to make it even if it was six months away."

Mam didn't seem happy with that, she was clearly looking for backup to have more time to prepare for the big day. She caught my eye over the table and pointed a finger at me thoughtfully.

"That reminds me Kit I invited your mother," she began, "I thought she might be too busy like, but she says she can make it. Isn't that great?"

"Leighton will be thrilled," I remarked, avoiding the question. I definitely wasn't ready to see Mum again so soon and if she was here at Ty Gwyn there was no chance of checking on Henri.

"Well everything's all right then, isn't it?" Blod said triumphantly, "Bampi, you'll have to take me out today to see about flowers."

"Oh good," Idrys answered, "I was hoping there'd be even more work to do today than usual."

Blod put her arms around his neck and gave him a big kiss on the cheek before strutting out of the room. Idrys watched her go, rolling his eyes.

"Bloody women eh?" he remarked to Bickerstaff.

"Don't get me started," the doctor replied.

I huffed at both of them, but they were actually right about Blod, if not women in general. All Bickerstaff had done was ask the big question, now his very life was in Blod's hands. All in all he didn't seem to mind, in fact his bad moods were lifting more quickly than they used to, giving way to more frequent happy moments as well as some very thoughtful ones where he let Ness talk his head off about everything under the sun.

After lunch the men cleared out of the room slowly, leaving me with Mam and Ness. I propped myself up at the sink to dry the cups and plates as she washed them, watching her rosy face as she focused her eyes out of the window on the frosty winter scene in the distance.

"I bet it'll be snowing by Friday," she mused, "Blod won't have thought of that."

"I suppose you have to let them do it their way," I mused. Mam gave me a knowing nod.

"It's funny how she's come back round to him," Mam said as she scrubbed out the butter tray, "I think he was about twenty five when he arrived yur, strapping young doctor from England, you know. All the girls were mad on him back then, Blod too. She talked on forever about his big blue eyes; oh I was sick of it!" She passed me the tray with a shrug. "And now yur we are, five years on and suddenly they're in love. It's a mad world, innit?"

"Very mad," I agreed, thinking about all the mad things that Mam didn't even know were going on.

"She went off him for ages, said she hated him," Mam continued, putting down her things and wiping her hands dry, "She'd never go to the doctor when she was your age, not even when-" She caught herself, looking at me carefully for a moment. "Well, not even when she really needed him. But he always came yur if we called him, you know? He's been very good to our family."

I dried the last of the dishes and sorted myself out, turning just in time for Ness to bump into my crutch. She rubbed her head for a moment before she started to smile again, looking up at us with her huge blue eyes. Mam picked her up, inspecting the place where she'd hit her head carefully.

"And what do you think of your sister getting married eh?" she asked, bouncing Ness in her warm arms.

"I like Steven," Ness said with a grin, "He's going to make me a house for Dolly."

"Is he now?" Mam asked. Something changed in her usually peaceful face as she studied Ness again.

"Why you looking at me?" Ness asked, suddenly wriggling to get away.

I realised all too late that Mam was putting the pieces together, looking at Ness's face from every angle, scrutinizing her tawny hair, blonde at the ends, and her oval eyes the wrong shape for the Price gene pool. I watched wordlessly, unable to act because I shouldn't have known anything, not even that Ness didn't belong to Mam. The older woman set the little girl down and straightened out her apron.

"Look after her a minute Kit," Mam began, her voice suddenly low, "I'm just going to have a chat with Steven."

CHAPTER TWENTY-SEVEN

Discoveries

Whatever happened between Mam and Bickerstaff meant that they spent the rest of the day in separate rooms after their little chat. But the wedding hadn't been cancelled and Bickerstaff hadn't been strangled, so I thought that was probably about the best that we could have hoped for given the collection of secrets Blod had been keeping from her mother for the last five years. I was worried that Blod and her husband-to-be might have thought that I'd given the game away, but they were both so temperamental anyway that it was hard to tell if much had changed. I decided to put them out of my head the next day, leaving them to their frantic planning whilst I considered my options for checking on Henri.

His meeting was somewhere around one o'clock in France which would be twelve at Ty Gwyn. It was an awkward time for a Saturday, right when I'd be expected to help prepare and then eat lunch. I came to the conclusion I would have to beg off with a sore stomach after I'd eaten something, perhaps catching the end of the secret meeting or at the very least getting to Henri when it was all fresh in his mind to tell me what was going on. I had a feeling that everyone would want to make excuses to get away from the lunch table anyway today, the memory of the tension at breakfast did not promise a peaceful meal at midday. When the time came I was right and I was excused without anyone complaining, clunking up the stairs under the pretence of lying down in my room. I tried my best not to make my footfalls sound too eager on the echoing stone steps.

Henri was alone in a small back room filled with brown cupboards, sitting at a table where a huge black cat was stalking towards him. It's fluffy face and curious eyes filled my vision for a moment as Henri's smooth hand went out to tickle the cat under its chin. It curved its neck; I felt its soft fur pushing against Henri's wrist as it came closer for more attention.

"Hi kitty, kitty," Henri said.

Hello, I answered.

He laughed out loud, still fussing the cat. "You picked a good time," he mused, "if someone comes in at least I can say I was talking to the cat."

You're not in the cupboard then?

Henri shook his head. "I've been told to wait. Someone's coming to that window to take me... I don't know. Somewhere new."

As he spoke of the window he looked up from the cat to show it to me. A large pane framed in black was ajar, leading out into what appeared to be a back alley.

No meeting then? I asked.

"I think this 'someone' is taking me to the meeting,"

Henri explained.

Has my mum been to speak to you? He shook his head again. The cat watched him with interest, curling up under his touch.

"I stopped hearing from her a couple of days before you found me again," he said quietly.

There was something troubling about the way he felt, like he was trying to withhold his feelings from me. His heart was beating faster than usual, but every muscle in his body was straining as if to stay forcibly calm.

Out with it, I demanded, *you can't hide from me Henri Haugen. What's wrong?*

He shook his head and let out a defeated sigh, removing his hands from the cat to run them through his mess of dark hair. It was then that I felt the feelings pour out, the nerves running up and down his spine, the heavy weight dragging down his lungs, making me feel like he was drawing laboured breaths up from his boots.

"The Germans shot some people in the square this morning," he said solemnly, "they were Resistance collaborators, like the people who are helping me here." His throat ran dry at the words as he tried to go on. "I heard the shots."

You'll be out of there soon enough, I soothed, but I could feel the lump in my own throat choking my thoughts.

"If they catch me here, they'll think I'm a spy," he said, his hands starting to tremble. The cat became skittish, slowly backing away on the table. "Then I'll go the same way."

You're leaving soon, Henri. I wanted so desperately to be there, to hold him and give him more comfort than just my hopeful words. *This person, the meeting-*

"But that's just it," Henri said, growing angrier, "this man who's supposed to be on his way to take me. He's a spy too."

"I'll thank you not to say that quite so loudly," said a whispering voice from behind us.

The voice was smooth and definitely English. Henri froze, looking at the window where he'd been expecting the man to appear. It was wide open; he had passed by totally unnoticed. I felt the hairs on the back of Henri's neck rising up into the cold breeze now streaming in from the back alley.

"Turn around then boy; let's take a look at what the Gaullists have sent me."

Henri gently rose from his chair, the cat making a dash for freedom out of the open window. It felt like Henri wanted to follow it; he fought to keep his legs from shaking as he turned around. The man who stood before him was tall and slim, his dark brown hair swept into a wave. He was suited all in black with a French moustache curling above his smiling lip. I let out a gasp. When Henri's eyes found the smiling man's face an explosion of emotions filled his chest. We both stared at the figure in shock for a few moments before Henri rushed forward, throwing himself into the fellow's arms.

"Mr Bavistock?" he cried in disbelief, thumping the back of his old teacher as he wrapped an arm around his waist.

Henri, I murmured, my heart hardly beating. *His name isn't Bavistock.*

Henri stepped back from the man's embrace, taking him in again, listening hard to my strained, panicked voice. *That's my father.*

Dad looked thinner and older than when I had seen him last, but the sparkle in his brown eyes was the same as ever. He smiled at Henri a while longer, but soon raised a brow. He looked funny got up as a Frenchman, under different circumstances I might have laughed at his fancy collar and curly moustache.

"Who were you talking to just now?" Dad asked, "I don't think it was Gail?"

Pieces of my past were slowly starting to come together. Dad had been posing as a tutor in Norway, perhaps for a long time before the war had even started. He and Mum were both working for the government, and she had led Henri to him. Who better to help him escape than a British spy? I couldn't quite get my head around the idea of my mild mannered parents doing all this despite the overwhelming evidence now staring me in the face.

Answer him, I told Henri, *tell him I'm here.*

Henri swallowed dryly. "It's your daughter, Mr... Cavendish. I was talking to Kit."

My father smiled, his shoulders dropping a little. "Is she still there?"

Henri nodded.

"In that case her mother did a damn fine job of

keeping her out of the war, eh?"

Charming, I said to Henri, *considering being so deeply involved in the war seems like a family tradition I've been missing out on.*

"Pardon me sir," Henri said, his heart recovering slowly from the shock of everything, "but your daughter is a smart girl, capable and resourceful."

Dad came closer to Henri and clapped a hand on his shoulder warmly. "I always liked teaching you, Henri," he mused, "you're a respectful boy. I once thought you'd be a good match for Kit, actually. I suppose that's where the phrase 'be careful what you wish for' comes from."

He was certainly the man I remembered, no matter how strange he looked in foreign clothes. Dad was always rattling off old proverbs to Leigh and me whilst we rolled our eyes at each other or pretended to yawn. It was odd to see him speaking that way to Henri. They had a whole history I didn't even know about, but I supposed that it was fortunate that they already knew and liked each other a great deal. I could feel his familiar hand on Henri's shoulder like it was resting on my own, and no matter how bitter I'd once been about him leaving us all, I had missed him so much.

"We'd best be moving off," Dad said, retuning with a cat-like grace to the window. He stuck his head out and had a look around. "Kit, you can stay if you don't distract Henri. I need him to focus, ready to do whatever I say if we get into a crisis."

"She agrees," Henri said before I could even reply.

Walking the streets of the little French village was like watching a scene unfold at the cinema. There were a few Germans in uniform gathered on the street, my father doffed his hat to them and said something in faultless French as he and Henri passed them by. The bright grey stones were wet with tiny snowflakes that were falling and dissolving the moment they touched the ground. I noticed as we walked that Henri's ragged trousers had been replaced for a smart suit and polished shoes. He looked as though he was some sort of junior version of Dad, trailing behind him a little as he suddenly weaved a path down a side street through some market sellers braving the icy winter air.

Eventually we reached a canvas truck that reminded me of the first time the Germans had arrived in Oslo. In the front was what looked like a German officer, but when my father brought Henri up to the window of the truck, the uniformed man put his window down and spoke with a Yorkshire accent.

"This the one George?" he whispered, looking from my father to Henri. He gave us all a kind smile.

Dad nodded. "Let's get to the meeting place, Cliff."

"Ja mein Herr," Cliff replied with a chuckle.

Both Dad and Henri looked around, checking the deserted little street before scurrying into the back of the canvas van. It was dark and murky, but Henri found a bench to sit on as Dad opened a flap that let in some light as well as Cliff's voice.

"Home James," he joked.

"Yes milord," Cliff answered.

"Are you still there Kit?" Dad asked, turning back to Henri in the semi-darkness. He nodded for both of us. "I might as well fill you in on the way. You're going to help us with a little operation we've got going to free some other chaps, then we'll pack you all off back to Blighty in a submarine. Sound good?"

"Getting back to Britain sounds good sir," Henri answered. I could feel inside his body that he wasn't so keen on the rest of the plan.

"We've been organising a big breakout in the POW camp a little north of here," Dad explained, "so when the boys come out I'll need you to help direct them into hiding until we meet the rendezvous for the submarine."

Are we near Toulouse? I asked. Henri repeated my question to my father.

"Yes," he said slowly, "What have you been up to Kit? What do you know?"

I told Henri about Ieuan Price and the Wing Commander and everything I could remember from sitting in on their meeting. Henri repeated it as best he could, though I seemed to be thinking the words a lot faster than he could say them. Dad listened to his stunted ramble carefully for the important bits.

"My, my," he said when the story was told, "you do get around my girl. But this is brilliant; we've been trying to get a psychic contact in that camp for weeks. You could help us! Ow!"

Dad suddenly held his hands up over his ears like something loud had happened, but the truck kept rolling along on the quiet road. He grumbled to himself as he rubbed at his head, suddenly holding his hands up.

"Okay, okay," he said, looking back to Henri and me, "apparently your mother thinks that's a very bad idea."

Mum was there in his head. We three were all together for the strangest of reunions.

Well tough, I said to Henri, *I'll be there whether you like it or not.*

Henri chose not to repeat my words exactly. "Would it really be so dangerous for Kit to just pass a few messages?" he inquired.

My father sat and listened quietly for a moment, then sighed. "She's not a baby any more, Gail," he reasoned. I could well imagine my mother's heated replies going straight into his brain. "She was bound to come into this sooner or later, at least I'll be there to guide her."

There was more silence, then Dad slowly started to grin. He had always won the arguments at home too. He gave Henri and me the thumbs up, I could feel Henri smiling, his chest bathed in relief.

Told you nothing would stop me, I whispered to him. His smile widened.

"Oi," said my dad, pointing a finger at us, "no lovey-dovey talk while I'm sat here. This is serious business. You kids will have to do as you're told if we're going to make this op a success."

"We will sir," Henri answered for us both, "just tell us what to do."

Dad nodded at something we couldn't hear. "All

right," he said to Mum, "yes dear." Then he turned to us, his dark eyes glowing in the dim interior of the truck. "We'll be at the meeting point soon. The plan's going to be mostly in French. Do you speak any?" I knew he was talking to Henri, who shook his head. "In that case you just watch and nod your head enthusiastically. I'll translate it all for you two later on. Shall we say five o'clock Kit?"

I'll be there, I promised. Henri repeated my words, still smiling.

"See you then," said my father, winking as he gave me his old familiar grin.

CHAPTER TWENTY-EIGHT

Giving In

I could hardly process how I felt when I returned to Ieuan's room at Ty Gwyn. Everything in my world had collided in one big jumble, filling my head with all sorts of new ideas that didn't marry well with the old ones. I had resented my father for more than two years for his abrupt departure, but now so much of his sudden leaving made sense that I couldn't make peace with those old feelings of rage. What's more he'd stood up for me, given me the chance to do what Mum was so desperate to keep me away from. Mum, I now realised, already had one person she loved exposed to the horrors of war every day of his life, I was starting to understand why she was afraid of me going the same way.

I rushed onto my crutches and out of my room, intending to find Idrys and tell him the good news, when I found Leighton sitting alone at the top of the stairs. He had his head on his knees and a slump in his shoulders. I clonked my crutch to let him know I was there. When he turned to face me his looks were pale and confused.

"Are you all right Leigh?" I asked.

K.C. Finn

I wanted to sit down beside him on the top step but it was a little too ambitious a move. I had visions of toppling down the stone staircase and landing with a crunch at the bottom, so I settled for reaching down to pat his head before edging away again gingerly. Leighton took the hint and followed me back to my room, sitting down on the bed with me.

"Blod and Doctor B are snogging," he said with a ghastly look on his face, "It's disgusting."

"I don't want to know," I laughed, patting his knee. "That's not what's upset you is it? I know the atmosphere's a bit funny today, but everyone's very busy with the wedding." Not to mention the dam full of Price family secrets that was fit to burst and flood Ty Gwyn.

Leigh shook his head. He looked more thoughtful than I had ever seen him, usually my little brother was fairly empty-headed, concerned only with where and when his next meal was coming and how best to play and fill up the time until it was served. Today he looked pensive and a little sad. I hugged him to me and he wrapped his arm around my back.

"We'll see Mum soon," I offered, "You can have the day off school for the ceremony, you know."

"That'll be good," he mumbled against my side.

"What's up?" I asked again, "You can tell me Leigh. I won't be cross."

He shook his head and pulled away. "I think I had a funny turn, that's all. I feel better now."

"It wasn't a fever, was it?" I questioned warily,

305

thinking of Mum and her little visits to his mind.

"No," he said certainly. I breathed a sigh of relief. "It doesn't matter."

He got up to leave and gave me a smile, but it looked a little forced. I caught him by the wrist before he could escape.

"Tell me if you feel like that again," I urged him, "Don't keep it secret."

"Course not," he replied; smiling a bit more genuinely, "We don't have secrets, apart from you thinking I don't know that you kissed Henri. A lot."

"You little git!" I shouted with a laugh, but he was already running away from me.

I sat giggling on the bed until a guilty kind of sadness washed over me. We don't have secrets, he had said. But I did. Big secrets. Tears threatened behind my eyes as I realised I was just like Mum and Dad, hiding everything from Leigh, pushing him out and ignoring him when I needed to. It was easy to do. Actually, it was so easy I hadn't realised how I had lied to my brother every day of his little life, spied on him, even messed with his head when I was younger. I made a silent vow to myself that I would give Leighton the truth after the wedding, once Mum was away again and couldn't interfere. He deserved to be prepared for the madness that awaited him in his future.

The plot to help the escaping prisoners of war was

simple and it would be highly effective if the whole thing came off according to plan. Dad had been taking it in shifts to dig out the sturdy tunnel with other members of the Free French Resistance, those who called themselves Gaullists because they believed in the political leader Charles De Gaulle. The tunnel was secured with wooden splints, poles, girders and anything else that had been donated to the cause by collaborating villagers. It began in the barn of a farm not too far from the camp itself, the place where Henri had been taken to the meeting, and in another day's time it would connect with the underground attempts that had been made by the Wing Commander and his men under the floorboards of their bunk house.

That was, if I did my part of the operation correctly. It had become my job to go to Ieuan and tell him that Dad and the Gaullists would be using a bird call underground to let them know when they were close to making the tunnels connect. That way the men in the camp would know which way to dig. The only real potential problem with the plan was if Ieuan didn't believe the voice in his head. If I wasn't convincing enough and he threw a fit or thought he was going mad, it might alert the German guards and the whole operation could go up in smoke. A tangible pressure lined the back of my throat, making me feel queasy at the prospect of being the sole reason that everything went wrong, but I agreed confidently to play my part in the plan.

The time came to do my part quite late the next evening. I found Ieuan sitting at a table with some of the other prisoners with a handful of playing cards that he wasn't looking at. Occasionally one of the men threw a card down, but none of them appeared to be playing a proper game. They were all watching the clock above the door to their barracks and looking out at the silhouette of an armed soldier standing right outside their door. I had never seen the solider there before. Something was wrong.

"Right chaps, lights out." The Wing Commander was standing by a little brass switch. "Into bed until the evening inspection's passed."

The captured fighters moved as one, obediently throwing themselves into their beds. Ieuan wriggled out of his uniform under the covers and screwed up his trousers and jacket, shoving them into a pack that was waiting under the bed. The lights flickered off. All was still. I took my opportunity to begin.

Mam wouldn't like you treating your clothes that way, Ieuan.

He jumped like most people did when they first heard my echoing tone in their mind. The fellow on the bunk above Ieuan's told him to shush. He lay back down staring up at the underside of that bunk, but now every muscle in his body was pulled into tense knots, nerves trickled like an electric river up and down his sides.

Don't talk, just listen, or the others will think you've gone mad.

I felt him let out a tiny laugh. He clenched his fists.

I know, I know that this is strange. But don't you know my voice? It's Kit. I'm here in your room at Ty Gwyn.

Ieuan's face was screwed up in thought; he rubbed

his chin where I felt a layer of ginger fuzz had been growing. Suddenly the door to the pitch black bunk house opened and Ieuan closed his eyes, plunging us into further darkness. I heard a set of footsteps echoing around the beds, the familiar click of jackboots that I wished I didn't recognise so well.

Bloody Germans, I told Ieuan, *but don't worry. I know about the Resistance digging in to help you. I'm here to help too.*

Being told not to worry didn't seem to do anything calming for the body I was in. Ieuan had started to sweat, his heart forcing out rapid beats. The footsteps of the inspecting solider walked away again and soon after the door closed. Ieuan opened his eyes again, now adjusted enough to the dark for me to make out other soldiers climbing silently out of their beds. Ieuan did the same, but his legs were now shaking as he put his bare feet into his boots and picked up his pack of clothes.

Please don't be scared, I tried in a calm tone, *you're not going mad. I'm the one with the strange abilities, not you. You'll be fine after this. I'll never put words in your head ever again, I swear. Okay?*

He nodded a little in the darkness and I breathed a sigh of relief.

"Price, you lead us in," the WC said.

Ieuan gulped and saluted the superior man, then marched to the very rear corner of the bunk house where the opening to the concealed tunnel was. In the dark I could just make out that the other men had removed the floorboards in the space, leaving a gaping pit below which

Ieuan leapt into. He landed on crumbly earth, his body still shaking.

The Resistance are going to give a bird call so you know which way to dig.

He didn't respond, but he set off with purpose, crawling down into a wide chamber before entering a tunnel slightly to his left. I could feel its damp freshness wetting his skin as he crawled in, picking up a spoon and a tray as he passed by its entrance. The murmurs of other men behind him started to pick up.

They're counting on you Ieuan, I said happily, *so listen for the birds.*

Again he showed no sign of response, but continued deep into the murky tunnel, his knees scratching on exposed stones. When he reached the tunnel's end he stabbed his spoon into the wall with great force and little but a second later there came a squawking like the cry of a crow. Ieuan's ears twitched, he looked around for the source of the noise. It was fairly loud; Dad had said he was sure they were very close to the desired bunk house.

Dig Ieuan, I encouraged, *dig towards it.*

Ieuan's nerves were as shaky as ever, but on he dug. The crow called again now and then, getting louder and louder until I was sure it was right beside our heads. In the darkness a loud scrape like that of a shovel caught my attention somewhere near Ieuan's hands.

They're here for you, they're breaking through.

The crow called once more this time the whistle it was coming from was right beside us. A shovel broke through the thin layer of earth and caught Ieuan on the hand with a painful stab. He winced and pulled his hand back, using the other to scrabble through the now collapsing wall of dirt until a flashlight and a face came into view. Dad's face.

"Hello boys," he whispered, "come on, it's this way."

Ieuan, relieved, passed the message back to the others in the line, then started crawling over the mound between the two tunnels and into a much larger, well-supported space.

"I see you got the message about the bird call," Dad told him with a cavalier wink.

I could feel that Ieuan's expression was horrified, but I stifled my amusement at Dad's attitude. He couldn't feel how scared the young man was or couldn't remember how frightening it must have been the first time my mother put her voice in his head. Through Ieuan's eyes I watched Dad crawl on casually in the wider tunnel, his huge muddy boots threatening to kick us in the face.

"Keep to whispers 'til we're out of the camp boundary," Dad instructed, "shouldn't be long."

Tell him your name, I urged Ieuan, *I've told him about you. He'll help you get back home to Mam and Blod.*

"Sir," he whispered, catching up to Dad so they were almost side by side as they crawled, "I'm Ieuan Price sir."

"You're acquainted with my daughter Kit," Dad answered with a nod, "Is she with you now?"

I could feel how much he didn't like the question, a bolt of electricity shot down his spine as he tried to answer.

311

"I… Her voice is…"

"It's all right," Dad said. I could see his little grin illuminated by the flashlight hanging from his shoulder. "Don't even try to explain it. In fact you'd be better off forgetting this whole night once you're home and dry."

"Yes sir," Ieuan murmured, taking a look back to see the row of happy men trailing behind him.

"Hang on," Dad said, trying to crawl with one arm as he fumbled in one of his pockets, "we're at the camp limit I think. I need to give a call to say we're coming through."

Tell him I could do that, I pressed to Ieuan, thinking that I could nip over to Henri at the tunnel's end and let him know.

Ieuan hesitated too long and when he did begin to speak Dad was already using the crow call again, giving three bursts in a row of the baying call. The second he did there was a great eruption of noise like something heavy was falling somewhere and a second later something unbearably sharp hit me. Dad covered Ieuan's mouth instantly, masking the horrifying scream that he would have let loose. A searing agony made my stomach twist as I saw my father's horrified face. Ieuan tried to move and I felt its cause.

A long blade.

Straight through his shoulder.

Ieuan struggled to breathe as the blade, which had been stabbed down into the tunnel from above, twisted behind his shoulder blade and made me feel like I wanted to vomit. I felt every moment of his unbearable pain. I could hear the frantic whispers of the men behind him now realising what had happened. They were retreating, leaving us there to die. The blade retracted and this time Ieuan bit hard into the dirty skin of Dad's hand so as not to make any more noise, but the puncture left him breathless and weak. The tunnel was getting darker all the time; all panic had run out of Ieuan's body, leaving only a sickening, unending pain.

Somewhere in the top of his chest was something still out of place. Even though the blade had gone, I felt a sharpness, a foreign body sticking into the back of his shoulder blade. It was horrid, I felt like I wanted to reach in and tear it out, but the ache of the object was too deep to get at. I didn't know if Ieuan felt it too, there were so many wild and agonising sensations swilling around his frantic mind.

"Dear God," Dad whispered, grabbing us by the torso. He struggled along, pulling Ieuan onto his back so he could crawl with him down the tunnel, but it was little use. My vision was almost gone; all I had were Ieuan's ragged breaths, growing weaker by the second as he lost the ability to breathe.

I snapped out of his head desperately and fled to Henri, finding it hard to change from the dark scene to the faint light of the cosy little barn. My words came so loud and frantic into Henri's head that he leapt a mile from the tunnel opening where he had been waiting.

Henri, oh God Henri please help them! I tried desperately to collect my thoughts for the proper words. *Dad... Ieuan's been stabbed. Dad's trying to carry him. He can't manage. He might be dying. He can't breathe. And they might stab down again!*

Every terrifying thought that hit me came out in a jumbled mess in Henri's mind and though there was fear in his heart he jumped head first into the tunnel mouth and starting to crawl down in at once. All the training on his hands and knees with Sergeant Cross in Essex had paid off; he scurried down the dark tunnel like a rat, I could already hear Ieuan's desperate gasps and Dad's effort-fuelled grunts echoing back at us. They couldn't be far away. If Henri got to them and pulled them out in time, things might be okay.

My vision began to fade, but this time there was no cold shiver to mark that my psychic trip was coming to an end. Instead I felt a wet sort of a heat all over my face as the sight of the tunnel dissolved and when I came back to Ieuan's little room in Ty Gwyn I was soaked all over in a cold sweat. A headache slowly made itself known in the back of my skull and my eyes shot open as the all-too-familiar sensation of a fever kicked in.

"Mum!" I shouted furiously.

You've done well sweetheart, she promised, *but you really can't see this next part.*

"No!" I protested. My eyes shot to my door as Idrys poked his head in. I had woken him up. "Please don't put me under! Not a fever, please!"

There was a pause, but my headache raged on. The dark room was already growing black as I felt Idrys put his smooth, dry hand on my clammy head.

I'm sorry, love, but I just can't trust you not to go back there.

In all fairness, that was exactly what I wanted to do, but I struggled all the same until the world became one big dark bubble once more.

CHAPTER TWENTY-NINE

Touch And Go

Mercifully it was only the next afternoon that I came round. Idrys was there watching over me, so I told him everything I could as floods of tears poured down my face. His expression had a ghostly pallor to it when I was done; his calloused farmer's hands were trembling. He took me downstairs as soon as I was able and we piled into Bickerstaff's room where he and Blod were sat on the bed sharing his lunch. I didn't know when or how Idrys and the former doctor had realised that each other knew about my gift, but there seemed no need for a preamble. Idrys launched right into the tale of Ieuan's injury and made me repeat it to Bickerstaff.

"Could he survive that Steven?" Idrys urged, "Is there any way?"

Blod clutched Bickerstaff's arm tightly, her lip trembling as she took in the shocking news. Bickerstaff considered things very carefully for a moment.

"When Henri was approaching," he asked gingerly, "was he still breathing?"

I nodded furiously from the chair Idrys had dropped

me into. "I could hear him… gasping." I shut my mouth quickly as my stomach gave a lurch. I took a few breaths in through the nose to calm down.

"Oh God," Blod said, burying her head against her beau's shoulder.

Bickerstaff was largely ignorant to everyone's pain, his mind consumed by matters medical. I could see the process of his thoughts behind his huge eyes. His breathing became sharp as he thought things out.

"It could just be a collapsed lung, but not a punctured one," he suggested, "if so he'll make it."

"And if not?" Idrys asked, biting hard on the knuckles of his clenched fist.

"If not I don't think he'd be breathing loud enough for Kit to hear him from that distance," the former doctor replied carefully. For once his emotionless face was extremely useful; its blankness seemed to calm everyone down. "Remember it's only one lung that's been affected. He's got a fighting chance if they get him to proper care right away."

"But we don't know if they have," Blod pleaded, surfacing from Bickerstaff's now soaking wet shoulder.

"They seemed to be very well organised," I offered, "I'll bet they have medics and all sorts."

"But you don't know that, do you?" Blod snapped at me with damp eyes, "You didn't see any yourself?"

I felt exhausted and defeated. "Well, no but-"

Blod made to shout at me but Idrys waved a serious finger at her. She shut her mouth slowly and sniffed in her angry sobs. At last Bickerstaff seemed to realise her pain and put an arm around her. She sank into the side of his body in silence.

"Even with the most basic equipment, it could still be done," he said in a low tone, "if they get him to a doctor in time."

I was taken back upstairs to rest and I hoped that perhaps my sleeping mind would take me back to the Resistance, but had no luck. I was out cold for another few hours of sheer blackness until I managed to haul myself out of bed for dinner. I dressed this time and clunked my way down the stairs, feeling confident that I was rested enough to go back to Henri for an update as soon as the meal was over. To hell with what my mother had said, I hadn't done enough until I could give Blod and Idrys better news.

I froze in the doorway to the kitchen. Mum was sat in my space at the table, fretting over a hole in Leighton's school jumper. When she turned and smiled at me I could see all the sadness and apology in her face. Nothing she had done was out of spite, but I couldn't bring myself to smile back at her. I said hello to her in a quiet, flat tone and settled myself in a seat a bit farther away.

"You're early, Mum," I commented, trying to sound bright as I eyed Mam stirring up the gravy, "The wedding's not for three more days."

"I had some time off, so I thought I'd come and lend

a hand," she explained.

"Very kind of you," Mam said. She turned and beamed at me. "Oh your mum's brought the most beautiful flowers and real chocolate for the cake! Blod's going to flip!"

I shot Mum a glare. What a bald lie it all was. She was here to keep tabs on me so I couldn't go against her will again. She knew that I knew, I could tell by the way she looked down at the table, unable to keep meeting my eyes.

As the rest of the family settled in for dinner, the mood became tenser still. Idrys and Blod hardly touched their food and Bickerstaff was lost in thoughts so deep he didn't even notice Ness stealing all of the potatoes from his plate. Idrys kept looking at Mum with a glint of steel in his eyes, waiting for Mam to spin out the last of her chatty conversation so he could strike with a line of his own.

"I believe we have someone in common Gail," he said in what seemed like a casual tone, "I knew your father, Reginald Arkwright."

"My goodness," Mum replied with half a smile, "what a small world it is, with Kit coming to stay here, of all places."

"Good job she did," Idrys added quickly, "she's been a godsend this girl."

"Here, here," said Mam, oblivious to the real conversation happening beneath the words, "very useful to have around."

After dinner Idrys persuaded Leighton to help Mam wash up with the promise of a trip to the cinema, which left the rest of us free to coerce my mother into the little sitting room. Bickerstaff and I were the last to arrive as we limped along at the rear, taking up the whole sofa between us and our crutches. Mum was outnumbered, but she gathered herself with a deep breath as Idrys closed the door.

"I'd been to check on things just before I got here," she said, giving the old farmer an apologetic look, "your grandson is still alive."

"Thank God," Blod muttered, putting her pretty face in her hands. Bickerstaff reached out and rubbed her knee gently, but his face was still totally focused on Mum.

"Where are they treating him?" he asked.

Mum bit her lip. "On a submarine, I'm afraid."

"Are you mad, woman?" Bickerstaff blurted, "A pressurised space is no place for a man who's been stabbed through the chest!"

"We didn't have a choice," Mum pleaded, "if the boys hadn't got on that sub, the next one we could arrange for England would have been after Christmas. There's nowhere you could hide a man in Ieuan's condition for that long, he'd have died."

"Do you at least have a proper doctor?"

Mum nodded. "There's one on the submarine. It's a fully manned vessel, lots of people trained to help with injuries."

"Getting stabbed isn't usually the speciality of doctors who practice underwater," Bickerstaff griped. He thumped his one remaining leg hard. "God I wish I could look him over and advise you."

Mum's gaze snapped up, her eyes suddenly brighter. "Actually you can."

I wasn't privy to the full details of how it worked, all Mum would tell me was that there was a way for psychics like us to pull another person's consciousness into our heads and take them with us wherever we went. She had done such things with Dad all year, letting him snoop on people and places with her across the whole length of Europe to gain information to help the Free French. She had never tried it with anyone but him though, so she took Bickerstaff away with her to another room to try it out in private. Astonished as I was that there were yet more things I could learn to do with my powers, I was bitter that she wouldn't let me see how it was done. I had a feeling she would be reluctant to teach me anything that would allow me to get into more trouble during the war, so I made a mental note to see if I could figure out the method with Henri sometime in the future.

After his first consultation with Ieuan, Bickerstaff was visibly shaken and practically green in the face. He had to lie down for a little while before he was collected enough to tell us what he had seen and even then his speech was stunted and breathy. Ieuan was in a critical state but there was every chance he could still survive. He had been pierced clean through the chest but the blade had only brushed against his lung, puncturing the chest cavity and causing it to temporarily collapse. Medics had been able to re-inflate his lung into a weak but working order, the problem now was the risk of internal bleeding. Ieuan kept suddenly rupturing inside his chest and the medics aboard the ship were finding it hard to keep stemming the blood and they had not found the source of the bleeds. Bickerstaff had recommended some medications based on what they had on board the sub to help his circulation, but the treatment he really needed wasn't available on board.

"If they don't find the source of the bleeding he'll need a transfusion soon from the continued blood loss," Bickerstaff explained in his usual emotionless voice.

"Or he'll just bleed to death?" Blod asked, her hand on his shoulder. He just nodded at her. "Then what can we do?"

Everyone started talking over each other, but I heard none of it, my mind reeling with something that Bickerstaff had said. The source of the bleeding. The thing that was causing the ruptures. I thought hard about everything I'd seen and felt that awful night in the tunnel.

"Stop," I said loudly. Everyone fell silent. I looked to the former doctor as I gathered my words carefully. "Could some kind of object stuck in his shoulder be causing these rupture things?"

"Definitely," he said with a nod, "What do you know?"

"When I could feel it all happening," I gulped dryly, "The blade came back out and he started to find it hard to breathe. But there was something else, something sharp under the back of his shoulder. I felt like I wanted to pull it out of his body."

"An obstruction," Bickerstaff mused.

"A piece of the blade left behind pr'aps?" Idrys suggested.

The men slowly started to nod. Bickerstaff leapt up, totally forgetting his fake leg until Blod came to steady his wobbling form. He approached my mother unsteadily and took her arm.

"We have to go again, now."

It was hard to believe that between all the life and death conversations a wedding was slowly coming together in the background. Everyone who was in on the plan to save Ieuan operated in shifts to cover for one another, doing their special duties like pressing clothes and arranging flowers whilst whispering updates to one another from Mum's latest trip to see how he was doing. I wasn't allowed to see anything, of course, so I spent the next three days passing on messages and quizzing Bickerstaff about what was really going on. When Blod wasn't around he was willing to tell me the truth: Ieuan had almost died the first time they tried to remove the foreign body in his shoulder. Things didn't look good.

It was the night before the wedding that I sat in Blod's room with her, helping her put her hair into overnight rollers for a perfect set of blonde curls at the chapel the next day. We were talking about simple things, nice distracting things like how pretty Ness would look as a flower girl and how we could put some flowers over my crutches to make them look less hideous in the photographs, when suddenly Blod fell silent. I knew she had returned to her worries about her brother, so I kept quiet too and tried to finish her hair. I had just put the last roller in when she exploded into a fit of tears.

"How am I supposed to go and have the happiest day of my life?" she sobbed, turning to me with anger in every muscle of her face, "Ieu's dying. He's dying and we're yur doing nothing!"

She slammed her fists down on her bed and I caught her by the wrists to calm her down.

"You heard what Mum said," I tried to soothe, "that sub is due to surface in England tonight, where all sorts of proper doctors and equipment are waiting." I rubbed her wrists with my thumbs. "He's made it this far."

Blod nodded a few times, scrubbing tears from her eyes roughly.

"It's lucky you were there to feel that bit of blade that got stuck," she said quietly, "or he'd most likely be dead already."

I thought bitterly about Mum not wanting me to be there at all, how if I had just done as she said and stayed away, Henri wouldn't have even known to rush down the tunnel and help them to get out. The thought of Henri sent a pang straight to the centre of my chest. Suddenly I wanted to cry too. All the horrible things he must have seen and now he was all alone on that submarine, time ticking away until he could set foot on safe ground once more. When he left for war I had promised to be there always, but now we were truly apart.

The door to Blod's bedroom opened and a breathless figure clunked in, shutting it behind him.

"Oi!" Blod cried, her hands rushing to her hair. "You're not supposed to see me now! It's bad luck!"

Steven Bickerstaff heaved with the effort of hauling his false leg and crutch up Ty Gwyn's stairs for the first time, but when he looked up at us he was grinning like a madman. He shook his head, gasping for breath.

"No love, it's the best luck," he began, clutching his chest, "they got the blade fragment out. The sub's surfaced in Cardiff docks. He's stable."

Blod leapt off the bed so fast she nearly knocked me to the floor, rushing to Bickerstaff and throwing her arms around him. He wobbled precariously and held onto her, trying to keep himself steady as she kissed him all over one side of his face in utter joy.

"Cardiff's in South Wales, isn't it?" I asked.

Bickerstaff nodded as Blod let him go. "It's a fair drive, but Idrys says we'll go down tomorrow right after the wedding and see him."

Blod settled herself beside me again on the edge of the bed, clutching my hand for a moment. "Thank you," she began with a huge grin, "both of you. You've done so much. Now get out of my room! I've got a sack-load of beauty sleep to catch up on for the morning!"

The Mind's Eye

She pushed and shoved our limping forms from the room, but we took her enthusiastic brutality with a smile.

CHAPTER THIRTY

Thirty Paces

Bickerstaff pretended that he'd had a letter from a colleague in Cardiff General Hospital so that we could break the news about Ieuan to Mam. I was front row centre to see her reaction and she didn't disappoint me. First she attacked Bickerstaff with a hug so fierce that he actually fell right over on his backside after she let him go, then she ran around kissing each one of us with joyous tears pouring down her cheeks like some great waterfall of relief. She picked up Ness; already half adorned with her flower girl outfit, and swung her around the kitchen until the paper roses that had been tacked to her skirt came flying off in all directions, covering us all in pink petals. As a final act, she burst outside to shout to the heavens and thank God himself, only to find herself ankle-deep in the first full drift of December snow.

"Ooh!" Ness cried, running out after her to play in the white blanket all over the yard.

Leighton followed suit, throwing himself face first into a huge drift that had piled up outside the nearby barn. I looked out at them with a nervous kind of joy in my heart.

I had never actually walked in snow before. I hauled myself out gingerly, stepping down into the cool, powdery stuff, feeling my feet make a deep print before I set out with more confidence. I looked back at my tracks after a while, the crutches making it look like two peg leg pirates were walking side by side. Even Blod came out to enjoy the drift without moaning about what it might do to her shoes, throwing a snowball at Bickerstaff that he deflected with his false leg, which almost came off totally from the impact of the throw.

The whole contents of the house were still outside in the fresh morning when a lilting voice called over from the path:

"Oi! I thought you lot had a wedding to go to?"

All heads turned to see Thomas racing towards us in his fine navy uniform, his bags discarded in the snow. He went straight to Mam, turning the tables on her for once as he half picked her up in his excitement.

"Oh Thom! Ieuan's home!" she exclaimed, delighted to have another person to tell, "He's in hospital in Cardiff!"

When Thomas pulled away from the hug his young face was a picture of shock. He looked around to Blod and his grandfather, both nodding to help him accept the good news. It took quite a few moments, but eventually it all sank in. He swore quite loudly, but nobody told him off, then threw himself backwards into the snow and laughed up at the morning sky. Ness leapt on his stomach and covered him in slush, which to Mam and Blod's horror was also all over her dress.

"You little mochyn!" Blod cried, pulling her away from Thomas and dragging her up to see her soaking wet hem.

And that was when the real work of having a wedding began.

The preparations had been hard, but they were nothing compared to organisation of the big day itself. The ceremony was at the chapel at half past twelve but it was gone nine by the time everyone was dried off and breakfasted after our time in the snow. Mum was a whirlwind of activity, shooing Mam away from the kitchen for her to get ready whilst she took over making the sandwiches and sorting out the other foodstuffs for the party at Ty Gwyn straight after the service. A visit to Cardiff or not, Mam would never let anyone set off with an empty stomach.

It was my duty to help Blod get into her dress, but everything was such a blur and a rush that I spent most of that time close up to it adjusting hems, fixing broken seams and resetting her golden curls once we'd secured her veil. In fact I didn't actually stop to look at her properly until some hours later when we were outside the chapel with Ness, waiting for Idrys to come and walk her in. It was then that I saw the long, flowing white skirt of the gown. It was as bright as the snow all around us, something shiny in the material was reflecting the sun that had broken through the clouds above. Blod's perfect skin was like porcelain against the dress save for a pinkish glow in her cheeks as she stood catching her breath in the cold air.

"You look perfect," I told her, smiling widely.

"I should think so, the amount of time it took us." She was grinning, but clearly agitated. "He'll be in there, now won't he?"

I caught on to some of her worries and nodded. "Of course. It's not like he could get away, not at his speed. Even I could catch him."

Blod laughed out a few nervous breaths, clutching her bouquet that matched the paper roses on Ness's quickly-repaired dress. The little girl was looking up at the sky, watching the clouds break with her familiar look of concentration. Blod and I followed her gaze.

"I wish Dad could've been yur to see this," Blod mused quietly, "but at least we'll see Ieu tonight." She let out a little sigh. "I reckon every family only gets one miracle, and Dad would've never wanted it to be the other way round, for him to be yur and Ieu gone, so there you go."

"I think we've had a few more miracles than that, if you think about it," I added.

Blod nodded at me and squeezed my shoulder.

"I'm going to try and remember that, and be less snappy with you from now on," she said with a laugh.

"Good plan," I replied, "Save all the snapping for your husband."

We were still laughing when Idrys came out of the chapel and told us we were ready to go. Ness was lined up to go first, a basket of paper petals in her hands ready to scatter, then Blod would take her Bampi's arm to walk down the aisle. I couldn't really carry the dress's train and use both my crutches, but Blod had asked me to, so I was going to give it a damn good try. The first thing I caught sight of as we entered the church was Bickerstaff waiting in his bottle green suit. Unable to stop himself he was already watching his bride approach with the biggest smile I had ever seen him wear. If I hadn't ever met him before, I'd have sworn he was the happiest man alive.

A photographer followed the wedding party home after the service, which was relatively short after Blod had finished lecturing the preacher on cutting out the boring bits a few days prior to the event. Mam had insisted on having all the pictures taken on the pasture outside Ty Gwyn, especially now that the fallen snow had given us such a beautiful backdrop. While everything was being set up I took my chance and set off to escape up to my room. A day full of love and happiness had only made me think of one thing for hours on end. I barely had one foot on the stairs when I heard Mum appear behind me.

"I've checked on everyone and they're fine," she chided, "so no sneaking off. Come and have a sandwich."

I spun on my crutch and glared at her.

"There's no danger right now," I protested, "why can't I just have a chat with him, just for five minutes?"

Mum approached me slowly, something I couldn't

read behind those indigo eyes the same shade as mine. She rested her hands on my shoulders and broke into a smile that made me feel warm even though I was mad at her.

"Your father and I have had a talk," she began, heaving the words out almost reluctantly, "and he's right. It's time I let you go. I'm not going to stop you using your powers ever again. You've done so well with them, handled things so much better than I would have imagined." I felt her hands holding me tighter, like she needed me to keep her steady. "I've been looking after you so much for so long that I'd forgotten you would grow up sooner or later. I just want you to remember the warnings I've given you, they always apply, wartime or otherwise."

I nodded, starting to smile too. "Psychic or not, I'll always have your voice in my head," I answered.

Mum chuckled a little, her hold on me relaxing again.

"But that freedom starts tomorrow," she continued, "so please don't do anything yet, just for today."

"But why?" I asked.

"You'll see." My mother started to walk away with a grin.

Leighton came into the hall in his little waistcoat and trousers, rubbing his head. His hair was sticking up at a funny angle and Mum rushed to adjust it for him, but he batted her away. That pensive look was back on his face.

"Leigh what's up?" I said as I approached.

But he didn't have time to answer as Idrys's deep Welsh voice boomed through the house to call us out for the photographs.

"Tell me later?" I whispered to Leighton. He nodded gently, still nursing his temple.

We all lined up on the snowy ground at the edge of the pasture waiting for our turn to be called. There were several pictures of the bride and groom as Blod took full advantage of her big day to look as good as possible, then there were a few more of just the bride when Bickerstaff got sick of posing and left her to it. Eventually it was the turn of the bridesmaid, flower girl and page boy, which saw Ness, Leigh and I trying to pose with my clonking crutches in the way.

"Oh sod these things," I cried eventually, chucking them out of the shot and standing behind Leighton.

I leant on his shoulders to keep myself steady, surprised at how strong my knees were to keep me up. It was hard to miss Bickerstaff's medical mind assessing my stance from the side-lines, but he was smiling so I thought I must have been doing all right. Ness was the next problem, the wriggly little thing refused to stay still for the photo. It was only after some careful persuasion from Bickerstaff that she did as she was told, beaming up at the photographer like an angel even after her massive fidgeting episode. I had the feeling her would-be father had promised her a lot of lollipops for that smile.

Mum was smiling too at Leigh and I, I caught her eye over the top of the camera after the shot had been taken. Leighton was pretty sure he had blinked, so another take was in order. I rolled my eyes at Mum, but then I noticed she wasn't looking at me anymore. Her gaze was cast way past where we stood at the edge of the field, her smile widening every moment.

"Yur now!" Mam shouted with a pointing finger. "Who's that ruining our backdrop?"

I turned, still leaning one hand on Leighton to see two shapes under the shadow of the nearest tree. The larger of the two emerged from it and I was surprised to see my father carrying another man on his back. When the other man looked up from Dad's shoulder, his gingery hair and sparkling eyes gave him away despite the unusual paleness in his face. Mam screamed with delight.

"Good God!" Bickerstaff shouted as he realised who it was. "Are you entirely insane? This boy should be in hospital, not travelling two hundred miles up the country!"

Ieuan ignored him and waved with every bit of strength he had in him. Dad was fast approaching, flashing me a smile as he passed us to deliver the boy to his family.

"I'm sorry," he said to Bickerstaff, "but he wouldn't be told. He insisted on coming up right away even if it killed him."

Bickerstaff glanced at his new bride as she raced past him to join Mam and Thomas in crushing Ieuan from all sides. The former doctor shook his head, starting to grin.

"That's the Price family all over, I'm afraid," he concluded.

"It's Dad…" Leigh muttered, clearly stunned. He tapped my hands where they were leaning on him. "Let's go to him, Kit!" he pleaded, more excited than I'd ever known him be.

Dad beamed at us both as he came back towards us, but when he looked at me he pointed again to the tree behind me. The other figure was still there. I watched, open mouthed like a goldfish as the other person stepped out from under the branches' shadows, stretching his arms wide open, his messy dark hair flying everywhere against the wintery breeze.

"Thirty paces!" Henri shouted.

Slowly, I let go of Leighton's shoulders.

"No, no!" Henri shouted, half laughing, "Get your aids!"

But I didn't. I knew that it was an all or nothing kind of motion. If I started to run I wouldn't be able to stop or I'd be face deep in the snow. It was a soft landing, all things considered, so before anyone could catch me I put every bit of power I had into my knees and ran for it. The distance was much less than thirty steps when I was running, jarring every bone in my body as I streaked desperately towards Henri and his open arms. He watched in awe as I sped at him, wrapping me up as I fell into his arms, my knees finally spent.

He held me up and kissed me deeply, sending warm tingles out all over my face despite the cold air. I pulled him close, my arms around his neck as I felt his warm body next to mine. It was a while before either of us had breath again to speak, both grinning at each other like a pair of Cheshire cats, trying to think of the perfect things to say having spent so long apart. I had nothing, no words that could express the relief and joy and completely all-consuming love that was gripping me in that moment, but Henri looked me up and down and grinned, creasing his lovely chocolate eyes.

"You're wearing the dress I made you."

I looked down at myself; the navy fabric with the white polka dots was bright against the white winter scene around me. I shrugged happily at Henri.

"I was the only bridesmaid, so I could pick whatever I wanted to wear."

He beamed at me, his strong arms holding me steady again.

"And you chose this?"

"Always," I replied.

"All right Romeo, put the girl down."

My father had found us. I turned to find him being swiftly followed by my mother and Leighton who were rushing up with my crutches. I took them rather gratefully as my weak legs shook in the cold snow, grinning when Henri kept a warm arm around my waist still. Dad rested his hand on Mum's shoulder and she took hold of it tightly. Leighton stood in the middle of us all, smiling at everyone, until his stomach gave a huge echoing growl.

"I think that means lunchtime," Henri observed as the rest of us laughed.

We set off as a group at my slow pace back towards Ty Gwyn, where the newly reformed Price family had bundled Ieuan into the wheelchair to take him inside. Leighton steadied my walking on one side with Henri on the other until we too were back at the kitchen door. The smell of fresh cakes invited us in and Leigh broke free to attack them. Henri turned to me and kissed my cheek softly.

"I love you," he whispered.

"Love you too," I mouthed, eyeing my Mum and Dad carefully.

Once Henri too had gone inside, Dad stopped Mum and I from following. He gave me a sombre look; his dark eyes open wide with thought.

"This war's not over, you know," he said quietly, "Henri will have to go back into service soon." I gulped; it was the last thing I needed to hear on such a happy day. "But," my father continued, "I was thinking of pulling him into my department, given his experience so far."

"Henri, a spy?" I asked in disbelief.

"He'd make a fine one," Mum added, "but he'd need an assistant at home of course."

I saw them standing there together, but not as my parents any longer. They were an operational team, working side by side to rescue good men from the war and help occupied populations fight back against the oppression of the Hun. And now they were inviting me to be part of the family business, to learn how to really help Henri like I'd wanted to all along. I nodded furiously, unable to even say yes. Mum swallowed all her reservations, looking to Dad for reassurance. He grinned proudly at us both and gave a little nod, turning to lead us indoors.

No expense had been spared in collecting as much food as Mam could muster, gathering all our rations together to produce a splendid feast. When I found my place at the overcrowded table Leighton had a mouthful of cream and jam. His skinny legs were swinging happily as I sat down beside him, watching Mum and Dad trek off to the places laid for them at the other end of the kitchen. My little brother looked at me and his eyes widened suddenly. He dropped the food he was eating and waved his hand for my attention as he tried to chew and swallow faster than was humanly possible.

"Don't do that, you'll choke," I sat, slapping his back as he coughed, "what is it?"

When Leigh had finally got his mouthful down he cleared his throat, pulling my ear nearer to speak in a hushed voice.

"Kit," he began carefully, "you know that psychic stuff that Idrys told us about ages ago?"

"Yes?" I replied, my breath hitching in my throat.

Leighton took in a little gasp of his own, breaking into an excited grin.

"I think I can do it."

THE END

WRITING ABOUT IMPERFECT PEOPLE

The Inspiration behind The Mind's Eye

If there was ever an embodiment of the idea of the 'troubled teen', then it was me, but probably not in the way you'd think.

I wasn't, for example, a smoker or a boozer; I didn't stay out late or smuggle anything (or anyone) untoward into my room at home. In fact, I stayed in. A lot. I would come home from high school aged 15 and find myself crawling straight into my bed at four o'clock, out cold until gone six and still in my uniform with Mum calling me down for dinner. My entire life was a pattern of eat, sleep, school, sleep, eat and so on; not a scrap of energy or enthusiasm for life, waiting desperately for the time when I could throw off the shackles of the 9-to-4 school day and finally use what little pep I had to do something better with my life. A myriad of doctors and therapists told me that I was depressed and filled me up with drugs, packing me back off to school like that was the answer to my problems.

It took me a further four years to work out what

was really going on.

At age 13 I developed what I now know to be called Myalgic Encephalomyelitis (M.E.), a debilitating physical condition that attacks every major system in your body from the nervous and digestive systems to the musculoskeletal, hormonal and beyond. Between the ages of 13 and 16 (what some would call the best years of your life) I went from being a spritely, bright child to a surly, aching, exhausted teen who saw every morning as just one more day of pain coming her way. I dropped out of school and spent eighteen months trying to recover from what I was still being told was depression and anxiety, but no matter what I tried I just couldn't get better. I knew that there had to be another explanation; I just had to find a way to prove it.

For my 18th birthday I was taken away for a week's holiday. I deliberately didn't pack my anti-depressants, suffering a week of cold-turkey withdrawal in order to flush them out of my system once and for all. This is not a practice recommended by doctors and I don't advocate it, but it was the only thing I felt able to do at the time. Coming home from that holiday I had a fresh perspective on my physical health, realising that I was never mentally depressed, but that my body was the one letting me down. I had an illness and it took me another whole year before I met a doctor who could put the label M.E. to my symptoms.

Armed with this knowledge I returned to college and then went on to university, all the while making my way through different doctors and different treatments until I could find one who would push to get the diagnosis

I so desperately needed. I was 22 years old when the letter finally came to tell me what I had been suffering from for the last nine years. It was a relief, but also a sadness, the final confirmation that I am living with a condition that has no known cure and will be likely to affect me for the rest of my life. At the point when I received that letter in November 2011, I felt as though the life I had been wading through suddenly needed a new purpose and a proper direction, something I would still be able to achieve if and when my condition worsened.

So I started to write.

I have written several self-published books in the last twelve months and it has been pointed out to me repeatedly that each one of them contains characters that are physically limited, pained and/or mentally scarred in some way. This is no co-incidence, but it is something that was creeping into my work without a definite conscious knowledge; I think I simply found it more engaging personally to write about imperfect people. That was until I sat down to write my first novel for Clean Teen Publishing, entitled The Mind's Eye. In this book my central character suffers from Juvenile Systemic Arthritis, a severe and debilitating condition that presents many of the same musculoskeletal symptoms that I face every day. Whilst I am not always bound to a wheelchair, the immobility that my character Kit faces isn't just about her legs not working. The Mind's Eye is an exciting wartime adventure with paranormal fun, but at its heart it is also a story about a girl just like me, struggling to work out how to find a place in the world where she can feel valued and still be useful to the people she cares about.

Scenes within The Mind's Eye are a mixture of Kit's psychic visions of the Second World War interspersed with her own struggles in her home life. I have a feeling that some people might consider those latter scenes to be the 'boring bits', the 'filler' that has to happen between the tense, exciting action moments. To me, however, I could take or leave the incredible and heart breaking scenes of war, because the real struggle that touches my heart is that of a lonely young girl quite literally trying to stand on her own two feet in a world where all the odds are stacked against her. When you read The Mind's Eye, spare a thought for Kit and the life she has to lead every day, because her fictional creation represents countless other people out there who face physical and emotional struggles that ordinary folk can barely comprehend.

The real story of The Mind's Eye isn't that of the glorious Allies beating back Jerry, but of Kit Cavendish beating back the sentence that life has handed her with the newfound love and support of the people around her. It is a story that is very important to me and I sincerely hope it will find a place in your hearts too.

CPSIA information can be obtained at www.ICGtesting.com
Printed in the USA
LVOW06s1658240614

391479LV00006B/854/P

9 781940 534381